I0563628

DRACIAN LEGACY

REUTS PUBLICATIONS

CLARA STONE

DRACIAN
Legacy

DRACIAN · BOOK ONE

Cover design by Tiffany Rose
Cover art Copyright 2014 ninjarabbit-stock/ashensorrow on DeviantArt.com
Interior formatting by Ashley Ruggirello
Edited by Kisa Whipkey

Paperback ISBN: 978-1-942111-13-9
Electronic ISBN: 978-0-989649-93-3

REUTS Publications
www.REUTS.com

To my husband, Rajesh, who stood by my side as I started on this adventure! Who supported and cleaned the house and our super active son!

To my lovely Jay, who has been nothing but Joy! It was because of you I started this new journey. You inspire me to break the bounds and live life to the fullest.

To my wonderful Koda, who has been right beside me every night, snuggling his furry-self next to me. Thank you for your company and all the love during those long nights of writing.

PROLOGUE

A SINGLE COLOR FILLED MY VISION—BLACK.

The wind blew around us without mercy. One stubborn strand of hair flew free from my neatly styled bun, escaping the imprisonment of at least twenty hairpins to dance with the frigid air.

It was the exact opposite of my mood. I felt nothing, as if a black hole had sucked the life out of me. My eyes were swollen, my body refused to respond, and I was cold.

Deathly cold.

I shivered and tried to focus on Father Jacob.

". . . as we commit Jim and Irene Pernell to the ground; earth to earth, ashes to ashes, dust to dust; in sure and certain hope of the Resurrection. We enter this world with nothing and we leave . . ."

Three days had passed. Three days since this emptiness had entered my soul and refused to leave.

An arm curled around my shoulders, pulling me closer. I inhaled the smell of home and the only family I had left—my brother. Joshua. I leaned into his comfort, wrapped my arms around his waist, and looked blankly ahead as my parents were lowered into the earth.

Never to be seen again.

Lost forever.

"Temperance . . ."

My brother's warm hand gently squeezed my shoulder, drawing me back from my morbid thoughts.

"Temperance . . ." Father Jacob repeated softly. No one had called me that in a long time. He gestured us forward to pay our respects.

I stiffened, rebelling. *No. I can't. That's finalizing. I won't do it. I won't admit they're really gone.*

"Ren."

I looked into Joshua's amber-blue eyes, so much like mine. His face was cautious and composed, but his eyes . . . his eyes were strained with pain. Normally, he was a concentrated ball of energy—a six-foot-three, broad-shouldered Marine.

Today, though, he was anything but strong. Today, he would be easily overpowered by a two-year-old.

"Ren, we can do this. I need you, Killer."

"Okay," I said, my voice raspy.

I hadn't spoken in three days. I'd had no appetite since my parents were killed, no motivation to speak—only to cry. And cry I did. Today was the first time I'd left my room since the sheriff had escorted us to the morgue. Even the officers had had a hard time looking at us. Not many murder cases came along in Rocky Hills, Idaho.

My hand rested in Joshua's as I dared a step forward. Then another, and another. I picked up a fistful of brittle dirt and stood over my parents' burial ground. I refused to look down. So instead, I gazed at the individuals gathered to mourn our mutual loss.

"I'll protect her with my life. I promise." Joshua's voice cracked, his eyes locked on the coffins. Ten years older, he'd always sheltered me from anything and everything he could. That had a new meaning now.

He gave my hand a reassuring squeeze. With a wavering breath, I knelt, tears escaping onto the soft, green grass.

"I don't know . . ."

My throat hurt, and I didn't recognize my own voice. My surroundings blurred and every uncontrollable, incoherent sensation came rushing forward, urging me to speak, yet holding me prisoner.

"Momma. Daddy." There was so much I wanted to say. But nothing seemed to make it past my lips. I missed them too much; it hurt to even think.

I gripped the fistful of dirt like a precious treasure, refusing to let the grains slip through my fingers the way my parents had. Tears rolled down my cheeks, trying to wash away my sorrow and anguish. Joshua knelt, placing a hand on my shoulder, comforting me.

"It's okay. Let go," he whispered into my ear, kissing my temple. "It will get easier. I promise."

I believed him. I kissed my knuckles as heavy sobs escaped me.

Slowly, I let go.

CHAPTER ONE

A year and a half later . . .

"The Bobcats are gonna eat shit Friday night," Dean argued. He leaned back and extended his legs, not a care in the world.

"Evidence, D. Show me some evidence," Landon challenged.

"Their quarterback broke his collarbone back in July." Dean ticked off each point, finger by finger. "They lost to the

Windsor Eagles last year, by over sixteen points. And then there's me." He smirked. "There's no way we can lose. We're going undefeated this year, baby."

"Shit, there goes our chance at winning," Pey laughed. "A cocky quarterback that's hopelessly in love with himself. We'll be lucky if you don't stop every two seconds to check yourself out."

"Hey, I can't help that I'm *that* irresistible." He shot me a flirty smile.

I glanced at Pey. She tilted her head, arching an eyebrow, and mouthed, "*For real?*" Dean wasn't just in *love* with himself, he was stalker-obsessed.

"You're a man-whore, Dean. Man. Whore," Pey drawled.

Oh no, not this conversation again.

"I've got plenty of love, and I don't object to sharing." Dean shrugged and threw fries at Pey.

"The only things you share are horizontal surfaces. And cooties," Pey sneered.

"Hypocrite," Dean fake-coughed into his hand.

Pey smiled, teeth showing, and flipped him off. The situation was spiraling out of control. I looked to Landon for help and he shrugged, laughing.

Landon and Peyton had been dating since we started high school. That same year, Dean had dumped me for his newfound fame as a ninth grade, varsity quarterback, and the groupies that came with it. We'd been best friends before that. Now, I wasn't sure what we were.

"Just because you can't call dibs on this yummy, white-choc—" Dean started.

"Hey, who got the cheesecake?" I interrupted, taking a bite. I closed my eyes, savoring the smooth texture.

"Dean," Landon answered, smirking.

I stopped mid-chew, mentally cursing the gods that had invented such a succulent dessert. The last thing I wanted was to owe Dean, especially since I knew he'd use it as ammunition against me.

The bell above the door chimed. I looked up as a group of teenagers in long black trench-coats entered the café, bringing the warm, early-September air with them. They settled into a seat diagonal from us, and I could hear their slight accents. The one closest to me looked over his shoulder and winked. I quickly averted my gaze, heat rushing through my cheeks. He must have felt me staring.

My favorite song started playing in the background as I looked toward the entrance again. The bell chimed, matching perfectly with the song, as the door opened and *he* walked in.

There was something so familiar about him, but I couldn't quite put my finger on it.

Pey murmured something in my ear and giggled. I waved her off and continued to gawk shamelessly.

His brown hair fell partway over his forehead, casting shadows on his electrifying blue eyes. Black clothes and dark, heavy boots complimented his tall, lean frame.

He glanced toward our table as he slid into the booth next to his friends and his penetrating gaze locked with mine. A delicious smile appeared on his full lips.

I sucked in a deep breath, feeling something coil deep in the core of my existence.

Ah hell, this was bad. Double-chocolate-chips-to-my-hips kinda bad.

"Hey, Pernell, I've been meaning to tell you: you should ask for a reimbursement," Dean said.

I arched my brow, bringing my attention back to our table. He had his signature smirk in place.

"Looks like that cosmetic procedure didn't work after all," he finished.

Argh! He was like splinters under my nails. I had the sudden urge to touch his cheek with groundbreaking force.

"I could make a few changes to your body without any procedure . . . wanna see?" I challenged.

"Buuuurn." Landon covered his O-shaped mouth with one hand, pointing at Dean with the other.

"Oh!" Dean's eyes lit up in surprise, his smirk dissolving into an infuriating smile. "I can think of other things you could do with your body and mine." He winked.

My jaw dropped. Dean flirted with anything that moved, but he'd never directed a suggestive comment at me before. Not since the day he'd stolen my first kiss from me.

"Don't make me gag. I'd rather jump off a hundred-story building straight onto a knife."

"You know, Pernell . . ." He leaned in, gazing into my eyes.

A strange sensation stirred inside me. Attraction. Hate. Annoyance. Attraction.

Damn him.

"You look super cute when you get all worked up. If it weren't for that razor-sharp tongue of yours, I'd *suck* that cuteness right out of you." His gaze dropped to my trembling lips as he inched closer, licking his own.

Then he gave me his most arrogant smile and pulled back slowly, like he was trying to make a point. He took a bite of my—his—half-eaten cheesecake, looking smug. I swallowed the lump in my throat.

I wanted to smack him. Heck, I wanted to punch him in the face and say, "*Ha! In your dreams, buddy.*" I considered it for a moment. But instead of following through, I paid for my portion of the meal, including the cheesecake, and walked out, giving one last glance to the brown-haired, blue-eyed stranger laughing with his friends.

"Shit. You're such an ass, Dean," I heard Pey say.

My phone buzzed.

Pey: LET ME DRIVE YOU HOME.

Me: I'M OKAY. HEADED TO SEE MY PARENTS.

Pey: K. CALL IF YOU NEED ANYTHING. G'NITE, LOVELY.

CHAPTER TWO

SO FAR, SENIOR YEAR SUCKED ASS. A WEEK IN, FOUR CLASSES down, and I already had a reading assignment, a five-page paper, and a test on Monday.

"I hate senior year," Ella said. "We're placing our future in the hands of idiots."

"Not all of us are geniuses, Ella," I muttered, irritated by her attitude.

Dean placed his arm around her waist and pulled her into his lap. "Y'all are just jealous," he said, burying his face in her red locks.

"Stop." She playfully nudged him, giggling. "If you keep this up, my daddy's going to bring out his shotgun."

"Nothing I can't handle, sexy," he replied, dipping in for another smooch-a-thon.

"Nice," Landon said, joining us. He grabbed Pey and gave her a rather long kiss.

"Mmm, minty fresh," Pey purred.

"Oh my God, this is turning into a lunchroom orgy. PG, guys," I said, dropping my half-eaten carrot back into its Ziploc bag, nauseated. "I need to find a new set of friends who don't suck face every few seconds."

Pey winked. "I had to draw my blood, cut open a cow's eyeball, and endure a surprise quiz. And it's not even Wednesday! Sue me for having a *little* fun."

"You have Mr. Webet for biology? You'll love him!" Ella insisted.

"No, see, I love these fries. I love my hair up in braids. I don't and will never, as long as I live, love biology."

"A little dramatic, don't you think?" Dean muttered.

"Shut it." A few fries flew in his direction.

"How did the school man-whore hook up with the school geek, anyway?" Christian asked.

Dean leaned down and gave Ella another kiss. "A gentleman never kisses and tells."

"Well then, that shouldn't be a problem for you, should it?" I crooned.

He gave me the most endearing look. Heat crept up my neck and he looked away, chuckling.

Jerk.

With his jet-black faux-hawk, bright blue eyes, and gorgeous bad-boy looks, Dean was the most-wanted, hunk-a-dunk, sex-on-a-stick that strutted around school. Girls knew he was a heartbreaker, and yet they threw themselves at him. Some even claimed he was a sex god and being with him even for a night was worth the suffering.

And worst of all, he knew it. He knew how much he affected girls. Sometimes, I even thought he knew how much he affected me. I hated the fact that my heart fluttered when our eyes met, or when he smiled at me. Just like I hated how his touch sent a soothing sensation coursing over my skin.

As if.

I shivered. The hairs on the back of my neck stood on end and my stomach coiled tightly. A strong, pulsing presence prodded me deep in my core. Like the pull of a magnet, it called to an imprint on my soul. I searched the overpopulated area, looking for something—anything, really.

My gaze landed on a face I wasn't expecting. It was him—the boy from the café. His eyes shone a brilliant blue, like light reflecting against diamonds. But there was no smile, just a dark, smoldering stare that rose goosebumps across my arms.

What is he doing here?

"You need a rag to wipe off some of that drool, Pernell?" Dean asked.

"Shut up, douche." I turned to Pey and whispered, "What do you see over there?" I pointed toward the doors, hoping I'd imagined him.

Really. Really hoping.

A wicked grin formed on Pey's lips. "A damn hot, sexy hunk-a-meat, that's what. And he's heading our way."

"Crap."

I cleared my throat and counted to five, praying he would walk on by.

"Hi." My heart skipped a beat at the warm, hot-choco-late-on-a-cold-day voice. He was right behind me.

Filling my lungs with much needed air, I turned around. His mouth curled up on one side.

Holy lips, Batman!

Black cargo shorts, skater shoes, and a leather cuff watch had never looked hotter. His gray skull t-shirt hugged his toned body, showing just enough to tease.

Clean up on Aisle Three. Customer slipped in her own drool.

I cleared my throat again, feeling heat pool in my cheeks as I stood on wobbling knees. Seriously? Wobbling knees? "H-hi."

"Hi," he repeated. His blue eyes stared back at me, a faint smile on his lips.

My heart hammered against my chest as butterflies danced around in the pit of my stomach. *What the hell is wrong with me? I'm never the one to drool over a boy. Like never! And over a stranger? It must be the carrots. Yup. Definitely the carrots.*

"Where are *my* manners? I'm Pey, Ren's best friend. And you would be . . . ?" Pey asked in her welcoming-yet-protective voice.

I glared at her, hoping to burn her alive. Who needed a nose-butting best friend anyway?

Blue-eyes chuckled. "I'm Axel Knight."

Axel. Interesting name.

"*Sooo*," Pey drawled. "How do you know each other?" She arched her eyebrow with suspicion.

I chucked a napkin at her and turned to Axel, placing myself between them.

"What are you doing here?" Okay, that came out accusatory. So *not* what I meant.

Axel reached out, tucking a loose strand of hair behind my ear. I stared at him, my head spinning. That should have been creepy. It wasn't like we knew each other . . . did we? Maybe I'd met him before? He flashed a knowing, crooked grin. The type of grin that said he knew my secrets—even the ones I didn't know.

Hell . . . did I know him and just . . . forgot?

He walked around me and pulled out my chair, gesturing for me to have a seat. It didn't go unnoticed that he hadn't answered my question. I slid back into the seat, and threw a quick glance at Pey. Axel pulled a chair close to me—*very* close to me—and sat. My skin prickled at his nearness.

"I see you guys have met my boy Axel, here?" Tyler said, walking to our table, dragging a chair behind him. "He just moved in with my family to finish high school." There was something mischievous in Tyler's explanation. Like he was making fun of Axel.

"Dude. Don't ever call me 'your boy,'" Axel responded, elbowing him in the gut—a small, blue spark appeared on impact.

What the . . . ? I squeezed my eyes shut, then peered up at Tyler, wanting to know if he'd felt it. If he had, he didn't show it. He continued like nothing had happened.

"Yeah, sure thing, bro." Tyler chuckled, patting Axel's shoulder.

Everyone soon fell into easy conversations about Lacrosse, homework, and school gossip. I continued stealing glances at Axel, wanting to catch whatever it was I'd seen earlier again. Maybe it had been my imagination. But something in the back of my mind told me otherwise. It wasn't until Dean's questioning eyes lingered on me that I stopped obsessing. I shook my head before averting my gaze.

"I didn't know you were friends with Tyler." Axel's warm breath teased my ear as he spoke softly.

"Hmm?" I turned to face him and my nose slid against his chin. My heart raced with excitement. I dragged my gaze up, locking on his unnaturally blue eyes. Was I imagining the twinkling they emitted, or was it really there?

"Let's go!" Pey grabbed me by the elbow, pulling me to a standing position as she scooped up her cherry soda with her other hand. "We don't want to be late to Mrs. Older-than-dirt's class."

With an apologetic look toward Axel, I followed Pey out of the cafeteria. As usual, we took the long route to Ms. Crowne's Great Books class, pausing at our lockers, and then stopping by the bathroom before heading toward C Hall in silence. I started to think that maybe this was one of those times she wouldn't butt in, but I was wrong.

"Spill." She pinched her nose and crinkled her brows, trying to look pissed as she handed me the soda. I knew her curiosity was killing her, though.

"I don't want to risk detention for violating school property," I teased, batting my eyes innocently while I slurped the last of the soda.

"Ha! Nice try. I'd risk expulsion for some juicy details. Tell me how you know that sexy piece of meat before I get us both detentions."

I sighed heavily. "They'd be worthless detentions, because I have nothing to share," I insisted.

"I wasn't born yesterday, dork. Your stupid grin says otherwise."

I was grinning? I chewed on my lower lip, biting back a smile as we rounded the corner to our class. That same pulling sensation I'd felt in the cafeteria hit me like cool air on a hot summer day, raising goosebumps over my skin. Everything zeroed in on that summons and I scanned the room, searching for the source. The only thing out of place was Axel, sitting in the middle of the RHHS do-gooders, a shy smile lapping over his lips.

An irrational pang of jealousy consumed me. Not even a day and he fit in perfectly. I forced myself to ignore him as I took my seat, thankful for the two rows and three chairs separating us.

"Nothing to tell, my ass," Pey muttered under her breath, so that only I could hear. "If you don't want to tell me you guys hooked up, that's cool. Wait! No. That's *not* cool."

"What are you talking about?" I was genuinely confused.

She gave me her infamous, I'm-your-best-friend-don't-bullshit-me look. "You serious?" She lowered her voice and leaned into my space. "He left the café a few minutes after you did! Remember? The day Dean flirted with you and we all thought an apocalypse had started?" She raised her eyebrows. "You didn't know?"

I shook my head. "Do I seriously look like I know what the hell you're talking about?"

She shrugged and straightened in her seat. "I just assumed you two were hooking up since his friends stayed behind. I even saw him head in the same direction you did."

What the hell? I looked over my shoulder and caught him staring back, a confused smile on his face. I slowly brought my hand up, waved hello, and looked away, bouncing my left leg nervously. Had he really followed me?

My skin prickled with the same need I'd felt earlier, that same pull, but stronger.

Someone slid into the empty seat behind me. I didn't need to look back to know who it was. *What is it about this boy . . . ?*

"So . . . I did something to offend you." It wasn't a question.

I looked over my shoulder. Axel hunched forward to get closer to me. "No . . ."

"Then, I must smell awful," he said, taking a whiff from under his shirt collar.

I tried not to smile, but the corners of my lips twitched anyway.

"Aha! We have a smile," he teased. "A smile that beautiful should never be hidden."

My gaze flickered toward the parade of girls he'd been surrounded with seconds ago, and who were now shooting daggers my way.

"I think your *friends* miss you," I said, not bothering to hide my distaste.

"I'm exactly where I want to be," he answered. A range of emotions passed through his eyes. They felt deep, soulful, and familiar. Strangely like Dean's. In fact, they were so much like Dean's it was unsettling.

I glanced at Pey. She winked, a smile plastered over her face. "You okay there, Rey-Rey?"

"Peachy," I gritted between clenched teeth.

Pey snickered, her eyes twinkling. Behind her, I saw Rachel roll her eyes, a sneer twisting her features.

"Slut," Rachel coughed into her hand.

Pey shot up from her seat. I grabbed at her elbow, while Landon wrapped his arm around her waist. "Says the girl that spreads her legs wider than the state of Texas."

Rachel gasped. "You bitch!"

"Wow, your vocabulary amazes me. Is that what they're teaching at Sluts-R-Us these days?" Pey said.

Rachel squealed something indecipherable and lunged. But, somehow, Axel was quicker. He darted between us, his hand extended squarely into Rachel's chest, stopping her dead on her feet. At first, I thought he'd jumped at the opportunity for a boob grab, but after squinting, I realized that assessment couldn't be more wrong. Axel's hand wasn't touching her chest. It hovered inches from her body, a faint blue light flickering around his palm, holding her at bay. That couldn't be right. It was impossible. I squeezed my eyes shut, and then stared at him, willing him to look at me.

He didn't.

In my peripheral view, I caught a glimpse of Rachel's friends grabbing her and pulling her back. Axel's hand dropped to his side.

Ms. Crowne chose right then to walk into class, her monotonic voice carrying through the tension-filled room. "Settle down, children."

We hurried to take a seat before she started handing out detention slips like Halloween candy.

My phone buzzed in my back pocket.

Pey: U GUYS R NOT HOOKING UP?

I rolled my eyes. Seriously? After her near cat-fight with Rachel, she wanted to talk about Axel? I discreetly texted back.

Me: I PRMS U'D B 1ST TO KNOW.

Pey: HAVE U KISSED?

Me: I'D NEED TO DATE HIM TO KISS HIM.

Pey: SOOO NOT TRUE! U KISSED DEAN & U WEREN'T GOING OUT.

Me: LOOK HOW THAT TURNED OUT!

"Ladies, I have a strict 'no cell phone' policy," Ms. Crowne said. How did she do that? She must have been a super spy in her previous life. "On second thought, keep using them. I'm running low on supplies."

"You planning to sell those on eBay, Ms. C?" Hunter asked, snickering.

"Craigslist, Mr. Tucker," she said, leaving half the class's mouths hanging wide.

With a triumphant smile, she turned her back and continued writing, the chalk protesting against the board.

"Now. Your next book," she said, passing a couple books to each row, "is *Lord of the Flies*. Pick three of your classmates to reenact a scene of your choice. Due next Friday."

A collective round of groans erupted.

"I could add a five-page paper for your enthusiasm," she responded.

The next forty-five minutes moved at a snail's pace. When the bell finally rang, I quickly gathered my books and bolted for the door. But before I could manage a clean getaway, Axel called my name.

I stopped and pivoted around, Pey stuck to my hip like glue. I swear, sometimes she's more interested in my boring life than her own. Something about me not falling in the deep end like I did last year.

I felt that strange, pulling sensation coil in my stomach, growing stronger the closer Axel came. I tightened my grip on my books. He stopped before me, glancing to Pey, Landon, then finally to me. He looked unsure.

"I was wondering . . ." His eyes flickered to our audience. "D-Do you have any plans this Friday?"

Pey giggled and her elbow poked me in the kidney. I swatted at her, telling her to *back-off*. "I don't plan that far ahead, Axel. No teenager does. You should try it sometime. Spontaneity."

The corner of his eyes crinkled in amusement. "I'll plan for spontaneity the following weekend, then." He laughed. The next set of words rolled off him like a wave of warm honey. "But for this Friday, if you wouldn't mind, I'd like to take you out for coffee or something. 'Something' being the spontaneity."

My breath hitched. I tilted my head to the side and trailed my eyes up to meet his. They were glowing bright blue.

There it was again. How could no one notice? I couldn't be the only one, could I? Maybe I'd be able to pry some information from him if I got him alone. "Yeah, I'd like that."

"Great," he replied, obviously pleased with himself.

I smiled.

CHAPTER THREE

"I can't believe you bailed on me last night." Pey hooked her arm in mine, looking giddy. "You'll never guess what happened yesterday, after school."

"Um . . . you won the lottery?"

"Nope."

"Landon proposed?" I grinned, knowing that was her heart's desire. How many nights had we spent talking about her future wedding with Landon? Too many.

"I wish. But one—" She stopped, turning to me and flashing a crooked smile. "Ingenious. You know, I underestimated your slyfulness."

"Really? Slyfulness?"

She rolled her eyes. "You remember Jax?"

I nodded, not wanting to know where this was going.

"I think he's into you. Like, *really* into you."

"Pey . . ."

"No, listen. He wanted to know if you had a boyfriend, and if you were going to the fall dance with anyone."

"Ah, crap. I was hoping he'd given up." I looked at her, doubtful. "You told him I don't date, right? That I'm *not* going to the dance?"

"What kind of best friend do you think I am? Of course I did. I've got your back." We were almost to the cafeteria. "But I don't think he knows what 'no' or '*reeee*-jected' means. So I just wanted to give you fair warning."

She nudged me in the ribs and jerked her chin to the middle of the cafeteria.

"What?" I asked, annoyed—not at her, but at the whole Jax situation.

She pointed. Both Axel and Dean were looking our way. Dean winked as he played with Ella's hair.

Axel had an endearing look coloring his features, and I couldn't help but be drawn to him. Heat pooled in my cheeks. I inhaled a steadying breath, commanding my heart to slow down. He smiled like he knew how much he affected me.

"You should go back to sweats, like last year, if you want to stay unnoticed. I think guys are starting to take note, and you know how they think . . ." She wiggled her eyebrows. "With their di—"

I cut her off, shaking my head. "No shame, Pey. No shame."

She chuckled.

Last year was miserable, and I had no intention of going back to that.

Closing in on our usual lunch table, I took a seat across from Axel, next to Tyler. Pey made herself comfortable on Landon's lap, wrapping around him like a boa constrictor before diving in for a tonsil check.

"I swear, one of these days I'm going to disown you as my friends." I crinkled my nose. "Hope it's worth your PDA," I added, smiling politely.

"You know, Ren, if you're feeling left out, I could help," Tyler responded, with a toothy grin.

I huffed out a laugh. *Is he being serious?*

"Tyler," Axel warned.

I opened my mouth to say something like, "*I can take care of myself,*" but when my eyes connected with Axel's, I found a gleam of possessiveness. My heart fluttered like a caged bird trying to escape.

"She doesn't date, Tyler. You're out of luck." Landon's voice snapped me back to reality. *Date? Luck? What?* I glanced around the table, finally landing on Tyler. *Right.* His eyes twinkled with mischief and his lips twisted in an evil grin. He looked pleased that I was squirming under his scrutiny. *Uncomfortably* squirming.

"You know . . ." Tyler's lips flattened and he moved his mouth closer to my ear. "Making out with a non-datable girl is a complete turn-on."

"Argh . . ." I backhanded him in the chest, making him gasp for air. And I refused to apologize.

"I'd never hook up with you, even if you were the last living guy on earth," I said, immediately regretting my choice of words and completely grateful when the topic changed.

"Are we all in for the senior party Friday night?" Ella asked. "I heard it's going to be epic. Christian's parents are out of town, and . . . he has plans, if you know what I mean." She looked at Dean, licking her lips suggestively.

Axel eyed me. "Do you want to go?"

"Of course she does," Pey answered, the same time I responded with: "No."

Pey turned her puppy-dog eyes on me. "Come on, we've been talking about this, like, well . . . forever."

My gaze landed on Axel. He'd asked me out for the same Friday night. "I can't . . . ?" I waited for him to take the lead.

"Oh!" Pey exclaimed, like the light bulb had finally gone off. "Axel is more than welcome to join us. I mean, he's officially a senior."

I looked at him, willing him to say no. I wanted a chance to grill him and Pey was costing me that alone time.

Instead, he said, "Sure. Maybe we can go somewhere before?"

That idea cheered me up instantly, spreading a smile across my face.

Pey leaned in and whispered, "Now that Axel's going, you should have no problem, right?"

I glanced up to find Axel staring back, a playful smile on his mouth, his cheeks a bit flushed. My nerves jumped at his reaction.

There was something about him that had me confused, knotted, and all-out attracted to him. But what drew me most was the mystery that only I noticed.

†

Before heading home, I made a stop at my locker to exchange my books for the day. When I popped the door open, a note fell out.

Honey.

A smile crept onto my face. I knew exactly who the note came from. I shook my head, approaching Axel's locker, located in the last row at the end of the hall. Tearing a piece of paper from one of my notebooks, I scribbled my response.

You hate honey? I so *don't know you.*

I drew an elaborate sad face, including hair and ears and a few tear drops. Then I gave him a bit about myself:

Project Bandaloop. Marie.

I stood on my tippy-toes and pushed the note into his locker, hearing it hit the metal bottom with a soft *clink*. I smiled, unable to hold back. I didn't understand this over-whelming attraction to a boy I'd just met, but one thing was sure: I was finding him more irresistible by the day.

†

At around 8:30 that night, my phone rang. Pushing my homework off my lap, I rummaged through my book bag, making a mental note to find a better place for it than the bottomless pit.

"Hello?" I said, a little out of breath.

"Is this a bad time?" I recognized the voice immediately. My heart hit the walls of my chest with a screeching halt.

"How did you get my number?" *Stupid, stupid. He calls you, and that's what you want to know?*

Axel chuckled. "I paid a huge price to get it."

"What kind of price?" I couldn't keep my grin from col-oring my voice.

"I traded my soul to the devil."

"The devil, huh?" I teased. "That's a hefty price to pay for a girl's number."

"Some numbers are worth it. But yeah, don't ever trade with Tyler. He's one tough S.O.B."

I laughed. "I'm glad you called." My voice sounded for-eign to me—heavy and soft.

He paused. "I wanted to hear your voice."

The muscles in my stomach clenched in response. *Damn the butterflies.* "I got your note."

"I thought I'd share something about myself." I heard his unsaid words: *your turn.*

"You call one-word sentences sharing? I don't know if you like honey or hate it, or if you're the beekeeper." I heard him laugh. "So, I assumed the worst."

"And what was that?"

"You're a bee-killing honey-hater." I lay back on the bed, pushing my homework further away. No point in trying to work on it now.

"A *beautiful* girl like you shouldn't concentrate on such strong, hate-filled words."

He called me beautiful!

"That's what you get for leaving me with so little information." My voice came out flirty. I didn't do flirty.

"Well, for your information, I love honey and practically eat it with everything." I heard a smile in his voice.

"Good to know, Mr. Knight." The wind chimes by my window played a soothing melody.

"How are you?"

Should I tell him about Jax? "Do you know Jax Winholm?" *Damn it, mouth. I was still contemplating.*

"Yeah?" He sounded annoyed. "What did he do?"

"He's stalking me through my friends, wanting to take me out on a date."

"What did you say?" he asked, his voice guarded.

"He'd need to ask me for me to answer."

"W-What would you have said?" Was he actually nervous?

"What would *you* have wanted me to say?" I countered, feeling braver, daring even. I pulled a strand of hair from my messy heap-of-a-bun and started twirling it with my index finger. My heart squeezed with anxiety, waiting to hear his response. *Did he want me to say yes? God, I hope not. Not when he'd asked me to get "coffee or something."*

"I can take care of him," Axel said after a pause, "if he's a bother."

Well, damn. That wasn't what I wanted to hear.

I laughed, disappointed. "You sound like you belong to some sort of Mafia or gang."

He was quiet for a couple seconds.

Did he? I shook my head, feeling stupid at that thought. Axel looked too soft to be anything but a romantic. Sure, he had an unbelievably gorgeous body, and the way he carried himself spoke of confidence, but he wasn't a fighter. Not with the innocence that was radiating off him in tidal waves. He *had* to be more lover than fighter.

"I can't wait to take you out tomorrow night."

"You going to share your plans, or still going to try the whole spontaneity thing?"

The warmth from his laugh radiated through the phone, spreading a bunch of cartwheels in the pit of my stomach.

"I think I'll try it out a little longer," he said.

We made plans for him to pick me up around five p.m., so that we had enough time to do something before heading to Christian's party. I had to give it to him, he did hold on to the details of what we'd be doing pretty well. But I got one hint: "*Dress comfortably.*"

After that, we ended up talking through the night. I learned about him being home-schooled for most of his life, and how he'd come out here to spread his wings. He told me about how close Tyler and he had been growing up, and how, when the opportunity presented itself, he couldn't help but jump at the chance to move, especially when he'd seen me at the café.

I laughed at that. Sure! I totally didn't believe he'd wanted to transfer schools his senior year because of me.

It was surreal hearing him speak. I didn't want him to stop. There were so many things I wanted to know—like what the blue aura I saw was—but I figured this wasn't the right time. I didn't want to scare the cute boy by admitting I saw things no one else did.

Soon, my eyelids drooped and I was ready to doze off, but I fought to stay awake. I didn't want the night to end.

"*Meus Aeternus* . . . you awake?"

His voice . . . felt like a dream.

"Mhmm . . ."

"You need your sleep."

I mumbled something incoherent.

"I'll see you tomorrow. Sweet dreams, *Meus Aeternus.*"

"Mhmm . . ."

Then sleep dragged me under its spell.

CHAPTER FOUR

I WASN'T SURPRISED WHEN I WOKE THE FOLLOWING MORNING IN a puddle of drool. Gross, but expected since I'd fallen asleep slouched against the headboard of my bed. But despite only four hours of sleep, I felt wide-awake. A stupid grin spread across my face as I hopped out of bed and headed for the shower. In an hour and a half, I'd be gazing on a certain someone.

The grin stayed all through breakfast, my commute to school, and even as I walked to my locker. When I finally saw Axel though, it turned into a timid smile. We didn't have time to talk, so we waved shyly and headed to class.

Throughout the day, we glanced at each other, letting our eyes speak what our lips didn't.

After the final bell, I opened my locker and found another note.

Project Bandaloop? I knew you were my angel, Temperance Marie Pernell. Harnesses, flying, dancing. Sounds so . . .

I rolled my eyes.

April 12th, 7:38 p.m. Eros. Can't wait to see you tonight.

I really didn't know what to make of the first clue. His birth date and time? His first kiss? Or worse, the day he lost his virginity? *God, please don't let it be the last one.* Just the thought of him with another girl rubbed me the wrong way.

Folding the note, I carefully placed it in my backpack. Since I was going to see him in less than two hours, I didn't bother leaving a response.

I made it home twenty minutes after school and went for a run, music plugged into my ears. I needed to clear my head and give the anxious energy fluttering in my chest somewhere to go.

After a long, hot shower, I got ready, going through outfit after outfit, finally settling on something truly comfortable—a pink lace, off-the-shoulder top over a white cami, cut-off jean shorts and brown, calf-high boots. It screamed fun and flirty.

I applied the final touches to my makeup and peeked at my phone. 4:45. Axel would be showing up soon.

Fifteen minutes passed.

Then ten.

And then another fifteen.

Maybe he'd gotten stuck in traffic? I picked up the worn-out copy of Anne Frank's *The Diary of a Young Girl* from my nightstand. Flopping onto my cushioned windowsill, I fought the urge to call or text him and tried to read.

Instead, I found myself looking at my phone more than I wanted, wondering what could have happened, why he didn't call.

An hour and a half later, my phone finally chimed. I let out a deep breath, hoping against hope the message was from him.

Pey: Don't bail on me tonight or I'll hunt you down!

I smiled through my disappointment.

Even though I felt humiliated, I couldn't hide in my room. Why should I sulk over some guy I'd *thought* was different? I should have known he wasn't.

But no matter the excuses I gave myself, I knew the truth . . . the *real* truth.

Axel did something to me that no one else could. He made my heart race, my palms sweat, and my lips tremble with longing. He made me feel vulnerable and weak. The first boy to make me feel anything since Dean, four years ago.

And just like I did then, I felt stupid for falling for it. Again.

I wasn't going to let it ruin the rest of my night, though. I would go to Christian's party, and I'd forget all about Axel What's-his-face.

†

This is either humiliating or incomprehensibly humiliating.

I should've known better. Sitting in a circle with an assortment of horny teenagers never ended on a positive note.

My instincts, which I'd candidly ignored, had told me that much. Yet here I was, in the middle of a staggered circle, secluded among an eager group of waiting teenagers. I looked around, searching the crowd of bodies swaying to the pounding music.

Everyone was having fun. Except me.

I caught a glimpse of Pey straddling Landon, laughing and whispering in his ear. Her eyes twinkled jovially when she caught me staring. I glared back at her. She winked and looked pointedly at the boy sitting in front of me, his hand on my knee, waiting for me to make my decision.

"This is your lucky day, Pernell." Dean's voice purred with mischief.

"Give him a big, wet kiss, tongue and all."

"Shut up, Hunter!" I growled.

"Rules are rules," Serena said.

I looked up to see her lips twitching in annoyance. Seriously. I was the one who had to kiss him. She could wait a few seconds for her turn to play.

"It's fate, babe. Just kiss and get it over with," Pey called.

Fate, my ass. Easy for her to say. She wasn't about to kiss the douchebag. I was.

I'd naively thought Truth or Dare would be an easy game, that I had control over my emotions. But Dean had found my weakness. I never backed down from a challenge, and he'd easily provoked me into accepting a dare.

"Afraid you might fall madly, *irrevocably* in love with me?" Dean smirked. "I wouldn't blame you if you did."

I scoffed.

I knew this was just a game to him, the conquest of another girl. But to me, it was a gesture of something intimate, something that expressed your heart's desires. To say I was *pissed* would be the understatement of the century. I shot angry daggers at him, wishing one of them would hit him square in the eye, blinding him.

"Don't make me beg, Pernell."

I don't know what came over me. Maybe it was the frustration and pain from being stood up, or maybe it was the amount of alcohol in my system, but either way, I made up my mind: there was no way I was going to let this self-loving, arrogant, insignificant ass win.

I licked my lips, shoving my nerves aside.

Dean scooted closer. He must have guessed my choice. He cupped his hand around the back of my neck and pulled my lips to his with force.

I closed my eyes, feeling his warm lips move against mine—slowly, tenderly—exploring the bottom, then the top. He was gentle, and it left me wanting more.

Warmth seeped through me, all the way to my toes, making me light-headed. I'd never been kissed like this. He tenderly nibbled at my bottom lip, tilting my head in a plea to open for him.

I wanted to push him away, reject his advances. Because, deep down, I knew it wasn't really Dean's kiss I wanted. I wanted another blue-eyed boy who'd stomped all over my heart.

Axel stood you up! Dean is here and willing. Live a little. For once.

I scooted closer to him, kneeling between his legs, cupping my hands on either side of his face. He pulled me against him, placing his hands at the hem of my cami as he urged for access. He parted my lips and let out a throaty groan, his grip growing firmer, pulling me onto his lap.

Never in a million years did I think I would kiss him back. But I did. My heart beat faster as *I* deepened the kiss. He moaned. He was no longer gentle, and I was in control.

It felt dangerous. My insides ignited, leaving my body ablaze. His greediness woke something deep within me. His hands, my hands—they had no boundaries.

He gripped my waist tighter, making me quiver under his possessive touch. His lips curved against mine. I threw my arms around him, my fingers vigorously working through his hair. I tilted my face to give him better access to my mouth.

Nothing was enough. I could feel something inside me wanting to get closer to him, pulling and tying us together. I didn't understand. I couldn't. It didn't make sense.

He growled, biting and nipping at my lip, and blood rushed to my ears. I heard someone whistle and hoot from far away. I didn't care. I wanted him. I craved his touch, his kiss. I wanted everything from him, and it scared the hell out of me.

After a few more dazed seconds, I pulled back, confused. Our foreheads touched as we struggled to breathe, my chest flush against his, my eyes still closed. My head swam with incoherent thoughts. I wanted to kiss him again, so I leaned toward him, biting my lip. He met me for a feather-light kiss.

"I missed you," he whispered against my mouth. My heart skipped a beat. "Tell me you did, too." His voice was hoarse, deep.

Shocked, I opened my eyes. The whispers around us were growing louder. We'd just provided a full month's worth of gossip.

Son of a—

I pushed him and fell back on my butt. Dean's face flushed as a lascivious smile crossed it. He laughed, his head falling back. I scrambled backward before shooting to my feet.

"Dean's finally met his match," Hunter said with a howl of laughter.

I ran until I was outside, gulping in the fresh air. What the hell was I *doing*? Everything inside me buzzed. I felt so alive and . . . something. I didn't know how to define it. Dean was the only boy I'd ever kissed, and it had been nothing like that the last time. The intensity, the need. . . I didn't understand.

My throat constricted and I dry heaved with breaths that didn't reach my lungs. It was the summer before ninth grade all over again, and I'd fallen for it. Again!

Stupid. Stupid. Stupid.

"Holy preggers, woman." Pey walked through the front door, her face beaming. "What was that?" she asked, handing me my jacket.

I counted: *One, two, inhale. One, two, exhale.* "Thanks."

"Yeah, no prob." She eyed me suspiciously for a few seconds. "That was some kiss. Epic."

"Well, I didn't really have much of a choice, did I?" I said, my breathing returning to normal.

She laughed. "That was intense. If I didn't know *you*, I would've believed you guys were having sex right there, in the middle of the room."

"What? I wasn't . . ." My fingers went to my swollen lips. "Shit."

Pey put her arms around my waist. "No shit! I knew he had the hots for you."

"I need to go into the witness protection program. I'll never live this down." I groaned with a hand to my face.

She chuckled. "How about I take you home?"

"I will pay you a million bucks and do your chores for a month if you get me the hell out of here."

Pey bumped my hip. "Okay, I'm gonna hold you to that. Give me a sec."

She ran back inside, disappearing into the gyrating bodies. My thoughts wandered to how I'd reacted to Dean's lips as I caressed my swollen mouth. I shook my head and told myself it couldn't happen again. I couldn't let my feelings and frustration with Axel confuse me—if that's what it had been. That was the only thing that made sense, though. I was never this drawn to Dean. Sure, I'd had a crush on him and thought he was super attractive. I mean, anyone with a set of eyes would think the same. But it was never more than an innocent crush. That kiss . . . it was like I'd been high on hormones. Maybe it was all the coiled up feelings for Axel?

Eww . . . I really hoped I hadn't just kissed Dean that way because of Axel.

"Let's go." Pey's voice pulled me back to reality. "Just had to let Landon know I'm going home with you."

"That is the last party I'm ever going to," I said.

She laughed and hooked her arm through mine as we walked toward her car.

CHAPTER FIVE

"**W**HAT MISSING PEOPLE?" I ASKED, SURPRISED. THIS WAS THE first I'd heard about it.

"People from Salt Lake, Portland, and some smaller cities." Pey's eyes widened, and her voice turned low and spooky. "Some have even turned up dead. They think a serial killer's at work."

"That's freaky. And so close to home." I shivered, thinking about it.

"Oh, and did you hear about the old sugar factory in Nampa blowing up a couple nights ago?"

I shook my head, intrigued.

"Apparently, they found dead bodies mutilated by knives."

I rolled my eyes. "Well, aren't you just the bearer of morbid news today?"

"Believe it or not, the world is full of crazies." She shrugged.

"No. Really?" I gasped.

"Admit it, without me, how would you ever survive?"

"By living life in simplicity."

"What the hell does that mean?"

I heard a girl's voice squeaking with excitement and shushed Pey.

"It's going to be awesome. You can be my king, and I can be your queen . . ."

Warm, familiar tingles rose along the back of my neck. We rounded the corner to the hallway and the blood drained from my face.

"I'll make it worth your night. I can ride your *Dulcea*," Rachel finished. She stood with one leg between Axel's, her upper body super-glued to his chest as her manicured nails trailed down his arm suggestively. His hands were planted on her hips. My heart cracked open, slowly bleeding what little hope I'd had left from the night before.

"What the hell . . . ?" Pey stopped mid-sentence. "That bitch!" she gasped, taking in the scene in front of us as I backed away, turning.

My eyes stung as I ran in the opposite direction. I could feel Axel's gaze burning a hole in my back, but I didn't stop. I refused to let him see me cry. He'd humiliated me enough already.

I snuck into the nearest bathroom and stayed there, feeling like a complete idiot.

My phone rang. I ignored it . . . and the next dozen or so calls.

Why was I letting him have such power over my emotions? We weren't together. He was free to be with anyone. But all I could see was him standing there with Rachel. Had he ditched me to be with her? Good God! Did he sleep with her?

My mind wanted to make excuses, but I couldn't fool myself. He'd never shown me *that* kind of interest, apart from the innocent flirting we'd both done. Sure, we'd talked and shared information, and I'd stupidly thought we'd had an incredible connection. But maybe he'd just befriended me to make Rachel jealous. And now that he had her, I was nothing to him.

Oh. My. God. I slapped my hand over my face. How stupid could I have been?

"Ren, babe. I know you're here," Pey said, standing in front of the stall I sat in. "I can hear you sniffling."

I stilled.

"Argh! You're going to be sorry . . ."—she grunted as she crawled under the stall door— "because I'm going to hug you now."

She held me in silence, stroking my hair.

†

That night, I received another call from *him*, shattering my will to do homework. I gave up reading *A Tale of Two Cities* for my Great Books class and went to the roof outside my window. It was a cool September night, but not too cold. I saw Dean looking at me from his bedroom, talking on the phone. He gave me a small wave. I returned the gesture.

I lay back and tried to relax. I concentrated on the coyotes howling in the distance, pushing aside thoughts of Axel and Rachel. A slight breeze tickled my skin. The fresh smell of wood and late-blooming flowers filled my lungs as I took in a much-needed deep breath.

"Well, aren't you the happiest chipmunk in the world?"

My eyes snapped open and I glared at an upside-down Dean. He held a square box in one hand and two soda cans in the other. "How did you get in?"

"Your brother. He agreed that you needed to be slapped out of your misery." He winked.

Argh! "Go away, Dean."

"Then who's going to eat this extra-large Hawaiian pizza, and drink all this Crush?" he asked, climbing through my window onto the rooftop.

"Does it have ham and pineapple?" I asked, my mouth watering. My stomach growled in response.

He scoffed. "What kind of idiot makes Hawaiian pizza without those two things?"

I sat up, rolling my eyes, as he stared expectantly.

"What do you want, Dean?" I wasn't in the mood to play his games tonight. He was only nice when he wanted something.

"What? Can't I come to see how you're doing?"

I raised my eyebrow at him. *Really? Do you want me to answer that?*

"I know I haven't been much of a friend . . ."

I huffed a laugh.

"All right, fine. I've been a complete sadistic ass of a friend. Happy?" He shrugged.

"Very," I said, smirking.

He sat beside me. "But I'm here for you, Pernell. I don't like seeing you like this." He smiled. "Okay, all this emotional crap is bringing me down. Pizza?"

I happily took a slice. We were both quiet for a few minutes, enjoying the cheesy, chewy pizza. I took a big bite. Dean cocked his eyebrow and took a bigger bite. I took another one, bigger than his, almost choking myself. He laughed, falling backward.

"You're such a sucker for challenges."

"Shut up!" I said playfully, shoving him.

"Oh, you're gonna get it now."

Before I knew it, we were a tangle of limbs and laughs, not knowing where one started and the other ended. Dean lay on top of me, looking directly into my eyes, his expression stoic. He studied me for a few seconds, glancing to my lips and back up. He shifted his weight as he reached up to push a strand of hair behind my ear, brushing the back of his hand against my cheek and down my jaw.

Blood pounded in my ears. My heart raced, thumping erratically against my chest as I remembered our last kiss. I bit my lip as he leaned down closer . . .

And closer . . .

And closer.

I cleared my throat before I lost control of the situation. He stilled, a mere heartbeat away, and his breath playfully brushed against my lips. His mouth curved shyly as he pulled me to a sitting position with him.

What was going on between us? Every time we touched, something stirred inside me, nudging me to follow his lead.

"Remember that year you had a huge crush on Mr. Bean?" he asked, breaking the silence.

"Yeah. I think that was the same year you were drooling over Wonder Woman," I said, remembering the posters all over his room.

"Yeah." A dazed look crossed his face. "I would so do her. She's hot and, God help me, if I'd known the things I know now about womanly curves . . ."

"Eww, Dean." I gave him a playful punch. "Is that all you think about?"

He shrugged his shoulders. "I've got a Y in my DNA."

It felt natural sitting beside him, eating pizza. All too familiar. But everything was different. He'd changed. He looked so much older—stronger and confident.

"Dean . . ." I waited for him to respond.

"Mmmhmm."

"About that kiss . . ."

"It was just a game," he responded, looking away, the muscles in his jaw twitching.

Even though I felt the same way, hearing him admit it made my heart clench. *Could I be any more hypocritical?* Or, maybe I just didn't know how to handle *two* rejections.

After that, we didn't talk much, but I was glad to have some company. We ate the pizza in silence, listening to the crickets and occasional coyote. When I ran out of soda, he offered me some of his. I accepted, just like old times.

Then, out of nowhere, he wrapped his arm around my shoulder, pulling me closer to him.

"I meant what I said before, about missing you." He gave me a gentle squeeze.

I laid my head on his shoulder, taking another bite of my pizza. He dropped a chaste kiss on my forehead.

That strange, magnetic pull stirred in the pit of my stomach, making me shiver. There was only one person that made me feel that way. I moved away from Dean and searched the surrounding darkness.

My gaze darted across the street, combing the area of parked cars, then down both ends as far as I could see.

Nothing. It was too dark for me to make out anything or *anyone*. But I knew he was there . . . watching. My skin only prickled like that when *he* was around.

"You okay?" Dean asked.

"Yeah . . . yeah."

Disappointment nagged at me. I sagged back down to Dean's shoulder. Maybe it was just another of my stupid fantasies. Once again, my emotions had let me down.

Why would Axel care?

CHAPTER SIX

I WAS GOOD AT AVOIDING. AFTER MY PARENTS DIED, MY EMOTIONS had been so volatile that a thought, or a simple, *"you okay?"* were enough to set me off. The more I'd tried to control them, the worse it got. Evading human contact became my only saving grace.

I relied on that skill now, as I tried to steer clear of Axel. But it's hard to avoid someone when they're determined to get my attention. I didn't understand why he was being so damn persistent, since it was clear he'd gotten what he wanted, using me in the process.

But, thanks to him, Dean and I were close again, like the last four years hadn't happened and we'd always been best friends. Like we hadn't kissed twice, and I hadn't been rejected—twice.

We'd started hanging out at the arcade, the bowling alley, the movies, and several bonfires. I became his excuse when he wanted out of family activities, and he became my diversion.

But no matter what I did, or how hard I tried to distract myself, Axel was always on my mind. Mostly, I thought of ways I wanted to hurt him. But, if I was being honest with myself, I was also curious about the mystery behind the glowing hands and eyes.

I sighed and pushed my laptop aside. I walked to my window seat and pulled out my favorite book, intent on a relaxing read.

An enticing aroma floated into my room, interrupting my concentration. My stomach growled loudly. Setting the book down, I followed my nose toward the kitchen.

"Muskles?" I called.

"Out here, Killer."

I walked to the patio and gasped. Our backyard was lit up like the holidays. Tiki torches flickered, illuminating the yard with an inviting glow as music played in the background. Bowls of mouth-watering food in Mom's favorite china sat on top of red placemats, and tastefully decorated candles were scattered all around. Joshua, my usually unkempt brother-slash-guardian stood in a blue dress-shirt and faded jeans, grinning ear to ear with a white gardenia in his hand.

Gardenias were my mom's favorite flowers. She'd told us countless times about my father's marriage proposal in a garden full of white gardenias. He'd given her a gardenia ring in a magical gardenia flower. Heck, for as long as I could remember, she'd grown a garden that surrounded her with gardenias year-round.

When I'd asked her how she kept them alive all year, she'd smiled up at me, cupped my cheek with her hand, and said, "Magic." It was true. My mother had had a green thumb. I, on the other hand, killed one too many plants before she'd banned me from her greenhouse.

"All right, spill," I demanded as I skipped down the steps. I gave Joshua a quick kiss on the cheek.

"I felt bad for not being around much lately." He tucked the gardenia carefully behind my right ear. He then pulled out my chair and waited for me to have a seat.

"You gave up on your dreams to babysit me . . . you really have nothing to feel bad about," I replied softly.

He smiled, pushing my chair under the beautifully laid table. I served food onto our plates while he poured us drinks.

"Tonight, I wanted to celebrate and catch up." He handed me a glass and raised his own. "To us."

"To us," I repeated.

We ate our dinner, talking about everything that had happened over the past year, and I somewhat skimmed through my boy troubles.

"You know, I'd be more than happy to permanently stick my foot up someone's ass, if it'd help."

"I don't think that would work, seeing how you might need your foot to get around . . . and having it up someone's ass . . ."

We laughed and chatted until we could no longer ignore the crusted dishes in front of us. By the time everything had been cleaned and put away, the moon peeked through the clouds. Silence passed between us as we swung on the patio swing.

"I miss them." It was obvious to whom he referred.

"You want to go visit them tomorrow?"

"I'd like that," he responded.

"Hey, do you remember our neighbor's dog—the one that used to pee on your skateboard every time you left it outside—and how Mom kept saying you needed to start taking care of your possessions?" I asked, trying to lighten the mood.

He grunted, annoyed. "Yeah. I hated that mutt."

"Whatever happened to it?" I asked, out of curiosity. "The mutt, I mean."

"I have *no* idea." He emphasized the word "no" with a bit too much mischief.

"No!" I exclaimed, my hand over my mouth. "Did you, like, kill it or something?"

When he didn't answer, I poked him. "Muskles?"

He chuckled. "No, I just convinced the owner that if I ever caught that mutt near our house again, he and his dog would be fetching *their* missing balls."

"You didn't." I couldn't help but laugh, hard. I had tears in my eyes and my stomach hurt when we heard the doorbell.

"Were you expecting someone?" I asked Jóshua as I opened the front door, my laughter simmering to giggles.

Dean stood before me, his hand running through his hair, flashing his signature cocky grin.

"What are you doing here?" I asked as three more people walked up the stairs, talking and laughing.

"Who is it?" Joshua called from the kitchen.

"The Jensens," I yelled back. I hugged Cassie, Dean's sister. "What are you doing here so late?" Concern hit me like an edgy, creeping thief. "Is everything okay?"

I looked from Cassie to Dean to their parents.

"Everything's fine, Killer." Joshua walked into the room, grabbing Cassie in his arms and dipping her back for a dramatic, movie-star kiss.

"Eww," Dean and I said in unison as Joshua set a chuckling Cassie back on her feet.

"John, Sandy," Joshua said with a handshake and a hug. "Would you like something to drink?" he asked, heading back to the kitchen without waiting for an answer.

Oh, something's up all right.

Drawers and cabinets opened and shut with loud thuds. Silverware rattled and clanked. It sounded like pirates were taking over the kitchen.

"Would someone like to tell us what's going on?" Sandy asked, eyeing her daughter.

"That's my cue," Cassie said, pointing a finger in the air. She left the room and reappeared with Joshua and dessert a few minutes later.

Cheesecake, strawberries, and whipped cream. *Yum!*

"First, dessert," Cassie said. She and Joshua methodically handed out our succulent treat. They stood next to each other while we ate, holding hands and looking nervous, shifting from one leg to the other. As I neared my last bite, I noticed Joshua gently squeezing Cassie's hand.

"We have news," Cassie announced, looking at Joshua with a soft smile. "Joshua and I are getting married on New Year's Eve!" Her eyes glittered with excitement as the room burst into congratulatory voices. "In Nafplio, Greece."

Hugs and laughter filled the room, dessert forgotten.

"Dean, I'd be honored if you would be my wingman," Joshua said. Dean bumped Joshua's fist in acceptance.

Cassie looked at me. "And I want you to be my maid of honor."

Shaking off my stupor, I sprang out of my seat and jumped up and down, squealing like a five-year-old. "Yes, yes, yes, yes, yes . . ."

I hugged her, twirling her around as I hummed "Here Comes the Bride."

The rest of the night, our house was filled with music, laughter, dancing, and stories about Joshua and Cassie. They were perfect. A match made in heaven. With everything that Joshua and I had been through the past year and a half, this was exactly what he needed. What we *both* needed. My heart filled with joy.

A little past eleven p.m., I finally bid everyone goodnight and headed upstairs to my room.

CHAPTER SEVEN

"HEY."

I jumped, placing a hand over my racing heart. "Don't scare me like that."

Dean slouched against the doorway—at six-three, he fit perfectly—his hand nestled in his front pocket. He smiled, running his other hand through his messy hair.

Over the last few years, he'd certainly transformed . . . but his soft, blue eyes hadn't. They still drew me in with their familiar comfort.

He pushed away from the doorway, stepping into my room. "Not much changes in here, does it?"

My room wasn't girly by any means, but it was me. A full-sized bed, study desk, and loveseat occupied most of the space. To add color, I'd decorated with flowery designs in yellow and red, adding sky-blue accessories with lots of pillows. A homemade, wooden wind chime with blue crystals hung by the window, and several James Dean posters plastered the walls.

"I like consistency. I don't do well with change. You know that," I replied, turning back to my closet. "Now, if you don't mind, I'd like to shower and get to bed."

He walked over to the wind chime and gently ran his fingers through it. "You kept it."

He'd made the wind chime for my thirteenth birthday—the last gift I'd received from him.

"*It'll keep bad things away and remind you I'm here for you, always. Dean and Nellie, together—forever,*" he'd said, sweetly.

At the time, I'd thought it was the cutest thing any boy had ever said or done. Especially one I had a huge crush on. But a few months later, everything had changed between us.

Still, I hadn't been able to throw it away. It wasn't just part of my room; it was part of me. *He'd* always been part of me, no matter the distance between us.

I shrugged and continued to stare at my clothes with meticulous observation, wondering why he was acting so strange. He'd been in my room just last week . . .

"After all the bashing over the past four years, I didn't think you'd keep it."

"You know I don't hate you, Dean. I do, however, want to punch you in the face every time I see your stupid smirk . . ." I laughed. "But, since I'm not a violent person, I settled for verbal bashing instead."

When I turned around, giving up on the small talk, he was watching me. He nervously rubbed his temple and his brows creased. His entire person radiated apology—a look that didn't fit his features very well.

The next thing I knew, he'd closed the distance between us in two long strides, placing his hands over my cheeks and lifting my face so we were looking into each other's eyes. I didn't step back. His touch had always been soothing; there was no point in denying that I liked it.

"I've regretted one thing." Remorse poured from him, heavy and smothering. "If I could go back in time, I would redo that one moment. I don't know why I acted the way I did." He gave me a long, tortured blink. "I was a complete idiot to push you away. After that kiss, my *first* kiss—*our* first kiss—I freaked. I wanted to come back and apologize, beg you for forgiveness, but my ego . . ."

"So you thought if you made an ass out of me, you could feel better about yourself? How original."

His smile turned genuine. "There wasn't a single day I didn't regret it. I knew we were drifting apart. I knew I needed to do something. I wanted to, but I didn't know how . . ." He traced my cheek and jawline with his thumb.

"Well, men, on a basic level, are stupid. It's been scientifically proven . . ." My eyes locked with his—desire radiated from them in strong waves. My heart skipped a beat or two, and I let out a shaky breath.

Dean stared back at me, his eyes clouded and seductive. He leaned in, waiting for me to push him away. I placed my hands on his chest, unsure of my own wants and needs. I knew I shouldn't want this—not when my heart was so conflicted.

Before I knew what was happening, his mouth covered mine. He kissed my lower lip softly. Once. Twice. Three times. A range of flutters built in the pit of my stomach as his lips seared a path from my cheek to my neck. When I didn't push him back, he covered my mouth with his, kissing me with more urgency. He pushed my lips apart and his chest vibrated under my hand as he moaned slightly. He pulled me closer, between his legs.

My heart was screaming that this was wrong, but my body was responding to his touch. A strong, mysterious bond connected me to Dean, but it paled in comparison to the connection I'd felt with Axel. The way I'd been pulled toward Axel was unyielding, like I had no control. Like he was my gravity and I was his moon.

A wave of sadness washed over me. Axel was what I wanted, what I needed but couldn't have. I placed my hand over Dean's chest and fought every urge of my treasonous body.

"Stop. Please." I pulled back breathlessly.

Confusion dressed his features. His heart beat frantically against my palm. His eyes were clouded, his cheeks flushed. He looked painfully vulnerable . . . gorgeous.

I shook my head. "Dean . . . I-I can't." I pushed him harder, desperate for distance between us. "This isn't fair . . . to either of us."

A range of emotions crossed his face before a devilish smile settled. I knew that mask. It was the one I'd seen for the past four years. He took a few slow, deliberate steps back.

"Are you always this uptight?" he asked, running a thumb across his lips.

Argh! There it was—his need to be an arrogant ass. Another reason we'd never work. I'd never understand how he could switch from being such a caring person to being this selfish, egotistical asshat. I squared my shoulders and put on a brave face.

"You would've known if you'd stuck around," I spat and spun on my heels, facing away from him.

Dean and I were like a spark to gasoline. We could be beautiful from a distance, but together, we were disastrous.

"Look at me," he commanded, his voice laced with vulnerability.

God, he was worse than a girl PMSing. I turned to face him, my hands in fists. His features were soft and calm. He wrapped his arms around my waist, pulling me to him. "I'm sorry. I promise on my life, I'll never leave you again."

I wanted to scream. I was so sick of his hot-and-cold routine. I just wanted my best friend back, and wished everything else would disappear. But I couldn't form the words, so I didn't say anything. Instead, I wrapped my arms around his waist and placed my head on his chest.

He sighed.

CHAPTER EIGHT

I NEVER ONCE FELT LIKE I WAS TALKING TO A GRAVESTONE. IT felt real, like my parents were listening, watching, and comforting me. I knelt at their tombstone and noticed a fresh bouquet of gardenias. Joshua must have stopped by.

"Hi, Momma. Hi, Daddy."

A cold breeze passed through me. I wrapped my arms around my knees, pulling them to my chest.

"I miss you guys. A lot. Sorry I don't visit anymore." I paused, taking a deep breath. "Everyone's telling me I need to let go of this . . . talking to you instead of people. Living people."

I looked around the empty cemetery, noting the sky full of stars and the bright, full moon. I sat there, talking to them for about half an hour, telling them about my life—school, friends, Joshua—and my hobbies.

Unlike most kids my age, my relationship with my parents had been strong. I'd never shied away from spending time with them, nor had I discouraged them when they'd been in the stands, cheering or shouting profanities during my games. And on days when I'd needed reassurance, or a little push to continue moving forward, they'd always come through.

They'd been so much a part of my life that when I'd had sleepovers with Pey, my mom had joined in, watching movies and gushing about cute boys over extra-cheesy Hawaiian pizza.

Whenever I'd needed a good cry, or advice, she'd been there. I could still hear her words: "*No matter what choice you make, be true to yourself. That's all I'll ever expect from you. We'll always be proud of you, sweetheart.*"

My hand clenched around the amulet under my shirt. I pulled it from the fabric and fiddled with it between my fingers, remembering the day I'd turned six and my mom had put it around my neck.

"*What is this, Momma?*" *I asked.*

She knelt, a small smile curving the corners of her mouth. Her thumb ran over the face of the amulet.

"This is my gift to you, Ren. To remind you that, even if I'm not around, I'll always protect you." She kissed my forehead, pulling me into a hug, and then held me at arm's length. "Promise me one thing."

"Anything, Momma." I beamed, thrilled at the opportunity to make her happy.

"Don't ever leave home without this. Can you promise me that?"

I nodded, looking down at the present. "I promise, Momma. I'll never ever ever leave home without it."

She held up her pinky. "Pinky swear?"

"Pinky swear." I locked my pinky around hers and leaned down to kiss her cheek.

"I love you, Ren." She rubbed her nose against mine.

"Not as much as I love you!" I giggled as she started tickling me.

My stomach clenched painfully. My throat tightened, like thick fog constricted my windpipe. I got up, patting my hands on my butt, brushing any earthly residue from my white shorts.

"It's getting late. I'll come back soon." I promised, putting my hand on their tombstone before slowly turning away.

CHAPTER NINE

SLIPPING MY EARBUDS INTO MY EARS, I EXITED THE CEMETERY.
The revving sound of a motorcycle roared over my favorite song as I started to cross the street, but I couldn't tell which direction it came from.

A circular, blue-white light loomed, closing faster than I could jump out of the way. I screamed, covering my face with my arms as I braced for the impact. Right before the collision, the driver swerved, sending the bike into a tailspin. The rear fender smashed into me and I tumbled to the asphalt, butt first. Pain radiated up my back, followed by a second burst in my left elbow. I jerked my head up in time to see the rider finish the tailspin, screeching to a stop in front of me.

I bit the inside of my cheek as sharp, searing pain spread through my arm and warm blood dripped down to my wrist. Using my good hand, I pushed off the ground, only to lose my balance and fall. I blew my hair out of my face as I lay on the asphalt, cursing the lunatic rider.

A pair of heavy black boots appeared, along with an extended hand.

"No, thanks." I waved it away.

The stranger retracted his hand, shoving it into his front pocket. I tried to get up again, this time using both hands. I winced as the pain in my arm intensified and spread across my ribs. Shallow wheezing escaped my lungs and I grimaced. His hand reached out again and I glanced at the newly offered aid.

"Fine," I said, placing my hand into his open palm.

Awkwardly, I stumbled to a standing position before finally looking at the face of my attacker. Bright blue eyes stared back, a deep crease of concern between the eyebrows.

Axel? He rode a motorcycle?

Ah, holy hell!

"May I?" he asked, his features schooled. Like a good zombie heeding command, I absently extended my left arm toward him.

His black attire blended into the obsidian night. I watched as he studied my features before inspecting my arm. That unexplainable pull toward him grew stronger. The hairs on my neck rose. It was getting harder to breathe, and not just because my ribs ached like they'd been trampled by horses.

I'd never felt so naked in my entire life. I'd never been this mesmerized, captivated, or drawn to any guy. Heck, I'd been avoiding them like the plague until recently.

But he was different.

A range of emotions swirled in his irises. Hope. Happiness. Admiration. Desire. Fear. Sadness. And finally, composure. My cheeks burned with heat as disappointment flared, and I remembered all the reasons I'd been avoiding him.

I yanked my hand back and yelped.

"Ren." There was a desperate undertone to the way he said my name, his eyebrows pulled together.

Damn it. What was he playing at? "Don't. Just don't."

He stepped forward and I fell back a step. His shoulders sagged. "Let me explain."

"Explain what? That you used me so you could get in the sack with Rachel?" I chuckled cynically. "Or, wait! Let me guess, now that you're done getting in her pants, you want me to help you bag *another* girl."

His eyes widened. "It's not like that, Ren."

How dare he think I was stupid enough to fall for his crap. I was on fire, and the words just wouldn't stop. "Oh no? Then, please explain to me why I was stood up, and why I found you with *her* the next day? Explain that, smart ass."

"Okay, first of all," he started, fisting his hand in irritation. "I was not *with* Rachel. She came on to *me,* and before

I could push her away, you ran off. Secondly, I stood you up for a good reason." He looked past me and then back, letting out a deep breath. "I just can't tell you what that reason was."

"Yeah, okay." I rolled my eyes. "I don't know what kind of girls you were with before, but I sure as hell am not falling—"

He moved in a blur, closing the distance between us. I gasped in surprise, taking a step back. But he wasn't having it. He stepped into my personal bubble—really close into my personal bubble. "I know you have no reason to trust me. But right now is not the best time for me to explain my actions."

I opened my mouth to tell him to go to hell. But he cut me off.

"However, your injury . . . that, I can take care of," he said in a low voice, offering a crooked smile. "I'm sorry I hurt you."

Which hurt was he apologizing for? For standing me up, or nearly killing me with his bike? My stomach fluttered as my veins flared with renewed heat.

I blew out a deep breath. "What were you doing going that fast in a fifteen mile per hour zone?"

He smiled, amused. "I was trying this spontaneity thing a cute girl at school told me about."

I scowled.

"Are you following me?" I blurted, immediately wishing the ground would open and swallow me whole.

"Why would you think that?" he asked with an enticing smile.

Puddle of teenage awkwardness. Awesome.

"A question isn't an answer." I tried to sound irritated, but it came out in an unattractive wheeze-growl.

His face darkened, and his smile disappeared. His brows creased together.

Well, that wasn't the reaction I expected.

He grabbed my upper arm, pushing me behind him so quickly, I stumbled.

"Don't—"

"Hold that thought, *Meus Aeternus.*"

He crouched slightly, one hand on his hip, the other—palm open—facing away. It was a protective stance, but against what?

A nanosecond later, an SUV came screeching around the corner. The sky filled with a thunderous staccato—like hail pounding on the roof of a car.

My heart stopped as the scene unwound before me. Images of my parents' funeral filled my head.

No, no, no. Not another death.

Two guys in trench coats slid out of the passenger side, their guns aimed at us.

This is bad. This is very bad.

A volley of shots echoed through the air. I was a dead woman. I was sure of it. I took a step back, and then another, only to step on my shoelace. I stumbled backward, a stubborn scream building inside my chest, my heartbeat elevating out of control. The bullets froze in midair inches from my shoulder. *What the hell?*

Axel stood with his hand extended, his lips curved in a grimace.

"Bad move," he snarled.

The frozen bullets flew backward, hitting one of the coat-clad men between the eyes, the other in the gut. Two more attackers jumped out of the SUV, marching forward. One held a sword, the other, a spiky ball attached to each end of a chain.

What kind of stuff is Axel into? Medieval fight club?

They eyed each other, silently conspiring, before rushing straight at Axel. Their eyes glowed red, and shark-like teeth protruded from their mouths.

My eyes widened, and I recoiled in fear.

The attackers advanced in a blur, swinging their weapons and snapping their teeth at Axel. But he was faster and stronger than the two combined. I watched, mesmerized, forgetting about the possibility of getting ripped to shreds if either attacker got past him.

Axel easily dodged, kicked, and punched his opponents, sending them flying a good twenty to thirty feet. He drew two small swords from under the backside of his jacket. They looked like mini-me sword replicas, too dangerous for cuddles and too cute not to.

Axel pushed off the ground in one quick swoop—dust rising like a tiny tornado behind him—closing the distance between him and his assailants. The speed he traveled made him seem like a blur of blue light in the middle of a lightning show.

He wielded the mini-me swords with ease, blocking attacks and dancing around his opponents before he found an opening. Without hesitating, he ducked between the two men, plunging a sword into each. The men disintegrated, leaving only red, glimmering dust.

I clamped my hands over my mouth, stifling a sob. I trembled, unable to process what I'd just witnessed.

"Oh, God," I whimpered.

Maybe he's a serial killer.

Super. Nova. Serial. Killer.

Like the one Pey had told me about.

"*They found dead bodies mutilated by knives,*" she'd said.

Panic with a dash of bruised rib made it hard to breathe. This couldn't be happening. My mind ran a hundred miles an hour, but my body refused to move. *Damn you, Pey, for putting scary thoughts in my head!*

I dragged myself backward as Axel approached. He threw his swords onto the asphalt, then took one step at a time, slowly. He raised his empty hands, as if to tell me he meant no harm. I wanted to believe him, but at this point, things were unclear.

"I won't hurt you," he said in a soothing voice.

What the hell is wrong with me? Why was I still staring at him like an idiot? I should be running the opposite way, screaming at the top of my lungs. Not feeling attracted to a guy that had just . . . *murdered* four people. My heart clenched, and my head spun with confusion.

"I'm extremely sorry. . . . You shouldn't have seen that. . . . I'm normally more careful."

Normally? He'd done this before? How often? Hell, did it matter? He'd just *admitted* to murder!

Panic consumed me. But at the same time, I couldn't help but be hypnotized by his presence, as if I had no choice in the matter. What was it about him that had me so ensnared?

I looked past him to the still-running SUV. Images of the dead guys replayed before my eyes. I was in full-on freak-out mode. I didn't know who was worse—Axel, or the men he'd killed. "Who the hell are you? *What* are you?"

Axel ran a hand through his hair, his jaw set. "They would've killed us."

"Those *people* . . . they turned into red glitter . . ."

"Do hallucinations run in your family?" he mocked.

"Go to hell! Have a nice life," I said, tripping over my words. I was so flustered I couldn't think straight. I jumped up without his help, ignoring the pain shooting down my ribs.

"Nice life in hell?" he asked, amused.

I turned and walked away.

"Wait." He followed behind me.

"What? Calling me crazy wasn't enough?" I stopped and turned to scowl at him.

Axel's features darkened, taking on a dangerous glint.

Whoa! What did I say now, moody Frankenstein?

A metallic, crunching noise drew my attention to the culprit. A red knife peeked out from his closed fist. Blood trickled from his hand, making my head spin like I'd been swept into a whirlpool.

Axel turned, thrusting his open palm toward his attacker. Blue light pulsated into the guy's chest, sending him flying. He ran toward the assailant, grabbing one of his mini-me weapons on the way.

The guy blocked Axel's kick to his chest, answering with a roundhouse kick to Axel's head. Axel ducked, stepping and spinning under the guy's leg until he was standing right beside and slightly behind him. Snaking his free arm around the attacker's throat, Axel plunged the dagger into the guy's heart, leaving behind a pile of glistening, red dust.

My mouth went dry as I helplessly witnessed another act of violence. Fear spiked once again as Axel headed back toward me.

"Shit. This is going to be a problem." He chuckled, his eyes on his bleeding hand. "You're a distraction," he said pointedly.

Droplets of his blood hit the asphalt, red streaks coloring his open palm. I felt my fear evaporate, replaced by a compassionate need to help—like the last fifteen minutes hadn't happened.

"Oh my God. You're bleeding. That thing . . ." I started to say, pointing at the now barely visible dust.

"Goarder."

"What?"

"They're called Goarders."

Really? He wanted to educate me now? I reached for his hand, but he pulled away lightning fast, like I'd shocked him. I settled my hands on my hips. "You need to get that looked at, before—"

"Don't worry about it." He wiped the blood on the side of his shirt. "It's a small scratch."

"No freaking way! I know what I saw. You were bleeding."

He laughed. "Now you're seeing things, too?"

I scowled, my mind racing a million miles an hour. I couldn't seem to make up my mind between wanting to help him and wanting to run away. "I-I need to go."

"Wait!" He grabbed at my elbow and I jumped. "Sorry." He let go immediately. "Will you please just give me a chance—"

"I don't know *what* you are, but stay the hell away from me." I turned and ran off in a jog. I heard him calling my name, but I didn't care.

My mind whirled around all the times I had thought I'd imagined that blue stuff emitting from his palms. But tonight had confirmed it. I hadn't been imagining. It was all true. And somehow, Axel had the answers—answers I was running away from.

CHAPTER TEN

I COVERED MY MOUTH WITH THE BACK OF MY HAND AS ANOTHER yawn escaped. My mind felt like it had rolled around in a puddle of double fudge syrup. I couldn't focus on anything, my concentration shattered and useless. But after only three hours of sleep and six sugar-filled coffees, what was I expecting? A drug dealer in the middle of a police raid would be less jumpy than I was.

I clicked my phone to check the time—the clock above Ms. Martin's chalkboard never read correctly—counting down the minutes to when I'd have to face Axel.

I laid my exhausted head on the desk just as the bell rang and everyone quickly filtered out into the halls. All I wanted was to get five minutes of shut-eye. Ms. Martin had often let me spend time in her classroom when I'd needed to dodge the clattering chaos of the halls during lunch.

And today, I'd rather stay in here and take a nap than face *him*.

I jolted awake when I heard the door click shut. I'd fallen asleep. Deep asleep. With drool and everything. Lifting my head, I wiped my hand across my mouth.

Yuck! Very attractive. How long had I been out?

Hoping I didn't have leftover drool dried on my face or sleep marks from my desk and arms, I packed up my books, neatly stacking them into my messenger bag.

"I know you'd rather not see me right now."

I stiffened and my mouth went dry. What was he doing here? How had he known where to find me? My pulse pounded in my ears and my heart raced, but whether from excitement or fear, I wasn't sure.

"Ren," Axel said, his voice pleading.

I no longer cared how my crap got in the bag, I just wanted out. My heartbeat increased and sweat flooded the nooks and crannies of my palms. I didn't want to look at him; I didn't want to know what he wanted. All I could see was him killing, thrusting his weapons into those people without a moment's hesitation. Killing them without a second thought.

I'd never been a violent person, despite my bravado with Dean. I believed in preserving life, that violence never solved anything. Axel obviously stood on the opposite side of that spectrum. Hell, he'd seemed to enjoy every moment. I could tell from the way he'd moved, and the glint of glee as he'd shoved his sword into each of their bodies.

"Breathe, Ren," Axel said, rubbing the length of my back. "Just breathe."

"Don't." I jerked away, stepping out of his reach. "Don't touch me."

"Ren, please." He took a step toward me, stopping when I whirled back. His hands went up in a placating gesture, like he didn't want to scare his prey before he caught it. "I just want to explain."

"Stay the hell away from me, Axel." I shouldered my bag, my eyes darting to the door. Could I make it to the hall before he caught me? Better question, would he dare? "Just leave me alone."

"I swear, Ren, if you let me—"

"I don't care!"

"If I hadn't done what I did—"

"I don't want to hear—"

"They would have killed us. Killed *you*."

I ran for the exit, but he was faster. I squealed as he grabbed me and spun me around. My back hit the closed door. Terrified, I looked up into his blazing blue eyes. They churned with something I couldn't put a finger on. Was he going to kill me, too?

"Please, Axel." I shook beneath his grip. "Please don't hurt me. Just let me go. I promise, I won't tell anyone your secret." Not that anyone would believe me. Okay, maybe Pey would . . .

He let go of my arms, placing his hands on either side of my shoulders, trapping me. He leaned forward, and I wanted to be sucked into the door. "Are you afraid of me, Ren?"

I looked away, flinching. Words were lost. I couldn't breathe or swallow or anything.

"Answer me," he demanded. "Do I scare you? Do I look like a monster now? Am I *disgusting* to you?"

I wanted to shake my head. Because, even after witnessing what I had, my traitorous body still wanted to get friendly with his.

Stupid. Treasonous. Body.

"Let me go, Axel." My hands fisted at my sides.

He didn't respond, didn't move. Hell, he didn't even blink. The air thickened, and the possibility of my death loomed closer.

Get a grip, Ren. He wouldn't kill you in the middle of the day, where he could easily get caught.

I took a deep breath. My lungs overflowed with the smell of Axel—woodsy springtime. God, I was out of my mind. Even now, my stupid brain couldn't stop drooling over him.

He was so close that I could see the white in the inner rims of his irises. How had I not noticed that before? My body swayed toward him like it was the most natural thing to do as he continued to stare into my eyes, never blinking, never wavering.

I wanted nothing more than to throw caution out the door and press my lips to his. His eyes widened and an audible gasp escaped him as he jumped back, like I'd shoved him.

That was weird. Almost like he could hear what I was thinking. Oh, crap! Could he? I seriously hoped he couldn't.

Like, I'd-rather-chew-off-my-own-hand-than-have-him-know-what-I'd-just-thought kind of serious.

But he obviously wasn't human . . .

He didn't make a move. Instead, he just stared, confused shock flickering across his face. Taking the opportunity, I turned around and hightailed it the hell out of there.

CHAPTER ELEVEN

AVOIDING HAD ONCE AGAIN BECOME AN EXHAUSTING SECOND nature. I should have been handed a medal for the ways I'd dodged Axel over the past four days. But school was finally out for the weekend. I had two whole days of not having to watch my back. It was also Dean's birthday party. Maybe I'd even get a little wild.

Me, wild? Rrrright! Stepping out of my old Beemer, I took in the sight. The party buzzed with drunk, over-en-thusiastic teenagers. Music blasted, couples gyrated near the bonfire, and drinks were passed around. I recognized many from school, but others I'd never seen before.

This wasn't my thing. Why was I even here?

Dean.

I spotted Pey diving into a cooler, coming up with a brown beer bottle, and headed toward her.

"This is some turnout," I said, hugging her. She reeked of alcohol.

"Rrreeeee-Rrreeee!" she slurred, throwing her arms around my neck. "How is your night so far?"

"Oh, you know. I caught my brother and Cassie making out on the couch. I know they're getting married soon, but seriously? I'm just thankful I didn't find them in a more compromising position." I closed my eyes and shuddered.

Eww.

"They're both adults, and there's no harm in getting laid." She jabbed me in the ribs and wiggled her eyebrows. "You should try it sometime."

"Hi, baby," Landon said, snaking his arm around her and pulling her roughly into a kiss.

I looked away, feeling like I was prying.

"Hey, baaaabbyyy," Pey drawled, slipping into a giggle-fest.

"Will you make sure she doesn't drive home drunk?" I asked Landon.

He nodded, offering me a red cup. I declined.

A hand slithered around my waist, pulling me against a hard body. I squealed with surprise and looked up to find

Dean beaming down at me. His face shone bright as a freaking Christmas tree.

"Hey, birthday boy," I said, wrapping my arm around his waist and giving him a sideways hug.

"I think my birthday just got a whole lot better." He grinned and pulled me into a bear hug.

"Happy eighteenth birthday," I said once he stepped back. He left his hand curled around my waist.

What gives?

He looked down at me, his eyes swirling with emotions I couldn't read. He seemed slightly buzzed.

"Dance with me." He pulled me into the crowd without waiting for my response. He wrapped my arms over his shoulders and placed his hands on my hips.

"I didn't know you knew so many people," I rambled. "I mean, I knew you were popular, but—"

"You should really stop talking, Pernell," he cut me off with a devilish smirk.

I stuck my tongue out at him.

"I would've been happy if it were just the four of us, like old times," he said. His features softened as he smiled. "I'm really glad you came."

I knew which four he meant—Pey, Landon, him, and me. I gave him a quick smile. He pulled me closer, his arms engulfing me in a familiarity that was too comforting to protest. I laid my head on his chest as we moved slowly to the upbeat music. He no longer smelled like mud, or fresh pine leaves, or metal. I lifted my head, looking at him.

"You changed your cologne."

"You noticed." His eyes bored into mine, making my heart thrum fitfully.

"It's kind of hard to forget that muddy stink," I said with a jab to his rib.

Dean smiled seductively, his thumb caressing the nape of my neck, leaning down as if to kiss me.

"I have your present," I blurted, not wanting to encourage him.

He leaned his forehead against mine, his eyes closed. My emotions were running high and Dean's attentiveness wasn't helping. I knew there was something strong between us, and I knew neither of us could resist if the right opportunity presented itself. But . . .

"Are you nervous?" he asked. "You're trembling."

I shook my head.

"I-I . . ." I didn't know what to say, so I asked him a sincere question: "What are we doing, Dean? What do you want from us?"

I didn't know what I'd expected, but his silence wasn't it. With a heavy sigh, I put distance between us.

"Have a wonderful birthday, Dean."

He cursed under his breath. "Ren."

"No, it's okay." I smiled back. "Just . . . just forget I said anything, okay?" I wrapped my arms around his neck for one more hug before I turned and walked away from the crowd, feeling empty, confused, and frustrated all at the same time.

Dean. Was. Not. Healthy.

CHAPTER TWELVE

THE SOFT, MELODIC RHYTHM OF WAVES WASHED OVER ME AS fresh air filled my senses—just what I'd needed. A rock half my height and close to the water called my name. Getting comfortable, I sat with my arms around my knees and stared out across the lake. Moonlight gleamed off the mirrored black of rippling water. Simply enthralling.

The skin at the back of my neck tingled. I shivered in response.

"Hi."

My undeniable connection to him told me who it was.

Axel.

"I didn't think this was your kind of party," I said.

"It isn't."

I looked up and inhaled sharply. Axel's brown hair hung shorter than usual, and his bright blue eyes twinkled like stars in the darkness. I could deny it until I was blue in the face, but the boy was gorgeous. I could stare at him for the rest of my life.

I swallowed, hard. "Is that how you get girls to fawn all over you? By being mysterious?"

"Is it working?"

I stood, not really wanting his company. Part of me wanted to trust him, but other parts— the logical, sane parts—sent blazing alerts. He grabbed my wrist. Electricity surged up the length of my arm. I gazed at his fingers before trailing to his face.

His brow creased. "Please, don't go."

"I should."

"Stay." His desperate plea dissolved my strength and anger.

A few moments passed with only the sound of water lapping at the rocks filling the air. Between the nerves and doubt, and the hammering of my heart in my chest, I couldn't think straight. The silence felt oppressive. I had to break it.

"So—" I said, the same time he started with:

"I've been—"

I tilted my head and looked at him, a nervous laugh bubbling through me. Silence once again settled around us. He let go of my wrist.

"I've been meaning to ask you," Axel said. "What's the deal with you and Dean?"

I raised an eyebrow.

"What?" He shrugged unapologetically. "You guys dating?"

I laughed.

"Are you?" He pushed for response.

My heart pounded in my chest. I didn't know what to make of him. He'd begged for a chance to explain himself, and now that he had the opportunity, he was wasting it on something else?

"Why does it matter?"

"Come on, you can tell me. I promise, I'm really not that scary, and I'm a great listener."

"You *don't* scare me." Lies . . . half a lie. He scared me to a point, but he also excited me. My body and mind couldn't get on the same damn page.

He chuckled.

Anger flared. "I'm *not* scared of you."

"I believe you." He sighed. "You and Dean . . . it matters because I want to know you, Ren. Now that my dirty little secret is out and you don't want to talk about it . . . I, at least, want to know. That way, if you ever decide to be my friend again, I could maybe ask you out without feeling like I'm pining after a beautiful girl that's taken."

My breath caught in my throat. Did he just . . . ? Okay, time to move away from that topic. Maybe talking about Dean wasn't such a bad idea after all. It wasn't like I'd be giving him anything he couldn't find out just by asking anyone at school, including Tyler. Maybe then, I could ask more about him . . . maybe hearing his side of the story would be enough to untangle the ongoing war between my head and heart.

"We used to be best friends, Dean and me. Now, I don't know what we are. I've known him since we were in diapers. Landon, Pey, Dean, and I were inseparable until the summer before ninth grade. He kissed me one day—we were waiting for Landon and Pey—right as his football buddies walked by. They laughed at us, and he . . . pushed me and said, '*No way, Pernell.*' That was the first time he'd ever called me by my last name." Tight coils formed in the pit of my stomach as the memory played in my head.

Axel pressed his lips together, like he was trying to hold back a chuckle. I smacked his arm, hard, hurting my hand in the process. He didn't even flinch. What was he, the Man of Steel? *Geez*. Images of his merciless killing flashed before my eyes and I grimaced.

"I'm glad you think my miserable *first kiss* is hilarious. I'll never get another chance to do it right, you know?" I frowned.

"I'm sorry." His expression turned smoldering. "Maybe I could help erase that memory?"

"What?" I struggled to breathe for a minute, wondering if kissing a serial killer would be any different than kissing a douchebag. "Don't be a jerk. Tell me about your first kiss so I can be envious."

Axel raised his brows in surprise.

Ah, hell. Did the temperature just go up a hundred degrees?

"You know what I mean. Geez." I rolled my eyes at him. "Since mine was totally ruined, I make a habit of listening to other people's first kisses and resenting them."

He chuckled in a deep, husky tone, sending an uncontrollable shiver up my spine.

Wowza! I mentally fanned myself.

"Well, if it'll make you feel better, mine wasn't that great, either. I got prank-kissed—by one of my cousins, no less—during a wedding when I was eight years old. My first *make out* session was with the butt of a lemon, and it was caught on camera. You can only imagine the kind of blackmail . . ."

I was laughing so hard I didn't realize tears streamed down my cheeks.

"You know what . . . ? Thank you . . . that did . . . help. God, I can't breathe!" I placed my hand on my stomach as I hunched over, trying to catch my breath. It was becoming too easy to forget everything when he was close to me.

"Hardy, har, har . . ." he said.

After a few more minutes, I composed myself, jumping off the rock to stand with my arms crossed. "If it's any consolation, I've never laughed so hard in my life." True story.

"Nope, that doesn't do it for me." A sultry smile slid across his lips. "But I can think of another way you could make it up to me."

He moved so fast, I didn't have time to react. One second I was standing, the next, I was pinned against the rock. He held me captive like he had in the classroom, his hands placed against the rock on either side of my shoulders, boxing me in. I sucked in a deep breath, and held it for a few long seconds, afraid of what was coming next. His aggressive stance made my insides tingle. It was dangerous, being this close to him. Sexy. What had I gotten myself into?

"W-what are you doing?" I stammered.

My gaze dropped to his lips. He licked them in response.

"Yeah, good luck with that," I said before I could stop myself, very sure I'd just sent him a personal invitation to try.

I tried to duck under him, but he blocked my path with his freaky speed.

Damn it!

His gaze dropped to my cheeks, lips, and finally, my neck. *Hot damn.* My throat went bone dry and I . . . I . . . couldn't think a single coherent thought. Everything became insignificant. Minuscule. Non-essential.

My lips parted in anticipation.

His finger traced my cheek and pushed a strand of hair behind my ear. *Good God, that feels incredible.* A shiver passed through me, awakening every nerve in my body. My eyes closed like they had a mind of their own. His hand traveled down to my neck. His thumb caressed the hollow between my neck and jaw. I stopped breathing. I didn't think I could move if my life depended on it.

My heartbeat increased and warmth pooled in the pit of my stomach. His other hand slid down my arm to my hand, leaving a trace of sizzling fire where he'd touched. His hand snaked around my lower back, resting on the small amount of exposed flesh. I let out a sigh that sounded somewhere between a moan and a whimper.

I wanted to forget about the killing and his special gifts. I wanted to forget about Rachel and the fact he'd stood me up. I wanted to forget about Dean, forget about everything, just this once. My chest heaved erratically and breathing became impossible. I needed his touch, his mouth against mine.

I opened my eyes. His lips were slightly parted, like he was struggling to breathe, too. A trace of a smile hovered on his face as our eyes locked. He knew he was driving me crazy.

He leaned closer, his body almost pressing against mine. Our breathing sped up, in sync with each other. His lips were so close. So close, I could smell his sweet, minty breath dancing against mine. I closed my eyes again and tilted my head back, ready for him.

"Give me a chance to explain what happened," Axel said, no higher than a whisper, but it was enough to bring me back from my momentary bliss. Had he just cornered me so I would hear him out?

"I'd rather you not—"

"Please, let me—"

I put up my hand, stopping him from continuing. I was still trying to wrap my mind around that day.

"Ren," he said. It sounded oddly like a warning.

"No, Axel." I didn't trust myself to hear what he had to say, because I was sure I'd believe any kind of crap he dished out. Because I wanted what I'd seen to make sense.

A shiver ran across my skin and the air around us changed, becoming much cooler. Axel's features darkened, taking on that dangerous glint I was starting to recognize. He spun, crouching before me as he drew his daggers from the back of his trench coat—his body forming a barrier between me and . . . what?

I peeked around him and my eyes widened. A dozen pairs of glowing red eyes stared back.

Goarders.

Oh, God. No. Not now! Not again.

Axel's hand reached for mine, and without a moment's hesitation, he tugged me toward him.

"We need to run," he hissed. When I didn't, he squeezed my hand. "Ren, I know this is all very hard to believe, but we need to get you to safety."

I looked at the Goarders—five of them were rushing toward us, gaining speed, their sharp teeth snapping like they were biting the air.

"Please, trust me on this," Axel urged.

Trust? He was no more human than they were, and I didn't know who he was—who he *really* was. How could I trust someone who had the potential to kill?

A cold snarl drew my attention and one thing became painfully clear: it was better to follow Axel than run toward the Goarders. So I nodded.

Before I could take a deep breath, Axel pulled me into a sprint toward the trees, setting a grueling pace. My heart hammered against my chest as my arms and legs worked their hardest. Being an undefeated 400-meter state champion was finally paying off.

The brisk September breeze lashed against my face. My lungs struggled to provide the necessary oxygen to keep my body moving, and I almost tripped over the thick branches that surfaced unexpectedly. Twigs snapped sharply beneath our feet.

My lungs and throat burned as they worked hard to supply air. My legs grew weak and could no longer carry me. I stumbled to a stop.

"I can't," I gasped, bending over, placing my hands on my knees.

"Just a few more yards, Ren," Axel pleaded. "We just have to make it over there, to that threshold." He pointed to where a light flashed in the darkness.

I couldn't figure out why the Goarders hadn't caught up to us. If memory served, they were fast. Faster than I could run. I sucked in a deep breath and nodded to Axel. We took off. I concentrated on my breathing and my end goal, and not the danger behind us. As we approached the destination, we came to an abrupt stop. He let go of my hand and caressed my burning cheek.

"Go!" he ordered. Or was that a plea?

I hesitated. A Goarder came too close before I noticed him. I shrieked in fear and brought my hands up to protect myself. I waited a second, then two, before dropping my arms slightly. The Goarder was frozen a foot or two from me. His teeth were bared and his snake-like tongue darted out like he tasted the air.

I stifled a scream.

Axel shook my shoulder. When my eyes met his, he said, "I promise, I'll be right behind you. Go, now." His eyes darted to the Goarders and mine followed.

My entire body perspired and I fought the urge to hurl. It was like watching a movie in slow motion. My ears became muffled and all I could see was the danger Axel was in.

He opened his mouth to say something.

"I've got her," someone said. I felt as if my ears were stuffed with cotton. A pair of hands grabbed me under my arms and dragged me away.

A knot formed in my throat; fear bounced around in my chest like it wanted out. Then I heard metal against metal, and my own scream sounded foreign to my ears.

"Let me go!" I screamed. "Axel! Axel!"

"Shh, he's fine. There are others helping him," a female voice told me. "They can't hear or see you. I've cloaked you . . . er . . . made you invisible."

I didn't know who she was. I didn't care what she'd done to me. Axel was all I could think of. I was stuck between wanting to save him and running the other way. I noticed a crackle in the air, like lightning striking a pole to the left of him and I didn't think twice. I thrashed until I was free and ran like hell, screaming Axel's name.

"Axel, to your—"

I was tackled to the ground. *What the hell?* I rolled over to find a blonde-haired, button-nosed girl pinning me down, a finger over her lips to silence me.

"That was her," a thick, raspy voice said. "The human."

"She's nothing but a human," Axel responded calmly.

They were talking about me? I could see them, just barely. Axel's back was to me. Even from here, I could clearly read his body language, as if I had known him all my life. That was scarier than facing ten Goarders ready to rip out my heart.

He was close to losing his temper. His fingers twitched like he was dying to take them out. I saw the wind pick up speed and the air grew brisker, sharper.

The Goarder with the raspy voice looked normal enough, except for his black globe eyes. *Well, that's different.*

"Leave, Rolium," Axel warned.

Rolium sneered. "If memory serves, you are in no position to tell me what to do, Dracian. Especially after our last encounter."

Axel's fists clenched against his thighs. The wind grew painfully cold. Sand swirled all around us, and it was getting harder to see. What were they talking about? And what the hell was a Dracian?

"Yeah, well, last time it was just him and a dozen of you cowards," Tyler said, stepping from the shadows to Axel's left. His smile was menacing, and a tad excited as he drew a dagger from the back of his pants.

Tyler? Oh my god! He was a . . . whatever Axel was? How had none of us noticed that?

"This time, the playing field's a bit more even, don't you think?" He pointed to three others that stood near the dip toward the beach, ready to spring into action.

Rolium's smile disappeared. He growled. It sounded animalistic, a cross between a lion and a bear. There were only six Goarders and five of Axel's people.

"We shall meet again," Rolium said, his gaze falling in my direction before he and his Goarders disappeared.

The temperature abruptly returned to normal, and, as far as I could tell, no tornado was about to land near us. The immediate danger had passed. I waited, wanting to go toward them, but not wanting to be seen. Unfortunately, Axel had other ideas. He headed toward me the same moment goldilocks went toward him.

"You're okay?" I heard her ask.

He nodded. His eyebrows furrowed and a vertical line appeared between them as his attention turned to me. Without warning, he stalked in my direction, his voice stern and scolding. "Why didn't you listen and go, like I asked?"

I hated being yelled at. I crossed my arms over my chest and stared in defiance.

He sighed, and his serial killer persona drained away. "Are you hurt?"

I fisted my hands and clenched my jaw. I wasn't waiting for answers anymore. He either told me, or I was walking away. "What the hell just happened, Axel?"

He reached for my hand, but I stood firm. "Let me drive you home. Then, you'll get all the answers you need."

I nodded and stiffly followed him toward his car. "What about mine?"

"Dean will bring it back."

Dean? Dean and Axel were on speaking terms? I shook my head as I slid into the car. He shut the door, pulled out his cell phone and walked to the driver's side.

"Yes . . . we'll be there in fifteen minutes," he said as he got in, hung up, and started the car.

He threw his phone in the center console before shifting the gear to Drive.

"Who was that?"

He inhaled deeply, his lean fingers drumming over the steering wheel. Instead of responding, he pressed down on the gas pedal, making the tires squeal in protest as we sped off.

CHAPTER THIRTEEN

THE ROOM WAS FILLED WITH FAMILIAR FACES: JOSHUA, CASSIE, John, and Sandy. My mind raced a million miles a second, but the words wouldn't come—it was like being stuck in thick foam.

"Why are they here?" I demanded, turning to Axel. "Why the *hell* are they here?"

"Because you wanted answers . . ." His eyes flickered to the audience behind me. Cautiously, he placed his hands over my shoulders and pivoted me around to face everyone else. "And this is where you'll find them."

Everything inside me swirled in confusion. My stomach churned and slushed like week-old sour milk. I backed away, right into a thick wall of muscle. I flinched, recoiling away from him. I didn't understand. What did he mean I'd find answers here? What did my family have to do with whatever he was?

Axel's warm breath fanned over my right ear as he leaned in and whispered, "It's okay."

No, it's not. But I couldn't move or speak. I felt cornered. I wanted to run, to hide from whatever was coming my way. But I didn't. I stood there, shaking, unmoving.

"We're here," Axel said quietly, "because everyone in this room is like me. We're Kshadria."

I blinked. His words—*everyone in this room is like me*— kept repeating in my head. Like him? But he wasn't human. At least, I didn't think he was with his ... special powers. And, if they were all like him ... my gaze found Joshua's.

"You ..." I accused my brother, but then realized that Cassie, John, and Sandy were still standing behind him. "All of you? Wait, does that mean ...? Am I ...?" I couldn't think properly. Too many thoughts and emotions rushed through me, making me nauseous.

My breathing came in short gasps. Sweat coated my palms and pain bubbled through me. I yelped.

"What's happening ...?" I fell to my knees, hugging my body as a burning sensation radiated through me and out the palms of my hands. My head spun. A blue aura flickered down my legs, but I didn't have time to analyze before familiar arms—Dean's arms—wrapped around me.

"Dean?" Uncertainty cloaked my thoughts. "What are you doing here?" Shouldn't he be at his birthday party?

A zing of shock traveled up my arm and into the core of my being. Like the tiny pores on my skin were being awakened one at a time and filled with a warm, soothing liquid.

"What are you doing? Let me go!" I jerked, trying to escape his arms. I flailed like a caged animal. Dean scowled, trying to keep his hold on me.

"No," he snapped back. "I can help. Let me."

However much I wanted to push him back, I couldn't. His cool hands pressed against mine as he laced our fingers together. Cool ribbons of relief flowed from his fingers into my skin. I felt the energy transferring between us like a soothing lullaby. I relaxed. The pain eased.

Slowly, I forced my eyes to meet Dean's. He had that stupid smirk on his face. I wanted to bitch-slap it off him, but instead, I pushed him away.

I didn't know what to make of all this. My head hurt. It had to be some elaborate scheme, a really bad April Fool's joke gone horribly wrong in September.

"I know this is hard to digest," Joshua started.

My head snapped to him as betrayal and anger coursed through me. "Hard to digest? Joshua, this is crazy talk. I feel like I've been dropped in the middle of a twilight zone."

Dean snickered. Of course he would. He was probably in on the stupid joke! My gaze flickered to Axel, the boy who'd promised me answers, and my lips twisted into a grimace. This was his fault.

"Maybe we should start at the beginning," Sandy suggested, a small, hesitant smile across her lips.

Axel sighed, his eyebrows pinching together. He looked like he was bracing himself. "Like I was saying, everyone in this room is a *Kshadria*. We're kind of like Asians, or Europeans, or African Americans, only our race is gifted with blue eyes, and the ability to control and command magic."

I raised my eyebrows. *Okay, I'll bite.* "What kind of magic?"

He cleared his throat and continued, "Charmers rely heavily on herbs to enhance their magical abilities, while Sorcerers use Reiki."

"Your mom was a Sorcerer. A hell of a good one, at that," John put in, smiling at the memory. "I've never seen anyone wield magic like she could."

Memories of the bright flowers and immaculate vegetable garden my mom had spent countless hours nursing flashed before my eyes. Rain or shine, hot or cold, those flowers never withered or died. Had she really been using magic . . . like she'd said? "What's Reiki?"

"Reiki utilizes a Sorcerers' own energy bank," Axel explained. I looked at him questioningly and he lifted his right hand. "Remember my stab wound from the Goarder?" He didn't wait for me to respond. "I used Reiki to heal it. I used part of *my* energy, *my* essence to heal myself."

"Huh . . ." I could feel all six pairs of eyes targeting me. Could it really be possible? I had seen the Goarders . . . but . . . "So, what are you? Are you all Sorcerers, too?"

"Your dad and I were born Sorcerers, but we pledged our allegiance to the Legion." John rolled the sleeve of his dress shirt up. He had five daggers tattooed on his outer arm. He smiled hesitantly. Axel, Joshua, and Dean all followed suit, revealing similar tattoos. Though Joshua's featured four daggers, and Dean's only had two.

"You're all part of this Legion thing?" I still couldn't believe that any of this was true. It just couldn't be.

Axel nodded. "Legions are an elite group of warriors that fight to protect our kind. Like the Navy SEALs or SAS in the human world. We're gifted with speed, strength, super healing, and telepathy."

"Telepathy. That's an awesome power," I said snidely. *Ah-huh. Right. Telepathy.*

He nodded, smiling. "It helps us communicate without the need for excess toys."

"I thought boys loved their toys."

His lips curved in an impish smile. He really did have a nice smile. I knew it wasn't the right time to be thinking about Axel's lips, but I needed to focus on something, anything other than the lunacy he was trying to sell me.

"What about you?" I asked, turning to Sandy.

She laughed. "I'm a Healer. Not as macho as them, but I've got my moments."

"And you?" I asked Cassie.

She shrugged. "Same as mom, nothing special. Except, I can also make people change their emotions. Like calming them down when they're upset or enraged." She crossed her arms over her chest and smiled sheepishly, glancing at Dean.

"There're also a lot of awful things out there, Ren. Goarders are the bottom of the food chain. They're mortals who were greedy enough to sell their souls," Axel continued.

"To whom? The Devil?" I scoffed, shaking my head at the bull-crap I was being fed.

"To the Telalians," Axel said, his expression serious.

"Who are the Telalians?"

"The exact opposite of our people. Dracia's been at war with Telal and his bloodline for generations—" he started to explain.

"Making you guys, what? Dracia-lians?" I interrupted, trying to piece together the details of their elaborate hoax.

"Draci-ans," Axel corrected.

"So, people sell their souls to these Telalians to become Goarders. Why? Why would someone be stupid enough to sell their soul?"

"Not stupid, desperate. Some people grow desperate enough to sacrifice themselves in order to save their loved ones."

If this wasn't all just a ruse, would I be one of those desperate people? Was I brave enough to sacrifice myself for someone else? I didn't have to think long before I found my answer.

Yes, I would. I would do anything to protect my brother, my family. Even if they, apparently, didn't feel the same—pranking me and all.

"How does it work?"

"Are you planning on making a deal with the devil?" Dean asked, that stupid smirk on his face again.

I glared at him.

"They don't turn just any human into a Goarder," Joshua offered, bringing my attention back to him. "They hand pick the ones that have the most potential. We think they target those that have no way out, are desperate, and are willing to do anything to get what they want. Their desire to sacrifice makes them strong, but the more tainted their soul is, the stronger they are when they're turned into Goarders."

"So they were once humans, with families and stuff?"

He nodded. I let that information sink in for few minutes. "Do Goarders have magical powers?"

"Yes. Proxys—Telal's direct descendents—are equivalent to our Sorcerers. We know for certain that the Goarders have strength and speed. We suspect telepathy, but since none of us have ever been one . . ." John gave me a crooked smile and shrugged.

"So, if Telalians can be created, can Dracians?" It seemed like an obvious conclusion.

"Making a magical being requires an Original's blood . . ." Axel sighed. "Synik and Bramuda, the leaders of Dracia, died centuries ago. Since then, we've survived through breeding."

I flinched at the word "*breeding*." It sounded so . . . animalistic.

"Arranged marriage," Joshua corrected, his hand wrapping around Cassie's.

"Breeding. Arranged marriage. To-mai-to, To-mah-to," Dean quipped.

"It is what it is," Axel said, almost like he was convincing himself.

Silence filled the air. Everyone waited to see how I'd react, if I would believe their elaborate story. Because that's all it was. A story.

I let out a long, labored breath and laughed. How stupid did they think I was to believe all this nonsense? "I don't know what kind of dream I'm in, but this is just too out of this world for me to even consider."

"How do you explain your encounters with the Goarders, then?" Dean challenged.

"Costume production," I fired back.

"Oh, really?" His lip curved into that dangerously cocky smile I'd seen far too many times. He moved, so fast I could only describe it as a blur. He snapped his fingers in front of my eyes and a flicker of red and blue ignited from the tips.

"What the hell?" I gasped in surprise.

He smirked.

"Get out of my face." I shoved him, but he didn't budge.

"Answer my question."

Dean seriously needed to learn about personal space.

"Strings, cables, and a lighter in your sleeve." I ground my teeth. "How many times have I seen David Copperfield pull mind tricks like that?"

"Well, then, you're a bigger idiot than I thought!"

"Dean!" Sandy and John said in unison.

Heat built inside me like an uncontrollable forest fire. That was it. I'd had enough. They'd taken this way too far. "Just because I'm not falling for whatever this stupid trick is, doesn't make me an idiot, you asshole!"

"Ren!" Joshua was at my side, his hand firm on my shoulder.

"Let go of me, Joshua." I glanced around the room, looking at the people I'd *thought* were my friends and family, and felt sick to my stomach. "If this is all true, why didn't I know sooner? Clearly you all know the so-called *truth*." I rubbed my hand against my forehead. "Never mind, don't tell me. Because—"

"Mom wanted to keep you away from all of this. As you got older, your magic would become stronger, and this was the only way she knew to protect you. To keep you safe from being found."

"Then I'm . . . ? I mean . . . I can feel . . ." I couldn't put my thoughts into words.

"Magic?" Joshua asked.

I nodded. *If what they were saying was even remotely possible, what had changed for me to feel magic now?*

"I *can't*. I just can't," I mumbled under my breath. It was too far-fetched, too unrealistic. "Excuse me," I whispered, heading toward my room.

"Ren," Joshua's voice traveled behind me.

"Let her go," Cassie's words followed his in a soothing tone. "She needs time to let this sink in. Give her time. All of you."

Fighting the fuzz in my vision, I dragged my lead-like feet up the stairs. With heavy limbs and an impervious heart, I softly shut the door behind me, leaning my head against it, and closed my eyes.

I'm not losing my mind. I'm going to be okay. I'm going to be okay.

I couldn't hold back the waterworks that followed.

†

The sun peeked through the mountains, stretching across the morning sky. Soft, luscious earth chilled the soles of my feet. I walked into the light, trailing my fingers over vibrant flowers that bloomed all around me. An old oak tree stood alone in the middle of the field. Rays peered through its branches, giving it the feel of angels descending from heaven.

"My dear Ren."

I jumped, startled by the greeting.

I turned to see a beautiful woman with flawless skin and a heart-shaped face standing among the flowers. She couldn't have been older than nineteen or twenty, but her bright blue eyes told me otherwise. She wore a white chiffon dress with one ruffled shoulder gathered by a stream of blue and white flowers. The empire waist hugged her curvy body and the skirt flowed softly to the ground. It moved like a beautiful arctic river as she walked with the precision and grace of a ballet dancer. The sun glistened around her, creating an aura, making her look like an angel.

There was something familiar about her. Cold air passed through me, causing goosebumps to rise.

"Nala," she said, extending her hand. I hesitantly took it. She smiled, looking at the surroundings. "Interesting that you are most comfortable here, of all places."

"What is this place?"

"Why, we're in Dracia, of course. Your motherland."

"Dracia? But . . . how?"

"You, darling, brought us here . . . with my help, of course."

I looked around again, taking in the vibrant scenery. This was Dracia? Even in my dreams, I couldn't get away from that preposterous story.

I raised my hands to find a glow surrounding my skin. I knew I should be freaked out, but for some reason, I felt connected. Calmer. I felt more in control here than anywhere else. The land's essence flowed through my bare feet like velvet ribbons.

"What does this mean?" I whispered, examining my surroundings.

I knelt beside a flower that looked like a hybrid between a lotus and an orchid. When I reached toward it, the flower stretched itself to meet my touch. The silky texture of the petals provoked an unfamiliar need to care for and protect it.

"It means the time has come for you to embrace your destiny."

I spun around, scowling. "Why can't you people leave me alone?"

"Because, Ren, you're destined to end the war, to stop the bloodshed and save us all."

"I'm what? I'm . . ." Words were lost to me. I didn't know if I believed what I'd been told. But me? Saving the world? Laughable. Completely, utterly laughable.

"I understand your reservation, Ren. But it is the truth. I've foreseen the future, and you *are* our savior."

I could tell she truly believed what she said. But I couldn't fathom the thought, even in a dream. I was a teenage girl, living a normal life, worrying about boys, and gossiping with friends. Not . . . whatever she and the rest of my family wanted me to believe.

"Perhaps if I tell you our story, it might ease your doubts." She paused.

Not this again.

"At the beginning, Telal, Synik, and Bramuda—the first of our kind—worked hard to build our race. They created a sanctuary for us—a place we could call home. They provided guidance, knowledge, and training. But then, greed and love consumed Telal, starting a battle that has spanned centuries and cost many lives." She gave me a weak smile.

"Telal was so obsessed with the idea of marrying Bramuda that, when she refused him, his actions brought the end of her life. After her death"—Nala's voice cracked, like she was swallowing pain—"Synik took it upon himself to protect those that needed his protection, moving forward with his sister's plans to continue building the Dracian race. But secretly, he was devoured by the need to avenge his sister's death."

The way Nala wove the story, I could *almost* believe it. Almost.

"Power is a beautiful thing," she continued. "It helps mankind continue forward, but it can also destroy when wielded incorrectly. Power is virtuous by nature. It's swayed by the holder, not the other way around." She sighed. "The story is told that Telal and Synik fought for over two centuries, each swaying power to their side equally."

I could imagine it, the battles, the slaughter. I shivered, not because of the story, but because I was finally starting to believe. Broken images, like pieces of shattered glass, flickered through my head. I couldn't tell if they were visions or memories, but they were out of order, fragmented, waiting to be pieced back together.

"They became savages." Nala's voice brought me back to reality—if this was, in fact, reality. "And many souls were lost until Synik was defeated. Immortality was at risk."

"So, you're immortal?" I asked.

Nala shook her head.

"No. We live longer than mortals, but we do eventually die."

The silence between us thickened. Everything I'd heard and seen started to merge together.

"One often meets destiny on the road you seek to avoid," she said with a smile. God, I wanted to stick a fork in it. "The time is nearing. You can't escape your destiny, Ren, only prolong it." Her eyes darkened and her smile faded. "Don't make the same mistake again, darling."

What did she mean "*same mistake again*"? When had I made a mistake?

"This time around, you aren't alone. You have someone to help you."

Did she mean Axel?

"You have a bonded. Love is on your side."

"Bonded? Love? What are you talking about?"

She stepped past me, her hands crossed under her sternum. She looked over her shoulder and blinked, then smiled. "You are so much like your mother. Bless her heart. The day before she left Dracia, she came to me."

I arched both of my eyebrows.

"Do you know what she asked for? Mind you, I don't typically interfere with fate . . ." She spun on the balls of her feet and locked eyes with me. "She asked me to help her hide you from fate's cruelty, to keep you from the responsibility of saving us from Telal's curse."

"And what does that have to do with bonded and love?"

"Haven't you ever wondered why someone has come into your life, Ren? Why you felt an uncontrollable attraction to that person, why being near them made you feel like you could face the world?"

I'd felt that around two people. And one of them had been ingrained in my life since my first memory. Dean. But it was easy to know why I was attracted to him. Hell, half our school pined after him.

"Dean was born to protect you, Ren. He was bonded to you—to serve you, love you, and stay loyal to you until his last breath."

"Dean's anything but loyal to me." Hadn't I learned that the hard way?

She smiled, like she knew a secret I didn't. "Dean is a complicated being. Don't let him fool you, or make you believe otherwise."

I groaned. Well, at least she'd hit *that* assumption right on the head.

"The balance is at risk, child. Don't waste more time avoiding what you can't. The cycle was set in motion at your birth. It doesn't matter what you believe; it only matters that you do what you must. Soon, your strength will be tested as others take your place in the universe—others that hold the most influence in your life. But no matter what happens, you must return home. *This* is where you are strongest."

CHAPTER FOURTEEN

A SOFT GLOW REFLECTED AGAINST MY EYES, PULLING ME FROM THE sanctuary of sleep. I groaned and ducked my head under my pillow just before my phone buzzed. I sat up and reached for my cell, charging on the nightstand.

I unlocked my iPhone and saw there were multiple texts, missed calls, and voicemails from Pey. All from last night. I shook my head. *So* not going there.

Pey: LANDON GAVE ME A PROMISE RING. AHHHH . . .

Pey: I EXPECTED MY BEST FRIEND TO BE MORE EX-CITED THAN THIS.

Pey: Joshua said you were still sleeping?

As I was about to call her, I received another text.

Pey: Ren, if I don't get a call right this minute, I swear to God, I'm coming over and beating the shit out of you.

Oh God, she was pissed. I sat up, scooting back against the headboard, and called her within two seconds.

"Since when did you become so violent, Pey?" I joked.

"Since I had a best friend that didn't answer my texts or phone calls. Oh, who are we kidding? I've got anger management issues."

I chuckled and rolled my eyes.

"Don't you dare roll your eyes at me."

Oh, how well she knew me. I smiled. "Coffee? My treat?"

†

"Oh my, a promise ring." I hugged my best friend.

"Can you believe it? He asked me last night, during the party. I was so surprised. I mean, I knew he liked me, but he *loves* me, Ren. This is un-freaking-believably awesome."

"What's not to love? How did you guys celebrate?"

She went into detail about how he'd taken her to Cheavoux de Boi, which required booking months ahead, all the sweet things he'd told her, and how he was going to join her in Seattle in the fall. I said my "oo's" and "ahh's" and gushed in all the right places, encouraging her.

"That's one hell of a night." I really was excited for her. "Ohmigod! Did you guys have sex?"

"No," she said, blushing. "We made *love*. And not for the first time, either," she added quickly, taking a sip out of her cappuccino.

"What?" I yelled, causing everyone at Starbucks to look at us. I quieted. "What? When did that happen?"

She rolled her eyes. "It's not a big deal."

"Like hell, it isn't. You lost your virginity and you didn't tell me?"

"I didn't want to overburden you when you were going through so much . . ."

I knew what "going through so much" meant—my parents passing away and my need to isolate myself. Guilt wrapped around my heart. I'd been so absorbed in my loss, I hadn't been there for her.

"I didn't think you were that naïve. It's not like we ever keep our hands off each other."

My eyes widened and I spat coffee in surprise. Leave it to Pey to make a joke out of something that was so important. "Seriously, I'm okay with not knowing where your, or, for that matter, Landon's hands have been." I traced my finger around the rim of my cup and looked back at her. "I'm sorry I wasn't there for you. It must have been scary."

She shrugged and crinkled her nose, grinning. "It was amazing, Ren." Her voice dipped low. "The first time was so memorable. He planned everything. He took me to McCall, and we went hiking, boating, and wakeboarding. By the end of the night, I was so exhausted, he pampered me with massages. When I came out of the shower, he'd lit the whole room with candles and laid a path of flowers for me to find him. When I reached the bed, I saw he'd written 'I love you. Be mine,' in red rose petals," she gushed.

"Aww, that's so romantic." I hesitated for a second, thinking. "I don't want to know the details . . . but . . . first time? You know, did it . . . ?"

"Why, Ren, if I didn't know any better, I'd think you were trying to lose your V-card."

I stuck my tongue out, giggling.

"It was amazing, and it hurt. Landon did everything he could, but there's only so much he could do, you know?" She blushed seven shades of red. "But, after that first time, it was like I was complete, and we were beautiful."

I cleared my throat, taking a sip out of my hot coffee.

"H-how did you know what to do?" I asked. Being naked in front of someone, letting them see your flaws and vulnerability, it seemed so nerve-racking.

"I didn't. It all just happened. We . . . *he* took his time and made sure I was comfortable. And there was a lot of touching—lots and lots of touching." She giggled. "I asked him later, and he said he'd researched about first-time experiences so he'd be prepared."

I raised my eyebrows, feeling heat creep up my cheeks.

"Now, spill. There's no way you're still a virgin after sleeping through the whole day."

"I *am* still a virgin, thank you very much." I let out a heavy sigh, wishing I could tell her everything. But I couldn't. Hell, I was still trying to make sense of it all. Instead, I turned the conversation back to her and Landon. I listened, half-distracted, my thoughts going back to the night before.

My legacy. Axel. Dean being my protector, my bonded.

Two hours later, Pey got a call from Landon. She looked so happy as she talked, laughed, and even blushed. We said our goodbyes so that she could spend some time with him, and I could be alone in my room. Away from the rest of the world.

†

Knock. Knock.

"Go away," I mumbled into the pillow. I was still pissed at Joshua. I'd made it perfectly clear, the last four times he'd tried to check on me, that I wanted to be left alone . . .

The door creaked open.

"Hey, you." Pey placed something on my study table and threw herself onto my bed. "Joshua *and* Dean called."

I pulled my head from under the pillow and looked at her patient smile. I threw my arms around her neck and burst into tears.

"Um, I love you like a sister, but don't get any of that snot on me, okay?"

I laughed weakly. "Sorry." I wiped my tears.

"What's wrong?"

Let's see . . . I was a non-human freak, and was expected to end a war that had started centuries ago. Oh, and I'd been lied to all my life by everyone I trusted, including Joshua. But I didn't say any of that.

Instead, I said, "Everything."

"Wanna talk about it?" She rubbed my shoulder.

Pey knew I would tell her when I was ready, so she didn't push me. Instead, she offered the next best thing: chick flicks and pizza.

"I'm game. Let me go freshen up." I sniffled, wiping the flood of tears from my cheeks.

I ran to the bathroom. Looking at myself in the mirror, I noticed how haggard I looked. My hair was worse than Medusa's, my eyes were bloodshot, and my face was caked with dried tears and snot.

"Argh."

Instead of a quick cleanup, I opted for a warm shower. A few minutes later, I changed into my Sponge Bob shorts and tank top, looking forward to the night.

"I swear my boobs are biggeerrr," I drawled, looking at Pey.

She was pulling on her Betty Boop shorts, changing into her nightclothes. "Well, it's about damn time." Pey whacked my butt, brazenly wiggling her eyebrows. "I was starting to wonder if your girls were ever gonna show up."

I jumped on the bed and rolled onto my stomach, my chin propped in my hands. "I think you've had enough boobs to cover both of us since sixth grade."

She crinkled her nose and hopped on my bed, a handful of DVDs in hand. "Well, don't be jealous, because . . ." she wiggled her eyebrows and started to sing, "My boobs bring all the boys to the parties; and they're like, it's better than yours; damn straight, they're better than yours!"

I burst out laughing and picked up a pillow, whacking her sideways. "Ohmigod! You did not just go there!"

"I sooo went there, girlfriend." She shoved a pillow into my body. "Don't be such a bitch, just because Landon is crazy about these babies." She cupped them, squeezing.

"Oh, Pey," I drawled. "I'm so glad Landon is into your boobs and not mine."

She giggled, falling back on my bed. "Me too, Ren. Meee too."

I joined her after I'd grabbed the DVDs. I studied each. "Which one are we starting with?"

"Is that even a question?" Pey asked.

I turned my head, and it was like we were twins born to two different mothers, because we both said the same thing: "P.S. I love you."

Giggling, I put the DVD into the player and hurried back to the bed with the cold pizza and popcorn.

When the titles started scrolling, Pey said, "I'm sorry."

"For what?" I shoved popcorn into my mouth.

"For not noticing you'd had a shitty day."

I shrugged, because I didn't know what to say and I felt like a complete fraud for hiding the truth from her.

CHAPTER FIFTEEN

"NUH-UH . . . NO WAY I'M GETTING ON THAT THING." MY VOICE trembled.

Axel had cornered me after school the following Monday, insisting that I needed to know more about who I was. He was so damn determined he'd threatened to make me listen to him, one way or another. So I, being the mature adult, and wanting to avoid whatever the alternatives were, finally agreed.

Unfortunately, I didn't know he was going to get me killed on the way to the truth. And the irony of it was, he wanted me to ride the same motorcycle he'd tried to run me over with. Its blood-red coating and black designer markings shone under the dazzling sunlight. The passenger seat was . . . well, there really wasn't one. I may as well have crawled onto his lap.

He handed me his helmet. "Come on, Ren, Dulcea is safe."

"No . . . wait, you named your bike *Dulcea*?" I laughed, momentarily distracted. "So that's what Rachel was insinuating."

"Shh . . ." He rubbed his hand over the glossy red finish. "She has feelings."

"Whatever. I'm not riding your *Dulcea*." Savannah and Rachel walked by just as those words slipped out of my mouth.

Kill me. Kill me now!

They looked to Axel, then me, and then back at him. Rachel glared at me and my cheeks blazed.

Axel graced me with the cutest little pout, completely oblivious to what had happened.

"Fine," I said. "But if my head splits open like a watermelon, it's on your conscience."

He smiled, a dazzling, shy thing that made me forget all the reasons I was supposed to be pissed at him.

My heart filled with joy. I wanted him to keep smiling. I liked it when he smiled. I liked it *a lot*, especially when it was . . . *because* of me. For me. I knew it was utterly ridiculous, but in that moment, I would do pretty much anything if it kept him smiling at me like that.

I took the helmet from his hands and placed it over my head.

"Where are we going?" I asked.

"Well . . ."

His cheeks turned red as he placed his hand behind his neck, looking nervous. There was nothing more gorgeous than that! My fingers fumbled with the straps of the helmet, trying to adjust it on my soon-to-be watermelon mush.

"Here, let me," he said.

He closed the distance between us. I stiffened and held my breath as he buckled the helmet under my chin. His fingers gracefully touched the skin along my jawline.

I studied him, wondering what he would do if I reached up and kissed him. He had to be a great kisser. I mean, who would have lips like that and not know how to use them?

You freak, get a grip. He kills for a living.

Mentally slapping myself wasn't enough, so I mentally drop-kicked myself in the gut.

"Now your pretty head is safe." He patted the helmet.

I let out a breath I didn't know I'd been holding. He smiled enthusiastically, crinkles drawing at the corners of his eyes. I gaped shamelessly at him as he straddled Dulcea.

His eyes locked with mine.

"One leg at a time, Ren. Here, first." He pointed to the foot pegs.

Okay. Here we go. I hesitated. After all, he was a very hot guy and my body was about to get up close and personal with his. I sighed deeply before carefully stepping on the foot peg and swinging over the seat.

"Hold on," he said, looking back at me with a twinkle in his bright blue eyes.

I nodded and placed my arms on his waist, trying to keep some distance between us.

His shoulders vibrated. Was he laughing at me?

"I don't bite. Unless . . ." He shook his head like he was trying to purge that thought.

Unless what?

He grabbed my wrists and pulled them around to the front of his stomach, bringing me flush against his back. I sucked in a surprised breath, my body humming at the contact. Everything around me zeroed in on him—his body against mine, his spring-like smell, his touch . . .

I cleared my throat.

He overlapped my hands on his abs—his rock-hard abs. My heart thumped against his back as I pressed into him even more. My thighs lined the length of his legs. I blew out another breath to shake off the nerves. What was going on? My hormones were on the express train to Lustville.

"Lean the same direction I do," he instructed in a hoarse whisper. He cranked the ignition and I could feel every rumble as Dulcea came to life, dreading the ride before it even began. He placed his hand on my bare knee to soothe me.

"I've got you, Ren. Trust me."

"I trust you," I whispered. I didn't know when or why, but that was the truth.

†

He parked the bike in the gravel next to the road and waited for me to dismount. Removing my helmet and handing it to him, I headed toward the walkway that led to a narrow, downhill path.

"Where are we going?" I asked, wrapping my arms around my stomach, feeling nervous and a bit self-conscious.

He hopped off the bike, secured the helmet, and walked toward me—every step measured and decisive. "Come. I'll show you."

I worried my lip. I knew these next moments would change my whole perception of the world, no matter where he took me. It was like my *Spidey senses* kicked in.

"You're ridiculously beautiful," he said, tucking a strand of hair behind my ear.

My heart pounded against my ribcage. *Why is he looking at me like that?*

His eyes stared into mine as the backs of his fingers gently grazed my cheek. I swallowed, hard. He dropped his hand and leaned in closer. His scent engulfed me, pushing everything else into oblivion. It was just him and me.

His lips moved seductively against my ear. "You'll love this place."

Sweet. Lord.

"You coming?" he called over his shoulder, chuckling.

One word snuck into my head as I trailed after him:

Addiction.

He paused, waiting for me to catch up, smiling that smile that could easily break millions of hearts, including mine. "Close your eyes," he instructed, grabbing my hand and leading the way toward a hollow surrounded by mysterious vines.

He was precise in providing instructions on things to watch out for—step down or up, move to the right or left.

His soft lips grazed my ear. Again. "Open your eyes, *Meus Aeternus*."

I think I just turned into a . . . yup, puddle of useless ooze. God, what was he trying to do to me?

I slowly opened my eyes to a breathtaking view.

The cave was large enough to hold at least a thousand partygoers. There was a little pond in the middle about ten feet wide; lotuses bloomed beautifully in the middle. Trees decorated the ancient walls with flowers I'd never seen. I could smell a combination of honeysuckle, jasmine, lotus, the breeze over pure water . . .

The smell of spring. The smell of Axel, I noted.

Words were lost in my throat. This was what heaven must look like. I was sure of it. I held on to Axel's hand as I ran forward to explore, pulling him with me.

"What is this place?" I asked, trying to figure out if it was real.

My senses were in hyperdrive. It felt exhilarating. Joyful. I looked up to find the last of the sunlight pouring through an opening in the ceiling—shining like angel rays. If gods were to descend anywhere, this would be the place. It was pure magic. And it felt like home. It had the same ethereal feeling I'd felt during my dream with Nala and Dracia—the same vibrant colors and smell in the air.

I turned around to find Axel staring at me, possibly concluding I was insane.

"What?" I asked, embarrassed.

I started to pull my hand back, but he tightened his grip. "It feels complete." *Now that you're here*, his eyes whispered.

I sucked in a breath, my heart kicking into high gear. That wasn't what I had expected him to say. My obsession intensified.

Great. Just freaking great.

"Thank you . . . for this. I don't think I've ever been so awestruck by nature—maybe in my dream about Dracia, but definitely not in real life."

He continued to watch me with a questioning look on his face. Awe colored his voice. "You dreamt about Dracia?"

I shrugged and took a seat by the pond. I ran my fingers back and forth in the cold water, creating a soothing rhythm. He walked over and sat next to me.

"After intervention get-Ren-up-to-speed-about-who-the-hell-she-really-is, I had this dream. It felt so real. I can't ever remember dreaming in color, or feeling the perfect texture of petals and the softness of earth," I admitted. "It was like I was there, physically. Hell, Nala even said I was there."

Axel's eyebrows rose, one of them disappearing behind the hair covering his forehead. "Nala?"

I nodded, chuckling, captured by the waves in the pond. "I didn't believe it. I mean, who would name their kid Nala, like the Disney character?"

"Do you now?" Axel asked.

"Do I now, what?" I turned to look at him. "Know people who would name their kid Nala?" I teased, knowing full well he was referring to my belief in his story. In my heritage.

He started to shake his head.

I smiled. "I don't have a choice. It's either that or I'm in need of a psych ward. And that's not an option. I don't look good in gray coveralls."

His blue eyes brightened a tad. "You always look beautiful, Ren. Always."

My stomach did a little flutter and my heart beat out of my chest.

"God is bipolar," I blurted, hoping to divert that gaze and his thoughts.

"What?" His voice was low and surprised.

"I mean, how can he create something as astonishing as this and also create those things? Goarders, or whatever." I shivered, remembering the blood-red eyes, sharp teeth, and snake-like tongues.

"Yin and yang, good and evil. It's the balance of life. It keeps the universe moving forward." He shrugged. "When the scales tip one way or another, nature takes control to balance it out. I think that's how we *Kshadrias* were initially born," he said carefully.

He leaned back on his elbows and looked at the sky peeking through the opening above us. I tilted my chin up, taking in the beauty. The sun had gone down, leaving us with millions of sparkling stars illuminating the sky.

Breathtaking. Beautiful.

I sighed. I looked toward Axel and our eyes found each other.

His were pale blue and clouded by conflict, like he was fighting an inner battle. Then his features relaxed. I saw the determination and knew his mind was made up.

"I want you to know me, Ren. I need you . . ." He shook his head. "*We* need you."

My heart did funny things. I knew it was stupid, since I barely knew the guy, but I couldn't control what my damned hormones wanted. I felt Axel's eyes travel along the side of my cheek, down to my shoulders.

"Do you age like humans?" I asked, attempting to change the subject. "Nala implied that you lived much longer than us humans. So . . ."

"The lucky ones." He half-smiled. "Most die fighting this never ending war, but the oldest of us lived to be in their four hundreds."

"Well, that's a long, boring life. Not to mention, lots of wrinkles." I crinkled my nose, thinking about how I would look at age four hundred.

His shoulders shook uncontrollably as he laughed, his mouth wide open. "You're seriously worried about wrinkles? You're such a girl."

"Well, I really don't think I could live with my wrinkly self for over three hundred years." He was laughing so loud I felt stupid. "What?"

"You're ridiculously cute. How did you ever survive being this gullible?"

I scowled at him.

"Okay. Okay," he said, raising his hands in defeat. "So, it's like this: humans start to wrinkle at about age fifty, right?"

"Give or take a couple years."

He nodded. "Dracians start to see wrinkles around two hundred-ish." He paused, shrugging his shoulders. "Give or take a few decades."

Oh. Duh! Stupid math.

But I wasn't ready to admit he was right. Might as well stay mad at him and math, and the person that had invented math, for good measure. Axel tried to get me to look at him.

"I'm sorry. I shouldn't have laughed. Forgive me?"

I looked away, acting like a five-year-old that didn't get her way.

"What can I do to make it up to you? Come on, Ren, don't be like that," he teased, offering his hand.

I raised my eyebrows.

"I thought a change of scenery would be nice," he explained, wiggling his fingers.

"Fine." I got up and walked away from him, trying to hide my mischievous smile.

"Ren, wait." He caught up to me and grabbed my hand. Electricity surged up my arm, jumpstarting the erratic beating of my heart. "Ren."

"What?" I intended to snap at him, but it came out as a longing whisper.

"You're going the wrong way." He grinned like a fool.

Shit.

Warmth built in my cheeks. Axel leaned in to the curve of my neck, his breath tickling my skin. I fought hard not to let my eyes roll back in pure bliss.

"Pink is a great color on you."

I was sure I turned bloody-red-tomato.

"Red isn't a bad color either," he laughed, letting go of my hand and turning to walk the other way. "Come on. You'll like this."

I followed in step with him as we headed back toward the cave's entrance.

"I want to show you some cool tricks."

"Oh, can you sit, stay, jump, shake hands, and roll over?" I asked sarcastically, clapping my hands like an excited little kid.

"That and more, *Amor Aeternus*," he teased, running his hand through his hair nervously. "I'm surprised how well you're taking all of this."

Considering I hadn't believed a word of it just two days ago, so was I. Maybe it had been Nala, or maybe it was because I'd had time to think and let the information sink in. But somewhere deep down, I was starting to *feel* the possibility of the truth.

His lips pressed together in a tight smile. "I was afraid you might never speak to me again, and possibly even get a restraining order."

"You're my ride home," I teased. "But I haven't tossed out the idea of a restraining order." I shrugged, smiling. "Where is home, exactly? Dracia, I mean."

"I'll give you one guess."

I searched through all the information I'd been given, but couldn't remember if anyone had said.

"I think humans call it the Bermuda Triangle," he responded.

My eyes widened in disbelief. "No freaking way!"

He chuckled, nudging my shoulder. I was amazed at how easy it was for me to be with him—talking, laughing, joking . . . it reminded me of when we'd first met, before I'd thought he was a serial killer, before Rachel. Before all of it.

"Come on, we're here."

He took my hand and I almost pulled back, still not used to the electricity that flowed between us. It was like our bodies were recognizing and responding to each other. Or maybe it was all in my crazed mind.

He led me around a curve of path that disappeared behind the trees. The smell of wet soil scented the surrounding air as we approached a rushing waterfall. The sound reminded me of the way most of us live our lives—rushed and chaotic.

I gasped at the spectacular view.

It resembled a mini Niagara Falls. We stood at the bottom as a cool breeze teased my senses. Kicking off my flip-flops, I sat on the edge of the bank and dangled my feet in, letting the cold water tickle between my toes. I sighed in satisfaction, once again getting lost in the beauty of nature.

"This is amazing." I glanced back at Axel, who was standing a few feet away, taking in the view. "Thank you!"

He walked over, kicking off his boots, and settled in next to me, placing his hand beside mine. Our pinky fingers touched slightly. "I'm just glad I could share this with you," he said, gazing into my eyes. Something inside me stirred. Acceptance or . . .

"I want to show you something. If that's okay?" he said, breaking the moment.

I nodded, feeling more willing to learn about my heritage than ever before. He jumped to his feet, angling himself toward the falls. He stood with his feet shoulder-width apart, his hands extended outward. The muscle in his jaw twitched as he shifted his weight, creating little circles with his hands. The duff on the ground began to shiver, rising toward his outstretched palms like puppets on a string, answering his every gesture. He choreographed beautiful swirling patterns with the fallen leaves, twigs, and flowers.

"This can't be real!" I rubbed my eyes, looking around at my surreal surroundings. "Can everyone do this?"

"Not everyone. Some of us are more gifted than others." Axel repositioned himself so he was facing the waterfall, his brows knitting together like he was zeroing in on a target. "Watch this."

He did a quick, wave-type hand gesture, like he was grasping at a fly—the waterfall ceased.

"Holy shit!" I squealed and clapped my hands, grinning wildly. "This is . . . wow!"

He smiled at my childlike behavior. "Hold that thought."

I looked at him, surprised. There was more? I watched closely as he balled his hands and moved them toward my head. He smiled wickedly as he slowly opened his fists. The waterfall roared as it surged back to life, tumbling into the pool below. Little beads of water speckled over me.

I gasped as the first cold drop touched my skin. "It's raining!" I squealed. "You're making it rain?"

Delighted, I opened my arms, inviting the drizzle into my embrace. I twirled with my face to the sky, eyes closed. When it stopped, I pouted. "I can't believe you just made it rain! You're my new favorite person. Okay, maybe after Pey, but you're definitely in my top two."

"What does a guy have to do to become your number one?" His voice dripped like warm honey.

"Wouldn't you like to know?" I mumbled, blushing.

He chuckled. "I didn't make it rain."

I looked at him, confused.

He twirled his finger around me, referring to my earlier question. "Part of my gift is not just controlling the air element, but controlling whatever the air comes into contact with. I can freeze molecules, combust them or move them . . . like I did with the water—diverting it from the waterfall to simulate rain."

"I can't believe you're actually showing me this." I took a seat at the edge of the riverbed, my feet dangling in the water. "I didn't think you would." Maybe a trick or two with illusion and mirrors. But this . . .

His lips curved at the corners in a boyish smile, his fingers running through his hair. He stared out at the waterfall instead of responding.

I realized I wasn't going to get much more so I went on to my next question. "Why didn't you just use your abilities on the Goarders, instead of your daggers? Clearly, you have the talent to blow things up. And don't say it was to impress me. 'Cause I'm not buying it."

He smiled, shyly, pink tinting his cheeks. "It's called a Tibt dagger." He pulled an object wrapped in blue cloth from his discarded boot and placed it on his palm for me to see. He crouched beside me, eyes glittering with excitement. "It's a mixture of Tungsten, Titanium, Iridium, a more lethal version of Botulin, and magic from an Original. The combination kills Telalians instantly."

"So, why not create bullets or some other type of fast-paced machine to kill them?"

He chuckled. "We do have advanced firearms that incapacitate them for several seconds, but with the Originals' blood in deficit . . ." He shrugged and sat down, his feet dangling in the water next to mine. "Besides, there's nothing more exhilarating than hand-to-hand combat. The adrenaline rush is indescribable."

His eyes were intoxicated as he talked about the thrill of action, a barely contained grin on his face. I'd never seen him look so alive. I wasn't sure how to feel about the fact that violence seemed to be like a drug to him. He tossed the dagger, catching it by the hilt and then the sharp end. I flinched several times, but he was clearly an expert at handling the Tibt.

". . . when he thinks he's got the upper hand, then, *bam*! You knock him out, taking him by surprise." His tone turned stern and deep. "It's the satisfaction that you and you alone rid that evil from the earth. Not with something else, but with strength from within."

His eyes grew wild, his brows furrowed, and a grimace dominated his normally serene features.

Suddenly, I understood. He wasn't a psychopath, intoxicated by the thrill of killing, he was a boy that had had to grow up too fast—too soon. He must have lost something dear to him. Like I had.

"What happened, Axel?"

He looked at me, his face unyielding, confusion flickering in his eyes. I watched him carefully, waiting for him to open up, to tell me his story. When he didn't, I tried to fill the awkward silence.

"I . . . you seem like a person that is . . . I don't know. You talk like you have nothing to lose. That you want to fight these monsters and . . ."

"You know what my greatest fear is?" he interrupted, his voice stern.

I shook my head, slightly afraid of this path I'd forced him down. I drew my legs up to my chest, encircling them in a tight grip, and placed my head on top of my knees, waiting.

"That I would die a coward. That when death and I see eye-to-eye, I would run the other way."

He sighed heavily before squaring his shoulders and facing me. There was hardness in his eyes, and the pain of losing people he'd loved. I could feel the weight of his responsibility—like he carried his entire race on his shoulders.

"I want to die with pride in my eyes, a smile on my face, and, if I can, taking one last Telalian with me. I want to die knowing I've saved another soul."

"Why?" My eyes stung. For his lost innocence. For whatever he'd been through to make him so hardened—like Joshua.

His voice trembled with painful emotion when he spoke. "Because I watched as they slit my mother's throat. She used her last breath to protect me, and I didn't do anything."

A shocked gasp escaped my lips. How could I respond to something like that? Sorry wasn't enough. What could I say to a boy that had watched his mother die? To a boy who blamed himself for her murder?

"How old were you?" I said quietly, my voice choked with emotion.

"Nine."

He'd been nine years old? Nine *years?* My heart broke for him. I didn't know what to say, so I offered the only thing I could that would put us on semi-equal ground.

"Both of my parents were killed last year."

It was still hard to talk about. I never did. Not with Joshua. Not with Pey. I didn't know if I could tell him my story. But I felt like he'd be the one person to understand the pain I still held.

"My brother and I came home after a night out." Words rushed out of my mouth without thought. My hand automatically went to the amulet my mom had given me when I was six. "My parents had been acting weird over the summer, like they were preparing for something. They finalized their wills, got their finances in order, and my dad gave me his BMW Z1 that he'd bought with his first paycheck. He never let anyone touch that car." The corners of my lips pulled into a faint smile at the memory, but it quickly faded as I continued. "I thought they'd finally come around to planning. They'd always lived for the element of surprise." My eyes went to my chipped nails, my heart heavy in my chest. "But that night, when the knock came and I saw the sheriff, I knew something was wrong." I paused, swallowing back the pain. "Joshua and I had to identify their mauled bodies. They were covered in cuts, bruises, and burn marks. The sheriff's department thought it was gang-related."

Tears welled in my eyes, spilling down my cheeks. When I looked at Axel's face, it was expressionless, except for his dilated eyes and pursed lips. He reached for me but obviously thought otherwise, drawing his hand back in a fist. He ran his hand through his hair and avoided my eyes. A flicker of something I couldn't identify crossed his face before he schooled it to be expressionless again. I took a deep breath and wiped the tears before continuing.

"It took me over a year to recover." I looked down at my hands laid across my criss-crossed legs. When had I changed positions? "It's been a year and three months since I've looked at anything that belonged to them, or even been in their room. I didn't let my brother or anyone else enter either. I don't want the closure. It's a stupid sentiment, I guess. But cleaning their room means I've accepted their death. I-I . . . I don't think I can handle that."

I turned away from Axel, wiping my tears. I felt ashamed for being so weak. He was so strong, and he'd mourned his loss by avenging his mother's death. I, on the other hand, sulked in misery.

"Ren." His voice was calm, inviting, and warm. I couldn't look at him. It took every ounce of my strength not to. He turned toward me, placing his hands on either side of my face, tilting my head up. A jolt of energy flooded through me, but I closed my eyes, refusing to look him straight in the eye.

"Please look at me."

His pleading voice stirred something unknown inside me and I gave in. I looked at his blue eyes, glowing with so much concern and care. How was he so strong? He'd lost so much, yet here he was, consoling me.

"Ren, you have nothing to be ashamed of. You hear me? Everyone mourns differently." He let out a deep sigh. "You, Ren . . . you're strong." He wiped tears off my cheeks with his thumbs. "I can't imagine losing both my parents. It probably would've sent me off the deep end." He chuckled weakly. "And I was brought up around death. You weren't and yet, look at you. You're still in one piece. Healthy, and smiling."

I gave a weak laugh. "You wouldn't say that if you'd known me last year." I sniffled.

"You're stronger than you think, *Meus Aeternus.*"

His eyes bored into mine, intense and ablaze, searching for something. It was both scary and breathtakingly beautiful. And I loved it. I was lost in a world where only Axel and I existed.

"Axel, I'm fi—"

My phone buzzed, shattering the moment. He dropped his hands from my face and sat back, watching as I pulled my phone from my pocket.

Pey: CALL ME WHEN YOU GET THIS. XOXO.

"It's getting late. We should probably head home." Axel got to his feet and held out his hand. Unlike the first time, I happily accepted his help.

"Thank you. Really. I've never talked to *anyone* about . . ." I said.

"Your secret is safe with me." He smiled, understanding. "But it seems we jumped the gun here."

"Um . . ." I was confused.

"We know each other's deepest, darkest secret, but not really anything else. I want to know more about *you*." He turned to me, once again looking at me with an intensity that excited me to the core. "I want to know you, Ren." His voice lowered as he said my name.

He wanted to know me. This gorgeous, absolutely imperfect man wanted to know *me*.

"I'd like that," I said, smiling.

A peaceful silence filled the space between us. It wasn't awkward, just serene. Neither of us felt the need to fill it with pointless jabber, and I liked that.

My phone buzzed. Again.

"Hello?" I answered.

"Where the hell are you? I've been trying to reach you all evening!"

"Sorry, Muskles." I shot a sideways glance at Axel, who stared at me. "I'm out with . . . a friend." I didn't know why I hid the truth.

"You're supposed to check in when your plans change," Joshua said, worry staining his voice.

A smidgen of guilt wrapped around my heart. "I'm sorry. I'll be home soon, okay?"

He let out a sigh of relief. "I called Pey, and when she didn't know where you were, I . . . never mind. I thought you two were joined at the hip?"

I rolled my eyes. "I'll see you soon, okay? And maybe we can talk some?"

He sighed. "I love you, kiddo."

"Who was that? Your *boyfriend*?" Axel asked, a different kind of tension coloring his voice.

I laughed, waving one hand in front of me. "Yeah, no such luck here."

"That's hard to believe," he mumbled.

My cheeks flared and my laughter died on my lips. "It was just my overprotective, underappreciated brother," I said, suddenly interested in my fingernails.

"You check in with Joshua often?" He smiled. "Don't get me wrong. It's cute."

"I should get home before he turns on my phone's GPS and comes to find me."

Axel offered his hand and I took it, feeling lighter than I had since I'd found out the truth.

†

"Thank you for a great evening. I hope I get to see you again, but only if you want to?" he asked, uncertain.

Of course I wanted to. *Doesn't he?* I shoved away my fear of rejection and pulled on my big-girl panties, taking a dive into bravery.

"Yes, even if it means the end of the world." I was surprised at my response. My face burned, and I looked away. "Thank you for helping me understand, and letting me ask all those questions," I quickly added, avoiding eye contact.

Axel hesitantly placed his hand on my cheek and drew gentle circles with his thumb. My heart took on an odd, excited rhythm and I closed my eyes, soaking in the feel of his warmth against my skin. My soul soared with the need to connect with his. But as he leaned in closer, the front door flew open. I turned around to find my brother framed in it, nostrils flaring. He crossed his arms over his chest, a hammer hanging loosely in his right hand.

Shit!

Axel dropped his hand, shoving it into the front pocket of his jeans, and took a step back, rocking on his feet.

"Give me a minute," I said to Joshua.

He gave a curt nod and walked backward, his eyes fixed on Axel.

"Sorry." I paused, sneaking a peek over my shoulder to make sure Joshua was safely out of earshot. "I think he thought you and I . . ." I looked down, away, anywhere but at him, blushing.

"You and I . . . what, Ren?" he asked in a low, controlled voice.

"You and I were . . ."

A slow smile appeared on his face.

"It doesn't matter what he thinks. He's just being a jerk." I looked at him through my eyelashes. "I'll see you around. Soon?" I asked, a little desperately.

"Yes. Even if it means the end of the world." He quoted me with that crooked grin I was falling in love with. "I'll see you soon, *Amor Aeternus.*"

My heart danced. My legs refused to move, but I forced myself to turn around and head inside. I heard the rumble of his bike disappearing into the night and knew he was gone.

I missed him already.

CHAPTER SIXTEEN

JOSHUA STOOD BEHIND THE KITCHEN ISLAND, HIS GAZE LOCKED on the front door as I walked through. Cassie hummed, working her magic in our kitchen. The aroma of rosemary and chicken filled my lungs. They weren't married yet, but with the amount of time Cassie had been at our place, she was already part of the family.

I walked into the kitchen and Cassie turned around, the corners of her lips curved up. "Hi, sweetie. Did you have fun?"

I mouthed, *"Am I in trouble?"*

She nodded.

Joshua's lips were pressed tightly together as he stared me down. "I expect you to be more responsible, especially now that you know the truth," he fumed.

I pictured real steam coming from his ears and stifled a laugh.

"Oh, I think we found Grumpy. Better let Snow White know." I tried to sound sarcastic, but it came out annoyed.

"Don't think you can get away by joking around, Temperance."

I flinched. The only time he ever called me by my name—my *full* name—was when I was knee-deep in trouble.

"You were out with a *boy* past your curfew, and you didn't text or call to let me know you were okay. Do you understand how worried I was?"

"Would you rather I'd been out with a *girl*?" I teased. "Why can't you trust that I can take care of myself? Besides, I was with *Axel*. And since you two know each other, you also know that he's capable of protecting me," I snapped back.

I regretted it as soon as I said the words. Of course, he'd worried. He hadn't known *who* I was out with, so he'd been right to worry. Besides, worrying was part of his role as my big brother. If not, he wouldn't have given up everything so that I could avoid becoming part of the *system*. I opened my mouth to apologize, but he cut me off.

"Like hell. You're still underage and living under my roof. That means you follow *my* rules. Rules that include you not spending time alone with Axel after your curfew. Which, by the way, just got bumped to eight p.m."

"Ohmigod, Muskles! Are you shitting me right now? You can't tell me what to do!"

His posture stiffened. He balled his hands into fists, like he was controlling his urge to lock me in a tower with a hundred guards to protect my virtue. I didn't back down. It wasn't like I'd done anything to be ashamed of.

Cassie stepped between us, placing her hand on Joshua's shoulder. "Calm down, Joshy. Ren is a responsible girl."

She turned to me, a cup in her other hand. "Your brother is just worried about you. He's got that protect-my-little-sister-from-the-male-species syndrome. He doesn't want you to make any hasty decisions. Right, Joshy?"

When he didn't respond, she elbowed him in the ribs. "Right?"

"Right." He gritted his teeth. Cassie walked toward me, handing me the cup of hot cocoa. I took a sip and winced as the liquid scalded my tongue.

"Well, you can tell your *fiancé* he needs to trust me. I'm not a person that sleeps with random guys." Not that I hadn't thought about Axel in that way. "Besides, Axel would never do anything to disrespect me."

"Fine. But we still need to talk about safe se—"

"Oh, no . . . don't you dare say that word." I shuddered at the thought of my brother lecturing me about sex. "That's one word I'd rather not ever—I mean, never ever—hear from you, Muskles."

"It's not easy for me to talk about it either, but better safe—"

I put my fingers in my ears and started singing loudly until his lips stopped moving and his hands came up in defeat. I saw Cassie's shoulders tremble, the back of her hand covering her mouth.

"I don't know how you keep up with this maniac, Cassie."

"Well, they say love is blind."

She put her arms around Joshua's waist and gave him a quick kiss. We sat down for dinner, continuing with small talk that had nothing to do with sex.

Thank you, baby Cupid!

"I understand," I blurted out.

Cassie and Joshua froze. Their backs stiffened, like someone had taped a support bar to their spines.

"I understand why you wanted to keep the truth from me. Even after Mom and Dad died," I told Joshua. "I know I sounded like an ungrateful child, but I understand. You were only trying to protect me."

Joshua lowered his fork and gulped down his mouthful of food. He reached for my free hand, pulling it between his. "I know I should have told you sooner. But I wanted you to have a somewhat normal high school life. I guess I just wanted the same thing as Mom."

"I get that. I just wish you guys hadn't kept this huge part of me *from* me." I paused, pushing loose corn to the side of my plate. "That's why I was late tonight. Axel was helping me understand my heritage. He even showed me what he can do. It was kinda neat." I looked up through my eyelashes, hoping to drive it home. "Don't be mad at him, Joshua. He's a good guy." And I sorta, kinda like him—maybe.

"I know," Joshua mumbled, averting his gaze. "But it's also my job to protect you from everything—natural or supernatural."

"I know." I loved him for that and wouldn't dream of having it any other way. He was my brother. Overprotective was part of his job description. "Oh, before I forget, I'm going to Chicago with Pey next month."

"Who else is going?" He dropped his fork in his plate.

"I don't know, but I promised Pey I'd be there on her big day."

He stayed quiet for a few minutes. I could see the wheels churning in his head and braced myself for another round of bickering.

"Okay."

"But—wait. What? I can go? Just like that?" My eyebrows shot high in disbelief.

He nodded hesitantly. "Just don't do anything I wouldn't."

I raised an eyebrow.

"Oh, you know . . . that the adult me wouldn't," he quickly added.

My brother's teenage years had been crazy—drinking, partying, and lots of trouble.

"Well, I've been thinking I'd get really drunk and have crazy, wild sex with every guy I come across." The look on his face was priceless. I took my plate to the sink. "Fine . . . only with the guys I really know . . ." I ran out of the room before he could say anything. I heard him growl and throw something into the sink that shattered to pieces.

"You know she's only joking . . ." Cassie soothed.

I really didn't get how she put up with his temper.

CHAPTER SEVENTEEN

OVER THE NEXT TWO WEEKS, AXEL AND I SPENT MORE TIME together as he continued to answer my questions. I couldn't believe I'd ever thought he was a serial killer. I'd never met anyone with the kind of chivalry he possessed—always polite, holding the door for me and others. One time, I actually ended up waiting a good ten minutes because he held the door until the last person had left the school. How could I not have fuzzy feelings for a guy like that?

Things between Joshua and I were back to normal. He was even starting to get used to the idea that my spending time with Axel might not be such a bad thing—as long as we were in the living room.

But today was different. As part of our getting-to-know-each-other-better scheme, he'd planned a surprise outing—no Dracian talk allowed. He'd picked me up at exactly three and wouldn't tell me where we were headed. He said something about living a little and spontaneity.

He parked in front of a huge warehouse labeled Karter Raid, turned off the engine and zipped out of the car, locking the doors.

"Stupid *Dracian*," I muttered under my breath. "Show off!" I yelled louder.

A sly smile tugged at the corners of his lips. He unlocked my door and pulled it open, extending his hand toward me.

"You've been beating me to the punch," he said as I placed my hand in his and stepped out of the car. He pulled me to him, slamming the door shut, and leaned me back against the metal. "I can't have you opening your own door, especially when we're on our first official *date*—as humans call it."

Date? We're on a date? I didn't know if I should jump for joy or have a nervous breakdown.

His eyes knitted together and he tilted his head to the side.

"That's what it's called, right? When a boy takes out a girl he really likes to have fun . . ."

I nodded. He grinned in response. My gaze fell to his delicious, full lips. There'd been many no-space-to-breathe situations since we started to get close, but he had yet to make a move. Sure, he'd kissed my forehead, temple, and even the tip of my nose, but never my lips. I daydreamed of the day his mouth would be pressed against mine. Maybe with an official date under our belt, that might happen . . . today?

"Come on." He grabbed a hold of my hand, leading me toward the entrance.

Once we were inside, Axel asked me to take a seat while he stepped up to the counter. He ran back to me with a huge grin on his face, handing me a helmet and red jumpsuit.

"I hear you're unbeatable in kart racing."

I cocked my eyebrow at him. "Oh, really? And who told you about my queen-of-kart-racing status?"

He pulled me to him and kissed the tip of my nose. "I would've never figured you for a racer." His voice dropped low and husky. "It's incredibly sexy."

I laughed nervously, feeling my knees weaken. "That's so not fair."

He rewarded me with his rare, boyish grin before hauling me into the arena.

"Ready?" he asked over the revving of the race karts.

I winked at him as the buzzer sounded and took off without a second thought. Sixty-minutes later—and after winning five out of eight races—our time came to an end.

"I can't believe you took me kart racing." I elbowed Axel teasingly in the ribs as we walked out of the building. "I had fun kicking your butt."

He grinned triumphantly. "And I loved watching you get all competitive. It's a win-win, really. Not to mention, you looked sexy as hell in that red jumpsuit and helmet." He opened the car door, waiting for me to slide in. "Are you up for the next activity on the agenda?"

†

Axel parked at a familiar scene. "Last stop," he said with a wink.

He slung a monstrous hiking bag over his shoulder and took my hand as we walked toward the falls—*our* falls.

But this time, he walked past the waterfall and up the trail, going deeper into the wilderness. The ground became rocky with small, loose gravel. Axel stopped, looking back. "I should have told you about the hiking."

"It's not so bad," I responded, then looked at the block of rock he stood in front of. "You wanted to show me a slab of rock?"

He chuckled. "Always the smart ass, aren't you?"

I shrugged.

"How do you feel about climbing up this *slab of rock*?"

Excitement filled me. It wasn't the usual size Dean and I typically scaled, but it was a good eight feet high. I grinned wildly. "You're lucky *slabs of rock* aren't what intimidates me."

Axel, always the gentleman, strung a rope to something solid at the top, then offered to help me up, which I refused.

I wasn't going to pass up a perfectly good opportunity to rock climb—however small it was.

When we finally reached the top of the trail, I knew why he'd taken me so far. The hike was well worth the risk.

A cascade of water rushed over the precipice of land quietly, crashing to the surface below, making the air around us cool, and glittering with moisture. Its serene touch mesmerized me, spellbinding me to its beauty.

"I couldn't think of a better place," Axel said, standing close behind me.

I nodded, drinking in the scene. My eyes absorbed each detail—the seclusion, yet fullness of nature, the flowing waterfall, the cloudless sky. Light shone through the tiny drops of water sprinkling like mist, causing a rainbow. I took a deep breath and smiled.

"Ren." Axel's voice was as smooth as warm honey. I turned my gaze toward him. From the bemused, slightly curious look he gave me, he'd been calling my name for some time.

"This is . . . wow . . . majestic. Words can't do justice to its beauty."

He smiled. "Ready for dinner?"

My stomach growled, as if on cue, and I grinned. "I'm famished."

He turned on his heel and started unpacking the food from his bag.

"You already set up?"

He winked. "You seemed so lost in the view, I wanted to surprise you. Besides, it took me less than a min—"

Something feather-light landed on my hand, successfully drawing my attention away from Axel. A beautiful orange butterfly with black and white spots stood on my knuckles. Slowly, I brought my hand to eye level, examining it.

"I should be jealous," Axel said, approaching me cautiously. "Did you know butterflies taste through their feet?"

As his hand neared the butterfly, it flew away. I laughed and leaned back on an oak tree, wrapping my hand around the mossy trunk above my head.

"And why would you be jealous, Alexander?" My voice sounded sultry.

His eyes turned dark blue, taking on a possessive gleam. I gulped. *This is new.*

He moved slowly, inching his body closer and closer, like he was floating on water. He placed his hands and legs on either side of my shoulders and hips. He had a wicked smile that made my heart skip a beat, curling my toes. I automatically placed my hand on his abs, feeling the ripples of his hardened muscles under his shirt.

He leaned toward me and inhaled deeply. His chest rose and fell, almost touching mine. His breath tickled my ear and a shiver snaked up my spine. He chuckled. I melted to the ground when he whispered into my ear, his lips grazing the ridges with every word. "Because you're mine, and sharing isn't part of my dictionary."

He kissed the curve of my neck and pushed himself away. Another first—his lips touching my neck.

He gave me one last look before walking backward, beckoning me to follow him.

"You hungry?"

"Yes." My voice was raspy. I *was* hungry. Hungry for something that wasn't on the menu.

He settled on the quilt and patted his hand on the space next to him. I sat, tucking both my feet under my butt, as Axel dug through the picnic basket for our food. I gazed out over the small canyon below, watching the waterfall crashing to the bottom. The horizon glowed with vibrant colors of orange, blue, pink, and a tad bit of green.

I took a bite of the sandwich he placed in my hands and all but slobbered all over myself. "Yum!"

I chewed, savoring the taste. A little moan left my lips before I could stop it and I mentally face-palmed for my lack of decorum.

"Sorry," I mumbled, swallowing the food. "This is so good. What is it?"

"It's a secret. But I'm glad you like it." He traced his thumb across my bottom lip, bringing it back to his mouth and licking with a light, satisfied noise. "What?" He handed me a Crush, shaking his head at my open mouth.

"Thank you." The can opened with a hiss and I took two thirsty gulps. "This is amazing."

"Come here."

He opened his arms, urging me to come closer. I gripped the sandwich in one hand and scooted closer to him using the other. He wrapped his arm around my shoulder and squeezed gently. I snuggled into him, placing my head against the curve of his neck and shoulder.

"Mmmmm . . ." I purred.

His chest rumbled against my ear.

"Laugh all you want, but this is one hell of a sandwich."

"I'm going to have to remember what I put in it."

"Wait, you don't know what you put in here?" I asked, surprised.

"No, I'm an unconventional cook. I like to throw in a little of this and a little of that."

"So you're an unconventional cook?"

"Do you have the repeat button turned on?" he teased, kissing my forehead.

I elbowed him in the chest, earning a chuckle and another endearing peck on my temple.

We sat silently and watched as the sun set, dipping low on the horizon and eventually disappearing. The air around us turned brisker. I felt warmth tug around my shoulders as a pair of arms engulfed me, urging me to get closer.

If only time could freeze in this moment.

I sighed.

CHAPTER EIGHTEEN

CASSIE AND I WALKED UP THE DRIVE, A HUGE BINDER FILLED with all the possible flower arrangements we could possibly need for the wedding clutched in my hands.

"Thank you so much for accompanying me," Cassie said.

"Are you kidding? I'd do this with you any day if it got me out of playing video games with Joshua." I hugged her tightly with one arm. "I'm so excited to have you as my sister."

Tears threatened to seep through Cassie's lashes.

"I know I can never replace your mom, but I'll try my best to be the role model you deserve, Ren. You can always trust me and come to me if you need anything. And I do mean *anything*," she said. It took me a minute to understand what she was referring to.

I laughed out loud. "Joshua's been nagging you to talk to me, hasn't he?"

She nodded. "He's worried. As am I. But I know you're a smart girl, and you'll make the right choice." She placed her arm around my shoulder as I snaked mine around her waist. We walked up the stairs toward the porch.

"Does he not trust me?" I asked. Axel and I had been spending a lot of time together and Joshua's glares hadn't gone unnoticed. But so far, all the touches, and even the kisses, had been so innocent I didn't see why he was so worried.

"No, that's not it. He just doesn't want his baby sister getting hurt. He's having a hard time because you and Axel are so intense. Joshua and I knew each other our whole lives, and we didn't get that intense until a few years back," Cassie said as she let go of me and opened the door, stepping inside.

"You have nothing to worry about. I swear. We just like spending time with each other. Nothing more." *Yet.*

We were immediately greeted by Joshua, beer in hand. "Hey. Did my two favorite girls have a good time?"

"Oh yeah. We had so much fun swiping your credit card. How much did we spend, Cassie? Five grand?" I teased.

Joshua wrestled me into a bear hug. "Well, nice to see you too, Killer."

"You suck." I looked over Joshua's shoulder to Cassie and said, "He cheats, Cassie. He uses his super army-training mojo to get his bear hugs. Watch out for this one."

He let me go with a kiss on my cheek. "Oh, don't be such a baby. You know you love my bear hugs, and one day, you'll miss 'em."

I rolled my eyes. "Puh-leeease. Egotistical much?"

"Hey." Dean stepped out of the kitchen, a Crush in his hand.

"Did you boys have a good evening?" Cassie asked, hugging her brother.

Dean nodded, planting a kiss on the crown of her head.

"Yup. Video games." Joshua pointed toward the game running in the background.

Cassie jutted her hip, placing a hand over it. "So, let me guess, the dishes are still in the sink, the laundry isn't dry, and we have four hungry tummies that needed to be fed ten minutes ago, but edible food isn't ready?"

"Nope." Joshua sauntered over to his fiancée and grabbed her hand, twirling her into his embrace. He wrapped his arms around her petite body and planted a kiss on her cheek.

She giggled, her hands on his chest, looking up adoringly.

"Dishes are in the dishwasher, laundry is folded and put away, and if nachos will satisfy the hungry, food is ready, too." He responded to each of her statements with a kiss to her nose, forehead, and finally, her lips.

It wasn't until their hands started to grab at each other that I decided to vocalize my reaction. "Eww!"

Dean groaned. "I know you two are past the screwing stage, but seriously Pernell, stop defiling my sister before I tear my eyes out."

"Dean!" Cassie pushed away from Joshua, breathless. "I don't complain about all the groping I've had to witness over the past few years. So, if you don't like what *my fiancé* and I do, don't let the door hit your ass on the way out." She swatted her brother's chest affectionately as she headed into the kitchen.

"I'm outta here," I said, heading upstairs two stairs at a time.

"Dinner in forty-five," Cassie yelled.

I slammed the door shut behind me. Grabbing a pair of Puss-in-Boots themed PJs, I headed into the shower. After quickly dressing in nightclothes, I wrapped a towel around my wet hair, walking out of my bathroom and into my room.

"Oh!" I jumped back, my hand on my chest like I was protecting my heart from falling out of it. "What the hell, Dean?"

He lay sprawled on my bed, unmoving.

"Dean?" I walked closer to him, removing my heavy, wet hair-wrap. "Dean." I nudged his leg with mine, throwing the towel over my study chair.

Dean shot up, grabbed me by my waist and pulled me down on top of him.

I squealed. "Let me go, you big oaf!"

"Do you ever wonder what would have happened if I hadn't freaked out when we kissed four years ago?"

I stopped struggling against him. He loosened his grip. His eyes were squeezed shut, like he didn't want to see my reaction.

"I used to."

"I still do." He opened his eyes, and their electrifying blue locked with mine. "I keep replaying how beautiful you looked that day . . . you still are."

"Dean." I pushed against his chest and his hold on me eased. I rolled to the side and sat up next to him, tucking my legs under my butt. I turned back to find his eyes closed. I needed to tell him about Axel, before this conversation got any more awkward.

"I need to tell you something—" I started.

He sat up, his lips grazing the corner of mine as he scooted closer. I shifted back. "It pisses me off how big of an idiot I was. That moment was so perfect and—"

"Dean." I tried cutting him off before he said something I couldn't hear. "It's in the past. There's no point in living on what ifs."

He looked at me from under his thick black eyelashes. Something inside me awakened. Little tingles rolled over my skin, soft, teasing, soothing—a feeling I'd been told was the bond between us. His hand reached up and I straightened, unsure of what he was doing. He paused for a second, his eyes never leaving mine. He tucked my wet hair behind my ear.

"I know." He took my hand in his, his gaze falling between us. I knew I should pull my hand back, but I couldn't. "Don't you think I know that?"

My heart thumped against my ribs. The need to feel his touch against my skin was getting stronger, like it was responding to some kind of call. He placed my hand over his heart.

"Do you feel that?" he asked, his voice low and shaky.

I nodded, confused. It was beating just as hard as mine was, the same needy, painful rhythm. Was this part of our bond?

"This is how it's been since that day we kissed. No matter how many girls I've been with, nothing ever makes me feel the way you do."

"Dean . . ." *God, please don't let this be the I-want-to-be-a-couple talk.* "I really need to tell you some—"

"Let me finish." He covered my mouth with his hand.

I'd had enough. He wouldn't let me speak and . . . and I couldn't do this right now. I scooted back, trying to stop him from saying anything further, and ended up falling off the edge of my bed.

"You okay?" Dean was by my side, his hands already scooping me into his chest. I struggled to free myself, but he wasn't having it. "What the hell did you do that for?"

I ignored his question and pulled back from his touch. "You don't get to do this. You don't get to come back into my life and act like the past four years didn't happen."

"I know I screwed up—"

"You didn't just screw up, Dean! You hurt me. You made me feel worthless. I trusted you, and you threw that away. I learned to live with it. And I'm glad to have you back in my life, but you can't just barge back in and think we can pick up where we stopped."

A flicker of pain crossed his eyes, but disappeared just as quickly. "Wait. What?" His eyes darkened. "You thought I wanted to talk about . . ." He threw his head back and laughed.

My face burned. I was so certain he'd wanted to. Had I misread him this entire time? "Now you're being a jerk."

"I'm sorry." He leaned forward. "I want to have that conversation. But tonight, I just wanted to tell you that I'm going to do whatever it takes to make up for my poor decision-making skills. I know you don't trust me, and I understand that. I *deserve* that. But know that I'll make it up to you."

"Oh," I said, feeling lame.

"Make no mistake though, we will talk about our future, our relationship."

I opened my mouth to respond, but he cut me off, like he'd been doing all night.

"Just not tonight." He wrapped his arms around my shoulders. My arms automatically went to his waist. He kissed my temple. "Not until you trust me again."

CHAPTER NINETEEN

THE NEXT MORNING, I WOKE FEELING SLUGGISH, NOT REALLY wanting to face Dean at school. Last night had been a mystery of its own. Dean had implied that he wanted to get back together with me, and that it was only a matter of time. But I couldn't let him live in that pipe dream. Not when our school could spread gossip like wildfire. I had to tell him about Axel and me. Before he found out from someone else.

I dragged myself out of bed and fell into my weekday routine. I jogged my six miles in record time, got home, got ready, and left for the day—dressed in a yellow, off-the-shoulder sweater, white cami, black cargo capris, and my favorite bamboo wedges.

On the way, I treated myself to a venti pumpkin latte and pumpkin bread. I rushed into school with only a few minutes to spare . . . gulping down my breakfast as I headed to my locker. Rounding the corner too fast, I lost my balance. But before my butt made contact with the floor, a pair of arms encircled me, preventing me and my hot pumpkin latte from spilling across the tile.

"You okay?" Axel asked, smiling.

He pulled me up, keeping his eyes on mine the entire time. A few passersby stared at us, but I didn't care.

I nodded with a wicked smile. "It's your fault."

"It's my fault you have two left feet?" he joked, leaning in for a quick peck on the cheek.

"Yeah, it *is* your fault. If you didn't look so good waiting for me, I wouldn't have tripped over myself," I teased, walking toward my locker.

He had an innocent look on his face.

"As if you don't know that half the girls at school are gunning for you." I pointed to the giggling, blushing group that had just passed.

He bit his lip, leaning down to my ear.

"Does it matter when *you're* all I can think of?" he asked in a heated whisper.

My entire body flushed and my insides formed tight coils. Axel was really good with words like that. He played me like an experienced guitarist, strumming every one of my heartstrings.

He gave me an airbrush of a kiss on the sensitive skin behind my ear before pulling back. I let out a quivering breath and my knees gave out. He wrapped his arm around my waist.

"I've got you." His voice was strained.

My heart thrummed with a different kind of vibration. He was as affected as I was. I groaned, dragging a hand down my face.

He arched one dark brow. "What's wrong?"

"You . . . know," I said, giving him my most seductive look, trying to distract him from seeing how weak he made me. And, damn it, he hadn't even kissed me on the lips yet! He was probably a terrible kisser. My eyes fell to his mouth as his tongue darted out to wet his lips. Yup, he'd be a bad kisser.

He chuckled, shaking his head.

Opening my locker, I exchanged my books. "You're just lucky I'm in a good mood."

"I like it when you get all giddy." He leaned in to kiss my forehead. "Let's go before you make me do something illegal and your brother comes after me with a butcher knife," he said, leading us toward homeroom, his arm wrapped around my shoulders.

"Oh, he wouldn't come after you with a butcher knife," I said, laughing. "He'd come after you with a machine gun to annihilate your boy parts."

†

Four long hours later, I caught Axel and Tyler in a heated argument outside the cafeteria. When Tyler saw me, he jerked his head my way and walked in the opposite direction, his face contorted with worry. I was baffled. Before I could ask Axel what that was about though, he spun me around, gracefully pinning me against the wall.

"I've been thinking about something." His mouth curved up on one side.

"Y-Yeah?"

He licked his lips, his gaze dropping to mine, hunger edging close to surface. "It's been a *very* long morning." His chest rumbled with a throaty groan.

He traced his thumb against my lower lip and down my neck, transferring a surge of electricity. Was this it? Was he finally going to kiss me? *Yes!* He leaned in as his hand trailed down my shoulder, over my arm, and finally rested on the hem of my sweater.

"Are you ticklish?" he whispered into my ear. His fingers found their way under my cami.

He softly grazed different parts of my body, making me giggle and squirm as I tried to block his relentless hands.

"Stop . . . Axel, stop . . . please . . ." I tried to free myself from his grasp, but it was futile. *Damn it!*

He let me escape after a few seconds. I ran down the hallway toward the cafeteria, laughing and out of breath. He followed me with a stupid grin. I pushed through the double doors and made my way to our usual table, taking my seat next to Pey.

"Why are you giggling like a two-year-old?" Pey looked from me to Axel as he pulled his chair as close to mine as he could.

"I'm not," I replied, trying to stop myself from grinning like a fool.

"Uh, yeah. You are," she insisted.

I rolled my eyes and pivoted toward Landon with a devilish smile.

Laughter boomed through the entrance of the cafeteria, announcing the arrival of the football team.

"Dude, that was inhuman!" Hunter howled, looking at Dean, awestruck. "Two hundred and sixty-five pounds on a bench press. Coach is going to be through the roof."

"Trying to lose weight there, porkie?" Landon shouted across the cafeteria.

"Working hard to get back in shape," Dean replied, obviously proud of his accomplishment.

"Good shit. Who ya trying to impress?" Hunter barked. "Your *girlfriend?*"

Dean gave me a quick glance. I looked away, only to be caught by Axel's quizzical gaze. I felt my cheeks heat. *Damn it.* I needed to find another table.

"You noticed?" Dean made a kissy face toward Hunter.

"Can't wait to get down and dirty with you, princess," Landon said, smacking Dean's butt.

I couldn't handle this conversation anymore.

"You guys sure you're not gay?" I asked. I looked at Pey and Ella. "Are *you* sure they aren't gay?"

"Aww . . . jealousy is cute on you, gorgeous." Dean walked over, giving me a hug and a kiss on my temple, shocking me and everyone else.

It got pin-drop silent. I swore I heard crickets.

It took me a minute to snap out of my shock and find my voice. "You're such a turd."

I pushed Dean back and put my hands on my hips. Axel's arm snaked around my waist, pulling me possessively toward him. He waited. The temperature rose ten degrees. I saw the precise moment realization hit Dean. Pain clouded across his features, turning his normally bright blue eyes to a darker shade of gray. His attention turned to Axel. They glared at each other, neither ready to back down.

I should have told Dean about Axel last night. But I'd been cut off both times I'd tried, and then, I'd been so shocked by his promise that everything else had kind of disappeared. I guess the cat was out of the bag now.

"Ren, you all packed for our trip?"

I could have kissed Pey for the diversion. I sat back down, cowardly ignoring the unspoken, primal war progressing behind me. I took a fry from Pey, placing it in my mouth and chewing deliberately.

"Yeah. When I told Joshua, he suggested not to do anything he wouldn't."

She snickered. "Yeah, like you could ever be that cool!"

"Just because you've had a crush on him since—"

A loud smack resonated behind me, followed by a thud and chairs screeching on the floor. My head snapped around to see what had happened. My stomach churned like week-old sour milk. People gathered around Axel and Dean, shouting and placing bets.

"What the hell?" I ran toward Dean. A chair lay next to him, his fingers tightly gripping its leg.

Did he . . . ? Did they . . . ? Oh, dear God!

I glanced at Axel. He stood a few feet away from us, clenching and unclenching his fists like he was ready to punch Dean again. His eyes shone bright, and a small blue aura emanated from his palms. I'd only ever seen him like this when he was in kill mode.

"That's strike one, rookie," Axel snarled, the muscles along his jaw flexing.

"What the hell did you do, Dean?" I asked, turning my attention back to him, tracing my finger across his bleeding forehead.

He continued to glare at Axel.

"We need to talk." I grabbed Dean's hand and Axel took a step toward me. "Alone," I said to Axel. Hurt crossed his features. Letting go of Dean's hand, I moved toward Axel, placing my hand on his chest. "Please, I need to do this."

Axel pulled me into a bear hug and pressed his lips to my forehead, lingering a bit longer than necessary. Like he was trying to make the statement that I was his.

Dean grunted in disgust.

"I'll be close," Axel whispered.

I wanted to be pissed—I felt like a bone between two dogs—but the look Axel gave me made me swallow my words. It was a mix of possessiveness and fear, like he was worried he'd lose me. So I fought the urge to roll my eyes and nodded. The sooner Dean and I talked, the easier it would get. I hoped.

I spun on my heel and pointed sternly at Dean. "You, caveman, let's talk."

Dean wiped his forehead with the back of his hand and followed me down the hall to the girls' locker room.

"What the hell was that?" I asked, pointing in the general direction of the cafeteria.

His eyes darted behind me and back. "A mirror," he answered sarcastically, his brows arched.

I glanced over my shoulder to see what he was talking about and my eyes narrowed.

A mirror. I was pointing to a mirror.

I turned back. "Ha, ha! You're a total jerk." I hit him in the chest with my fist. "Why did you attack Axel?"

"Do I need a reason to punch a rich, spoiled ass?" He smirked, not even trying to hide his arrogance. "Besides, I'm the one bleeding."

I ran my hands through my hair and tugged the ends, frustrated. I went into the bathroom and brought back a wet paper towel. I stood on my toes, dabbing it against his bleeding cut.

"If this is about us . . ." I sighed, bringing my hand back from his already healing cut. "We're in the past, Dean."

"Is it so disgusting that you can't even admit we kissed?" he yelled, finally losing his façade. "Do I sicken you that much?" He moved closer. His eyes flashed, cutting through me with anger, pain, and sadness.

"Don't you dare blame this on me. You're four frigging years too late."

He flinched.

"Just because someone else is showing interest in me, doesn't give you the right to—"

"To what?" he interrupted, his voice softer, more seductive.

He leaned in until our lips were inches apart. Familiar waves stirred over my skin. I stood my ground, glaring back at him. I wasn't going to let him or our bond intimidate me.

A group of giggling girls walked into the room, unaware of the scene about to combust in front of them. They froze.

"Beat it," Dean threatened, grinding his teeth. When they didn't move, he yelled, "Now!"

I watched as the girls fumbled around the locker room, making their way out. If a teacher found out I had a boy in here, I'd be in so much trouble. Shaking my head, I glanced back at Dean. His eyes flared with agony and jealousy.

"Are you afraid of me?"

"No," I whispered.

Truth.

"Don't choose him," he pleaded.

"Why not?" I fired back, feeling a bubble of pain crowding my chest. I knew why. He wanted a future with us. But I couldn't just sit around and wait for him to fix everything he'd done. He'd hurt me too deeply, and I couldn't trust him not to hurt me again. His interests in girls changed weekly. And then there was Axel . . . how could I deny what I felt for him on the chance that Dean might be sincere? "Just let it go, Dean."

His eyes were dangerously challenging, taking on a gleam of darkness.

My voice softened. "He's good for me. And I like him. A lot."

After what seemed like an eternity, he let out a labored sigh and tilted his head back. He growled and swung his hand in my direction, smashing it into the wall behind me. I stood there, stunned, staring at the hole he'd left. I'd never seen him so angry.

Before I could comprehend what happened, Axel stood between Dean and me, his body guarding mine.

"No," I said in a crackled voice. My throat felt dry.

"You fucking know I won't hurt her," Dean snarled, charging at Axel, his hand raised in a tight fist. His knuckles turned white.

Axel stood his ground, unaffected by his threats.

"Axel, it's okay." I grabbed his forearm and pulled at him, urging him to follow me. He let me haul him out hesitantly. "Dean would never hurt me." I looked into his flaming blue eyes.

"How do you know?" He flinched slightly. Anyone else would've missed it.

"We're bonded, Axel. He's meant to protect me." I truly believed Dean would never hurt me intentionally, no matter how pissed he might be. "Besides, we've been friends for far too long for him to do something that stupid." I cupped his face between my hands. "Let me take care of this my way, please?"

He nodded and leaned down to kiss my forehead. He then whirled around and walked away without turning back. I knew he wasn't happy with my request, but I was thankful he trusted me enough to let me handle it on my own. Somewhere in the back of my mind, my conscience screamed at me for making him upset. But, for now, I had bigger fish to fry. I squared my shoulders and spun on my heel, storming back into the locker room to Hulk, who apparently couldn't keep his temper in check anymore.

"Now, you listen to me—" I stopped in my tracks. Dean sat on the floor against the wall, his head back, eyes closed. "You okay?" I asked, my voice softer.

He didn't answer.

"I can't believe you're making me do this," I said, sliding down to sit next to him. I crossed my legs Indian style, tucking my hair behind my ears, and started playing with my chipped fingernails. "Dean, I'm sorry if I hurt you. That was never my intention."

He didn't look at me, or move. I didn't even know if he'd heard me. So I shifted to kneel in front of him, cupping his face between my hands, forcing him to look at me.

"I love you, Dean." His eyes lifted to mine, big and bright. "But I love you as my best friend. Even when we were apart, I cared for you. You have to accept that I make my own choices. I don't need another big brother looking after me."

"I'm not your brother," he said with revulsion. "You don't even know the guy, not like we know each other."

"We're dating, not getting married and having babies."

He flinched.

I ruffled his black faux-hawk playfully. He grasped my hands and placed them on his chest. His heart beat unsteadily.

"Up until now, I never had to worry about anyone coming between us. Now, here's a spoiled rich kid, born with a silver spoon in his mouth—"

"Nobody's going to get between us. I'm still your best friend, and you're still mine—even with all the years there was a gap." I stood, extending my hand to him and pulling him up. "Okay?"

He nodded, his shoulders slumping in defeat.

"I reserve the right to beat the shit out of him if he mistreats you, though," he said with a sad smile.

I opened my mouth to respond, but he cut me off before I could make a sound.

"I'm not negotiating," he said and walked out of the room.

"Douchebag," I called after him, feeling relief spread through me.

†

By the time I got home from the football game, it was nearly nine-thirty. The Bobcats had won, thirteen to zero. I was exhausted from the day's events and my throat felt sandy from too much screaming.

"I'm home," I called, throwing my handbag over the sofa and heading to the kitchen for some Gatorade. A note was stuck to the fridge.

"*Out with Cass. Don't wait up. Stuffed mushrooms in oven. Love you, J.*"

Scrunching the message, I threw it in the trash and pulled the food from the oven. My mouth watered and my stomach rumbled. Ten minutes later, I cleaned the dishes and headed to my room to shower. Just as I settled in, I heard a *tap, tap, tap* on my window.

What the heck? Rolling off the bed, I moved to the glass and looked down. Axel was bent over, searching for something. I pushed the window up just as he hurled a rock. I squealed in surprise.

"Shit!" Axel rasped.

Before it could take out my eye, I saw the small piece of rock freeze in mid-air, inches from my face. Ignoring that, I bent over the windowsill and asked, "What are you doing here?"

"Can I come up?" he answered, pointing to himself, and then the window.

I nodded. Before I could turn around, he stood in front of me, hovering in the air. I backed away until the back of my knees touched the top of my bed.

"Thanks for letting me come up." He looked at me with guilt and a shy smile.

Sure, no problem.

He snaked his arms around my waist and cautiously leaned his forehead against mine. I relaxed into his familiar masculine grace and let his warmth soothe me. He pulled me to him gently, like I was a delicate flower that needed to be protected.

I wrapped my arms around his waist and he tightened his hold on me. He felt so good, and knowing he was mine, that I could touch him anytime I wanted, sent a rabble of butterflies fluttering about my insides. I tilted my head and stared into his regret-filled eyes. My heart rate spiked with longing.

"I'm sorry, Ren," he whispered, lowering his lips to my ear. His breath teased against my sensitive skin and a shiver ran up my spine. "You have every right to be angry at me. I shouldn't have acted the way I did earlier. I shouldn't have put you on the spot in front of everyone. But it was . . . it's just that Dean . . ."

"I want to be angry with you, but I can't. I understand."

His grip adjusted, securing me to him. Was he worried I would push him away? He clearly felt possessive, acting like I was some sort of object to be claimed. But I'd probably act the same way if the roles were reversed. Besides, today had been a long day, and Axel was making an effort to apologize. I was tired of fighting what was natural. I was tired of being angry.

"I just wish I'd had the chance to talk to him before-hand." I'd had the chance, but I never took it. I'd tried to take the easy way out. So, technically, I was responsible for the way things had gone down this morning.

"I never intended to make it difficult," he whispered. "It was just that I know you have history with him, and the bonding, so I—"

"You thought I'd jump ship?"

His cheeks turned slightly pink. "I don't know what to think, Ren." His gaze traveled over my eyes, like he was study-ing them for answers. "All I know is I like you a lot, and I'm not ready to lose you."

"It isn't just because I'm supposed to be some sort of savior?"

His eyebrows bunched up in the middle and I ran my finger over it. "I liked you well before I knew you were the Echo," he whispered.

"Echo?" I asked.

"That's what we call you—the savior that rose from the pleas of generations to help free us from war." He traced his hand down my cheek, shoving a piece of hair behind my ear. "But, to me, you will always be that girl I first laid eyes on."

"Oh!" I let out a deep breath. I hadn't realized until right then that I secretly feared he thought that, that that was the reason he was attracted to me. But I *wasn't* just some tool aiding him in the fight against Telal. I could feel my lips curve into a smile.

He took my hand and placed it over his heart. "Feel that?"

I nodded.

"Every time I'm near you, every time I hear your voice, my heart's racing to be closer to you."

So why did I still feel unsure?

"*This is real, and I promise I'll do everything I can to make you see it,*" he said.

Heat pooled in my cheeks. "You will?"

His eyes widened.

It took me a few seconds before I realized he hadn't said that out loud. "Wait, did you just . . . ?"

"You heard me?"

I nodded.

He cupped my face between his hands. "You're amazing. You know that?"

"Wasn't I supposed to hear you?" I was confused.

"No, not really." He shook his head. "Only Legions can hear each other's thoughts. They undergo an oath ceremony that enables them to communicate through telepathy."

"Oh." My eyebrows knit together. "Why could I hear you, then?"

He shrugged. "I'm not sure. Maybe because you're the Echo? That would be my best guess, at least. According to the prophecy, the Echo is the most powerful Dracian to be born. Second in strength only to an Original, she'd have the ability to defeat Telal. So, maybe it was just your Essence doing what it's supposed to."

"Can I talk to you, too?"

He smiled at me, finally relaxing. "*Try.*" He spoke into my mind.

"How?"

"I had to have skin-to-skin contact the first time I did it, when I was thirteen. Like this." He placed his forehead against mine. "Now, think the thought you want me to hear. Picture sending that message to me."

I closed my eyes and let out a breath, picturing myself pushing the thought out.

"*Can you hear me?*" I asked.

No response.

"*Testing. One . . . two . . . three.*"

Still nothing. I let out a heavy sigh.

"*You can do this, angel,*" he said. "*It'll get easier. I promise.*"

"*Practice makes perfect,*" I said in a melodic voice. No response.

"*If you hear this, I'll put our mouths to good use.*" I looked into his eyes with hope.

"*Stop talking dirty when I can't hear you.*" He chuckled in amusement. "*I can tell by the way you're looking at me,*" he added.

Heat pooled in my cheeks. I took a deep breath, picturing myself connected to him, as if a wire bridged between us. Then I pictured myself transferring the message as the words formed in my mind. I saw them scroll down that wire toward his mind.

I sang the "Milkshake" song.

He chuckled. "'*Milkshake,*' huh?"

I pulled back, looking into his proud eyes. My heart fluttered. *He heard me!* I leaned against his forehead and tried again.

"*You heard me?*"

He nodded. "*I really want to kiss you now.*"

My stomach muscles coiled in response. I sucked in a deep breath and locked eyes with him. "*Then kiss me.*"

"*With pleasure.*" He ran a finger down my jaw. I shivered in his arms.

I wrapped my arms around his neck and pushed up on my toes the same time he leaned down, our lips connecting for the first time.

Whoa!

My world shattered into innumerable pieces. Nothing else could ever compare to this. We fit perfectly against each other, like a multilateral puzzle, complementing each other's contours with precision. It was like he was my other half—my body, my heart, and my soul soared from the connection.

His soft lips moved, caressing mine. First the bottom, then the top. I needed him with a demand so great, I felt it might never be satisfied. My fingers tangled in his hair, pulling him closer. He groaned and moved his hand to the nape of my neck.

Suddenly, I was pulled into a vision. *The two of us walked hand in hand, him whispering in my ear and making me blush ridiculously. Then I ran, him in pursuit, chuckling.* The vision shifted. *We were dancing at the beach, my feet on his.* Another shift . . . *we smiled at each other before we turned, back to back, ready to fight. Then, we were at the altar . . . then falling into bed, tangled in sheets, giggling, kissing, moving as one.*

Every vision flooded my senses, making it harder to breathe. But I didn't care. I pulled him closer.

Once the visions stopped, Axel pulled back just enough to speak.

"Did you . . . ?" His lips moved against mine.

"Yeah." I pulled him back to me, missing the pressure.

I didn't know if those images were my imagination, or if Axel had some kind of clairvoyant power and he was showing me our possible future. But whatever it was, I didn't care. I just wanted it to be true. All of it.

The door to my room flew open a breath before his lips touched mine again. Joshua stood there, a surprised look burning on his face.

Axel jumped back like he'd been electrocuted. I blushed, biting down on my lip. The room grew silent, and I saw a flicker of orange flame at the tip of Joshua's fingers.

Shit! Pissed off brother. A boy I kissed. Fire blazing. *This was so not happening.*

"Joshua," I stepped forward.

He raised his hand, silencing me while keeping his deadly stare on Axel. "What are you doing in my *baby* sister's bed-room this late at night?"

I wished I could crawl under my bed and snuggle with the dust-bunnies.

"I—"

"Hey, what's taking—" Cassie's eyes widened. "Hi, Axel." Her eyes darted from me to Axel, then back to me. She raised a questioning eyebrow and I silently pleaded with her. "It's kind of getting late. Axel, let me walk you out."

"Um, yes." His gaze darted to Joshua, then to me, with uneasiness. "I'll see you tomorrow?"

Awkward. "Yeah. See you tomorrow." If I wasn't being forced into friendship with the dust-bunnies. "Thanks for dropping off the—ah, my notebook." I picked up the closest book on my study desk and waved.

He didn't respond. With one final glance toward me, he silently followed Cassie out of my room.

"Joshua," I began.

"Don't even start with me, Killer." He walked into my room and suddenly, I felt like I was five again. "I trusted you, and this is how you repay me?"

"Joshua—"

"*Especially* when you knew I was planning on being late."

I flinched, feeling the cold slap to my face. "It wasn't—"

"How do you expect me to trust you, when—"

"JOSHUA MATTHEWS PERNELL!" I tried to make myself heard over his rambling. "Will you please just listen to me?"

His eyes widened.

"Good. Now that I have your attention." I sighed. "First of all, I didn't invite him over."

"So that—"

"Let me explain before you blow up the house," I said, pointing to his ever growing flame. "Secondly, he came here to apologize and he didn't know you weren't home." I left out the fact that Axel had climbed into my room through the window. "So technically, neither he nor I plotted the demise of your trust."

He scoffed. "He was going to apologize by defiling my sister in my own house?"

I groaned. "Seriously? I can't—"

"Joshy," Cassie called from downstairs. "Can you please come down here?"

He looked at me. "This conversation isn't over."

As soon as the door shut behind Joshua, I fell back on my bed, groaning. My phone buzzed.

Axel: I'M SORRY FOR GETTING YOU IN TROUBLE.

Me: ME, TOO. BUT ONLY BECAUSE WE WERE INTER-RUPTED.

I was definitely feeling a bit brazen.

Axel: IT'LL BE WORTH THE WAIT.

Axel: WHEN IT'S YOU, IT'LL ALWAYS BE WORTH THE WAIT.

I sighed, a smile etching my face as I hugged the phone to my chest.

CHAPTER TWENTY

"**How are you prepping for midterms?**" **I asked Pey as I** pulled the fifth maid-of-honor dress over my head.

"Argh . . . I may as well give up now."

"Me, too." We high-fived, chuckling. "Zip me up."

I turned to face the mirror and pulled the dress higher over my chest. "I guess there's no way to hide these babies."

"Oh, stop being such a whiner and flaunt those assets," Pey said. She held a gorgeous pair of strappy pink, five-inch heels and wiggled her eyebrows. Once they were on my feet, she said, "Axel's going to trip."

"On what?"

"On you. He'll be picking guys off you all night. Especial-ly . . . Dean." She winked at me. I ignored her last comment. "You're kidding me, right? Or are you really that dumb?" She rolled her eyes. "That boy has it bad for you. He looks at you with ridiculous, worshiping eyes reserved exclusively for you."

Yes, exclusive because he was my protector and we had a magical bond. If only she knew . . .

"Help me get out of this dress."

"Seriously, Ren. Dean is head-over-heels in love with you."

"Whatever. Even if what you're saying is true, it doesn't matter. I'm with Axel." After the cafeteria incident, our rela-tionship had become public knowledge and open to scrutiny.

"I know, but you and Dean would be totally hot, too."

We gathered our purchases and walked to the cashier.

"Remember that first kiss? You can't fake that kinda stuff."

Yeah, I remembered *that* kiss, only it wasn't the first.

"Did you find everything you needed?" the cashier asked politely.

"Yeah." I took a card from my purse. "We have one more bridesmaid and three groomsmen coming within the week. If they hand you this card"—I passed her a designer card I'd created for the wedding party—"can you charge my account for all their purchases?"

"Of course," she responded, taking my details.

"So, when are you leaving?" Pey took out her cell phone, smiled, and quickly stowed it away again.

"In about eight weeks." I took the receipt from the cashier and signed it, handing it back to her with a quick, "Thanks."

Picking up the bags, Pey and I headed out the door. I smiled, remembering Pey's words. Maybe Axel would be a bit stunned by my dress. Axel. My heart skipped a beat as a sudden thought crossed my mind.

"What is it?" Pey asked.

"I-I was wondering . . ." I didn't know how to ask her.

"Spit it out." Concern filled her eyes.

"Remember how we talked about your first time?" I asked, raising my eyebrows for emphasis.

"Ohmigod. Are you ready? Do you *think* you're ready?"

"God, I hope not! We've only been together for three weeks." I chewed my lip. "But, we've been . . . you know . . . making out quite a bit, and if we go to second base or third—wait, how many bases are there?"

She raised her eyebrow, amused.

"Never mind how many. The point is, when we do decide to cross that line, I don't want to look like an idiot."

She placed her hand over her heart and tilted her head slightly. "My little girl is growing up, *opening* herself up."

"God, Pey! Forget it. This was a bad idea." I turned around, about to walk away.

"Ren. Ree-Ree. Sorry!" She grabbed my arm and pulled me back. "Forgive?"

Like I could ever live without her. *But you'll have to soon,* a small voice reminded me. Stupid conscience.

"For the love of all things babies, always have condoms at hand, *especially* when you guys are going at it."

I snorted. "We aren't animals."

"You know what I mean." She waved her hand. "Anyway, rule one: condoms. Rule two: you have to relax, knowing that it might hurt the first time, and trust him not to hurt you . . . much. Rule three: touch, explore, and don't be shy. There's nothing more sensual than touch."

My mouth dropped open.

"And most important, rule number four: *condoms*."

"You already said that."

She smiled mischievously. "Exactly, it's important enough to state twice."

This was all too much, too fast. How could I remember all that when I could barely breathe around him? Maybe we could wait . . . a little while longer. Like *never*?

"Ren, don't worry about it. I didn't know much when Landon and I did it the first time, but now . . . wow." She blew out a shaky breath, grinning.

I noticed a familiar motorcycle parked across the street and grinned like an idiot. I hugged Pey, kissing her on the cheek. "Thank you! What am I ever going to do without you?"

"Probably die a virgin." She walked backward to her car. "Don't forget the Before Finals party two weeks from this Saturday. You know, in case you need to get permission from your *brother*."

"I think Joshua and I came to an understanding after *he* finally came to terms with Axel and me," I called after her.

"No shit!" she yelled, giggling.

Shaking my head, I waited for her to get in her car before I headed toward the motorcycle. *He* leaned against it, his arms crossed over his chest. His hair was slightly messy, and his eyes scanned me slowly from top to bottom. Even through his leather jacket, I could see the bulge of his biceps. His washed-out, boot cut jeans sat low on his hips. He definitely didn't look like a teenager. Which, I guess technically, he wasn't.

"Babysitting again, I see," I teased. "That's sad."

Axel's lips curved up in a grin that sent flutters through my chest. He pushed himself off the bike and closed the distance between us in three short strides. Placing his hands on my hips, he tugged me closer, his lips curving to one side.

"If babysitting you is sad"—he pressed his lips to mine—"then I want to be sad for the rest of eternity."

He leaned down, giving me the lightest airbrush of a kiss. My arms, still holding the dress, circled his shoulders. That was all the invitation he needed. He groaned into my mouth, deepening the kiss, making it deliciously yummy. He gently sucked my lower lip between his teeth. My breathing became shallow and my pulse raced.

"*I could do this forever,*" I told him through our connection.

He chuckled. "As much as I love this, we need to go."

He twined our fingers as we walked back to the bike. I bit the inside of my cheek, holding back the urge to pull him into another kiss.

"*Stop that. You're becoming a major distraction,*" I heard him say as a smile crossed his lips.

I reached over and ran my hand down the side of his face, kissing him before straddling the bike.

†

Axel parked outside a home I'd never seen. It looked like it was built to entertain—three stories, a huge entryway with decorative, wooden double doors, and a five car garage. Cars were piled in the driveway.

"Before we go in, there have been some findings . . ." Axel said, helping me shrug out of my helmet.

"What kind of findings?" I asked, turning my attention to him.

"A lot of movement . . . more missing people." Axel ran his fingers through his hair. "That's what we're here to talk about. That, and wedding security. Come on, let's go in."

"Where is 'in,' exactly?"

"My home," he said, opening the door. The corners of his lips turned up. "If you're lucky, maybe we can go see my room."

My heartbeat quickened. *His room. I get to see his room?*

". . . more will be joining us." A man in his fifties stood in the middle of the room, capturing the attention of everyone in it. He was physically fit—built like a linebacker, actually—with light white stubble running across his jawline. I wondered just how old he really was.

"Elijah," Axel whispered to me.

Oh. Elijah was the Dracian guardian for Rocky Hills, Axel had told me, and one of the king's most trusted advisors.

Elijah continued his speech, surrounded by familiar and unfamiliar faces.

"As many of you know, the missing people are starting to grab the mortals' attention. We need to do something to ensure they are kept safe. That means more patrolling, more risk for us."

"Have we found any clues?" A guy with red hair asked.

"Yes. We have a lead we're planning on following. But before I assign a team, I want to know everything there is to know." He looked to everyone in the room before his eyes landed on Axel with a quick nod. "We can't afford to lose anyone."

Murmurs broke out around us.

"Rest assured, we'll take every precaution to control the situation in a smart, strategic way." He waved his hand toward Joshua. "Now, let's talk about something we're all looking forward to: Joshua and Cassie's wedding. We're going to split into teams. Dimitri, Drusus . . ."

"How are we supposed to be confident if the D's are leading us?" Tyler said. "*Doom* is written all over this plan." He laughed, fist-bumping Marcus and Dean.

"Axel and I will lead the teams. Drusus and Dimitri's teams will be posted within a block of the wedding. Axel and my teams will be placed within and immediately surrounding the venue." He handed out plans to the leaders. "These documents detail expectations. Let's meet in private to discuss further." He eyed each leader, crossing his arms. "Make sure to debrief your teams soon."

I peeked at the documents in Axel's hand—a blueprint of the wedding venue with red and green lines, and arrows drawn all over. I chanced a look at Axel. He watched me, amused.

"What?" I asked him through our connection.

"You're on my team," he responded with a quick wink.

"And here I thought I'd have to throw a hissy fit."

We both laughed.

"Something you'd like to share with the group, Axel?" Elijah asked, while the rest stared at us. Axel shook his head.

"Why are you guys planning so much security for Joshua's wedding?" I asked Axel, after Elijah called the meeting to an end. "I mean, it's just a wedding, right?"

He hesitated, like he was deciding if he should tell me or not, but then answered, "It's a wedding where you're going to be in the spotlight, Ren."

What did that mean?

"We can't take any chances that you'd be an open target." He raised his eyebrow, hoping I understood the full intent.

Oh. My eyebrows shot high. He meant because I was the Echo, and they couldn't risk me getting shot at. "So, this is all for me?"

He nodded.

"Team leaders, meet me in my study." Elijah's voice boomed in the small room.

"I'll be right back," Axel said, before making his way toward Elijah.

"Whose team is she on?" asked a tall, slender woman with curly red hair. She sported faded, straight-fit jeans and a floral-print top covered by a trench coat that ended above her black, buckled boots.

"Good luck to whoever has her." Tyler chuckled as the multitude dispersed.

"Hey, I'm not *that* bad," I said. "And *she* has a name . . . Ren." I walked over to the redhead.

"Skye," she responded, shaking my outstretched hand. "Carson's twin sister," she added, pointing to the guy talking to Joshua and Cassie on the other side of the room.

"She's a kickass Legion," a familiar-looking blonde said, joining us. "And an amazing professor."

"Professor?" I asked. My brain strained to remember where I'd seen the blonde curls. She looked so familiar, but so . . .

"Well, yeah, how else do you think we younglings actually learn at the academy?" she responded. "By the way, we've haven't been formally introduced. I'm Lilly."

"Hi," I said, wiggling my fingers. "I'm—"

"Oh, I know who you are. You're Temperance."

"Ren," I corrected her.

She grinned, and I remembered. She'd been part of the team that rescued Axel and me after Dean's birthday party. The one who had cloaked me.

"You should see Professor Skye in action. She can put a three hundred, fifty pound man on his back in a matter of seconds," Lilly said in awe, rocking on her heels.

"Who can put who on whose back?" Dean asked.

Really? A sex joke?

Dean put an arm around Lilly and leaned into her. She blushed in record time. I raised my brow in surprise. *They know each other?* Of course they did. Dean probably knew everyone. He'd probably even been to Dracia. I shook my head, vacating the jealousy that hitched its way to the surface.

"Skye, I'd love to learn more about this academy," I said, turning toward her. "Being raised human and all, I don't know much about your world."

"It's your world too, you know?" Skye responded tenderly. She gestured for me to follow her and we left Lilly and Dean alone. Well, as alone as they could be in a room full of people.

She introduced me to the new faces as we made our way toward the backyard. After thirty minutes of chatting, I was quite impressed by her accomplishments. In the history of Dracia, no female had ever led the Legion program. Not only was she a brilliant fighter and Sorcerer, like her brother, but she was also one of thirteen council members that reported directly to the Dracian king. *The king!*

Talking to her, I realized there was still so much I didn't know about this new world. So much I didn't know about Axel. A pang of guilt and sadness consumed me.

Axel always went above and beyond to learn my likes and dislikes, and I didn't even know when his birthday was. Did he have any pets? What was the name of his best friend?

I was officially the worst girlfriend ever.

"I hope I'm not disturbing anything?" Axel asked, placing his hand at the small of my back. He gave me a quick, acknowledging smile. It felt so distant, so not him.

Axel and Skye fell into an easy conversation. They talked about home and old friends. I could tell he really missed his life in Dracia. It was in the way he smiled at the mention of certain places or people, and the detailed questions he asked. Jealousy overtook my guilt. I didn't know anything about him.

I mean, sure, I knew his ambitions and some of his likes, dislikes, and interests in the human world, but back home, what was he like? I didn't know him, not remotely as well as Skye.

"*No one knows me like you do, angel,*" he said, quieting my inner turmoil without glancing my way.

"Skye, it was great catching up. But if you don't mind, I'd like a word with Ren."

"It's always an honor." She bowed with respect, like she addressed royalty. For all I knew, he could be a freaking prince.

He led us through clusters of people, expertly dodging any interruptions. He took the rectangular metal stairs in the back corner of the room, pulling me behind him.

Two flights later, he stopped beside a door and said, "My room." I stepped inside as he grinned and closed the door behind me, locking it with a soft click. My breathing grew harder as guilt consumed me. It tasted bitter.

"What is it?" He placed his hand over my shoulder. I shook my head, not wanting to point out how lousy of a girlfriend I was. "Don't. Please tell me. I want to help ease your pain."

"I don't know you, Alexander. I mean, I do, but I don't know anything about what made you . . . you," I blurted. I turned around, holding his face between my hands, searching his eyes. I crushed my mouth over his, hungry for connection. His chest rumbled against mine. I pulled back. "I want to know if you had any nicknames growing up. What your favorite hobby is; your best friend, your family, your birthday, your favorite dessert . . . everything." My throat constricted with emotion. "I'm such an awful girlfriend. You find things out about me without me having to tell you, and I don't reciprocate."

"Where's this coming from?"

I dropped my hands from his face, frustrated, but he caught my wrists before they fell all the way. He tugged my arms, placing them around his waist. Then he cupped my face with his hands, exploring my eyes.

"While you and Skye were talking, I realized how little I know about you, how little I've tried to learn about your past. I'm sorry. I've been so selfish. I barely know you, and I'm . . . j-jealous that others know you better than I do." I looked away.

"First off . . ." He kissed the crown of my head and let his warm lips linger. The heat spread through me like the slow drizzle of honey. "The past is the past. But if you want to know, just ask. I want you to know everything about me, Ren, without a doubt. Second, jealousy can be a good thing." He pulled back enough to look into my eyes. "Because that means you want me all to yourself, and there's no better thought."

"What if I go all psychotic and start killing people in a jealous rage?" I asked, trying to lighten the mood.

"We'll tag team, and I'll help clean up the evidence."

I couldn't stop the little smile that crept onto my face. His finger traced my lower lip before his mouth captured mine, nipping and tugging playfully. He pulled back and I moaned with need.

"I used to be called 'flabby.' My favorite hobby is woodworking. My best friend is Dimitri. I have one brother, Alastair Felix, who's five years older than me, and my father is

Nicholas Walter. He's one hundred and sixty-three years old. And, as for my birthday, it's July first."

"Don't tell me you're in the three digits, 'cause that would be kinda gross."

"Will you not want me if I am?" His voice dipped low and seductive. "It could have its advantages." A sultry smile pulled back his cheeks.

I stopped breathing.

"I'm nineteen."

"Wow, your parents were old when they had you boys, huh?"

His chuckle awakened something deep inside me as my heartbeat gained speed. I had the urge to throw him on the bed and have my wicked way with him.

"It took them a lot of practice," he said, his voice low and suggestive. "We could start practicing now. I'm ready to submit to your 'wicked way.'" He grinned and I almost swallowed my tongue.

I thought he couldn't hear my thoughts unless . . .

"When your emotions are at their peak, I can hear your thoughts loud and clear, like thousand-watt speakers."

Heat rushed into my cheeks. "Oh!"

He leaned down, placing a light kiss on my right cheek, then my left. His thumb caressed the area where his lips had left a blazing glow. Why was I always the one thinking these things? I was so wrapped up in him and the world he created for us that I lost myself to him. His love consumed me so deeply, all I could do was absorb the warmth of its presence. God, I thought guys were supposed to be the horny ones. I needed help.

"Ah, hell no," he said.

His eyelids drooped as his eyes turned a darker shade of blue, staring into me like a lost man. His mouth consumed mine, and he growled with hunger.

Holy freaking hot.

"How can you feel so insecure? It takes every bit of concentration to control myself around you, not to kiss you every waking hour, not to touch you every second of my existence."

His breathing came in short gasps. He leaned his forehead against mine and he sent me an image—a very delicious image that threatened to catch me on fire.

"That's just the tip of the iceberg," he said. "There's nothing PG in my thoughts where you're involved. You awaken the beast inside me. These feelings and dreams and fantasies . . . I can't wait to make them *our* reality. To make you mine in every way." His voice was husky.

"So, what're you waiting for?"

God, I'm worse than a dog in heat!

"For the moment you're completely mine without any restrictions." Before I could ask what he meant, his mouth was on mine, taking my breath away.

My lips opened for him, welcoming him to devour me. He laid me on the bed, hovering above me. His hands explored the curves of my body, caressing and teasing. He found the hem of my shirt, and it soon found its way to the floor. My eyes rolled back in pleasure and a moan erupted from my throat.

I was drowning in the whirlpool of our world. I could barely breathe and everything in me ached to be released from the pressure pooling inside. I bucked under him, wanting to be touched more, wanting to be loved.

Want. Want. Want.

His lips left a trail of kisses on my forehead, nose, cheeks, jawline, and neck, all the way down to my navel. He sucked on the skin by my belly button before he went lower, kissing just above the waistline of my jeans. Then he came back up, leaving another trail of kisses along the way.

My hands trembled as I started exploring the hard planes of his torso. I pulled his shirt over his shoulders and threw it on the floor beside mine. His lips ventured to areas no one had ever touched, let alone kissed. Small gasps and moans escaped me. Then I felt coldness raise goosebumps across my body. I didn't feel any part of him on me and the emptiness made me more restless with each passing second.

I opened my eyes to find him staring back at me with intensity, releasing a million butterflies in my stomach and tingles all over my body. Blue and red ribbons of light swirled around us, illuminating the room. Axel's eyes darkened with desire, a deep need smoldering behind them. His lips curved up in lascivious smile.

"See something you like?" I asked, biting my lip, out of breath.

"Mmhmm . . ." He leaned down, kissing me before he placed his ear to my chest.

I inhaled a deep breath.

His arm snaked around my bare waist. "Will you stay with me tonight?"

"Yes." I wrapped my arms around him and kissed the top of his head. "But only if I can ask you twenty questions."

"Of course. Now you have nineteen left," he teased.

"Hey!" I playfully ruffled his hair.

We spent the majority of the night in a Q&A session. He answered my queries verbally and sometimes sent images of his favorite places, his happiest moments, and some crazy food called Alcur, which was a mixture of ocean creatures made into a main course. He promised it was the best food he'd ever tasted.

Yeah . . . not so much. I was definitely off the seafood diet.

CHAPTER TWENTY-ONE

I BUSIED MYSELF WITH CHEMISTRY HOMEWORK WHILE AXEL worked on official Dracian business. He used a see-through, all-in-one device called a D.C.S.—Defense Communication System—that allowed commanding officers to communicate tactical strategies and mission briefings. The level of access depended on the level of clearance—civilian, all the way to the king of Dracia.

I slammed my book shut and looked at him—waiting. His brows creased and his eyes narrowed as he moved his finger over the D.C.S. until, finally, he looked up and his gaze connected with mine.

"What?" His finger tapped the tip of my nose.

I sat next to him at the breakfast bar in our kitchen, rapping my foot on the barstool, wondering how I should tell him what I wanted.

"I'm thinking it's time you teach me self-defense."

He stiffened.

I pushed my book aside and looked at him through my lashes. "With my track record for attracting trouble, I'm bound to run into some kinda mess knowing what I know and hanging around you. I don't always want to depend on you to rescue me. Plus, you guys seem to think there *might* be some issues during the wedding."

He sighed and minimized the D.C.S., placing it around his wrist, where it instantly camouflaged into a leather cuff watch again. He laid his hand on my cheek, his eyes drilling into mine. "The extra wedding security is just a precaution. I'll keep you safe, Ren."

"What if you can't? You can't watch me twenty-four seven. You'd have to move in with me." I hopped off the barstool and stepped closer to him. I brought my lips to his ear and whispered, "Besides, training could be fun . . ."

"There's nothing more dangerous than a half-trained rookie who thinks she can defend herself." His eyebrows knitted together and his lips pursed in disapproval.

Damn, he's stubborn.

I placed my hands on his thighs, leaving a trail of kisses under his jawline. He groaned. I smiled, knowing his resolve was weakening. His breathing became labored. I rose on my toes, kissed his lips lightly, and pulled back to see his reaction. He sat up straighter, adjusting his jeans. Suddenly, I was pulled into his lap. The corner of his lip twitched and all kinds of bad thoughts ran through my mind. I flushed and bit my lip.

"Maybe I need more convincing," he suggested before dragging his nose from my cheek to the base of my throat. I moaned. He pulled away and I pouted.

"Damn, that's sexy."

"If you're trying to kiss up to me instead of agreeing to my one and only request, it's not working. Try again, Mr. Knight." I attempted to dismount.

He picked me up and placed me on the counter. He jumped off the barstool, pushed my knees apart, and stood between my legs. His fingers found their way under my shirt.

I gasped.

Fireworks exploded across my skin as he playfully caressed my waist. I found myself leaning into his gaze, wanting a taste of him. A smile formed on his mouth. He nuzzled his nose into the curve of my neck and pressed his lips against the sensitive skin under my ear, raising gooseflesh with his taunting, feather-light kisses. My head fell back and I trembled as heat coursed through me, desire consuming my every nerve. He pressed his lips against mine, caressing, massaging them between his teeth before letting me go. I opened my eyes and was ensnared by his painfully stunning blue irises.

"What were we talking about?" I panted, my eyes darting to his lips.

"How I'm dying to teach you to defend yourself."

"Right." I took a deep breath. "Let's start training tomorrow, then," I said, giving little pecks on his lips between each word.

"I'm looking forward to it, *Meus Aeternus*." He buried his face into the hollow of my shoulder. Warm, succulent kisses soon trailed wherever his lips traveled.

"You're really good at this," I whimpered.

"Anything to please you, my goddess."

I placed my fingers under his chin and tilted it up before settling my lips over his. What started as slow and methodical soon became a scorching fire that neither of us could control. I giggled when he pulled me to him, wrapping my legs around his waist. He kissed anywhere and everywhere but my mouth.

"You're a tease," I complained.

"All in good time, angel."

He dipped to my collarbone before conquering my mouth, like he needed my kiss to survive. He let out a deep rumble that vibrated through me, carried me into the living room, and fell onto the sofa with me on top of him.

"Now who's got the upper hand?" I asked devilishly.

I looked directly into his eyes and ran my hand under his shirt, tracing his chiseled body. His eyes closed and a visible shudder moved through him.

"That feels amazing," he whispered.

I leaned into him for another peck. He wrapped his arms around my waist, tugging me closer.

"Ahem."

Axel and I froze. I squeezed my eyes shut, praying I'd just imagined the sound. Axel peeked over my shoulder and let out a nervous laugh.

Don't let it be my brother. Don't let it be my brother.

I pushed myself off Axel, looked over my shoulder, and . . . let out a sigh of relief.

"What were you two doing?" Cassie asked.

My body blazed like it had been lit on fire. "Um, studying?"

Axel got to his feet. She stared at him, an expression between amusement and scowl coloring her features. He shifted his weight from one leg to the other, dodging her eyes.

"I'll see you later." He leaned down as if to kiss me on the lips and paused. He tilted his head up and kissed my forehead instead. "Bye, Cassie," he said, waving awkwardly to her.

"You know the rules, Ren." She turned to me, her hand on her hip.

She had that look my mother used to use right before I was grounded.

She's pissed.

"We weren't doing anything—"

"That didn't look like '*we weren't doing anything*' . . ." Her eyebrows rose high in disbelief.

I ran my fingers through my hair and pulled it forward until it covered my face.

"Listen, Ren, I know how it can be. I was a teenager once, too. If you want to talk about sex . . ."

I cringed.

"I'm here for you, okay? I trust you to be responsible."

I nodded.

She smiled and changed the subject. "So, I was hoping you could help me with something. I need your opinion." She waved the magazines in her hands, taking a seat next to me. "I've narrowed down the invitation designs to these twelve, but I can't decide." She looked at me sheepishly. "Since our colors are tea rose pink and white, these seem to fit best. Which would you pick?"

She passed the three catalog cards over to me. I slid down to the floor and laid them on the coffee table so we could get lost in the details of wedding planning. After a few hours of itemizing, only one thing remained.

"And . . . which one?" Cassie asked, holding two floral arrangement pictures in her hands.

"But I thought you loved lilies?"

"I do."

"Then, why gardenia as the main flower?"

"Because these were the flowers your parents had at their wedding. I wanted something that would represent them, so they could be with us even though they aren't there."

"Oh, Cassie." I fought back a sob. "I love you so much!"

"Don't be silly. They were as much my parents as they were yours. Now, pick one."

"This one." I pointed to the simple arrangement with pink lilies and just a hint of greenery peeking through the creamy gardenias.

My mother would have loved it, without a doubt.

CHAPTER TWENTY-TWO

"Oomph . . ." I hit the mat head first.

The training room ceiling came into view, red and black spots dancing above my head. I inhaled deeply.

That hurt like a bitch!

Everything except my face was on fire. Heat crept like a slow flame, boiling my skin. A pair of feet rushed to my side and a shadow obstructed the bright lights.

"You okay?" a deep voice asked, sending piercing tremors reverberating through me.

I'd gotten my wish—it was day ten into the training I'd practically begged Axel for.

"*It could be fun,*" I'd told him.

Ha! Well, the joke was on me. Axel the trainer wasn't as sweet as Axel the boyfriend. When we were on the mats, he had no trace of the fun, easygoing attitude I was used to. His demeanor changed, commanding devotion and respect without saying a word.

"Just peachy," I grunted.

Axel's features softened as he crouched in front of me. "For someone with no combat training, you're doing excellent." His voice filled with pride.

"I don't need an ego boost."

"You're getting better." He sighed. "And I'm not just saying that because you're my girlfriend, or because I'm afraid of the doghouse."

I rolled my eyes. Axel insisted on defensive training over offensive. So, every day, I learned to block, duck, roll, and avoid getting punched, kicked, thrown, or captured.

"You need to pay more attention to my body." He pulled me to a standing position.

"*That's* the problem." I winced at the aching pain in my back and shoulders.

"You're *not* okay, Ren." He reached for me with concern.

I waved him off.

My greatest distraction was Axel. Of course, it didn't help that he wore a sleeveless shirt, showing off his well-defined biceps, or that the athletic material hugged his impossibly perfect body. A tight coil sprang within, bouncing about my insides. Thank God he hadn't gone shirtless. *Yet*.

I stepped back and wiped my hands on my butt. "Again."

He gave a curt nod. "Concentrate." He tapped his temple. "Even the most skilled fighter will give something away." He settled into a fighting stance, giving me a chance to do the same.

We danced around each other, waiting to see who would strike first. A fraction of a second before his foot made contact, I noticed his eyes divert to my waist. I deflected the kick with a swipe of my arm and then ducked with a squeal as his left hook made its way toward my head. He was super fast—inhumanly fast. I sprang up, only to be taken down with a swipe of his foot. And, because I was so very talented, I took him down with me. Somehow, he managed to land on the bottom, taking most of the impact, but the fall still knocked the air from my lungs.

"Much better," he said, breathing easy, while *I* panted like I'd finished a marathon.

"Hmm . . . I agree." I licked my lips with a sly smile.

I leaned into him, wrapping my arms around his neck, my fingers buried in his silky brown hair, and kissed him. His mouth curved up in a smile as he kissed me back.

"Make-out sessions are part of combat training now?" Tyler snickered, stepping into the room. "Suh-weet! When do I get my turn?"

Axel growled.

"Go away, Tyler," I said.

"No can do, princess." I heard others step into the room, feet shuffling.

"I guess that's all the time I get . . ." I painfully separated myself from his embrace.

"I could skip prac—" Axel started to offer.

"You will do no such thing." As soon as the words left my mouth, my conscience glared at me, shaking her head. "I'll see you tomorrow?"

He pulled me closer, his hands resting on my waist as he gave me a smile that said, "*You're my world.*" My insides tingled as his warm fingers found their way under my shirt, lingering, caressing the bare skin. It was so full of care and longing; it felt natural—like it was exactly what he should do.

"Yes, even if it's the end of the world." He leaned into a kiss.

"Don't worry, princess. We'll take care of your boy-toy." God, how I wanted to cuff Tyler in the face. "Or you could stay. *We* could spar." He wiggled his eyebrows suggestively.

I scoffed.

"Marcus, Tyler—weapons training. Grab a staff," Axel instructed.

A tall girl with long black hair stood next to Marcus and Tyler. She wore skin-tight black pants and a tank that hugged her every curve. Her stance was confident, arrogance written all over her face. She stared at me with annoyance and something else I couldn't quite figure out—jealousy, suspicion?

What's her problem?

"Trinity, sword, then balance beam," Axel ordered.

Each gave a curt nod and headed to the weapons room.

Trinity paused, throwing a glare over her shoulder before she disappeared behind the boys.

Yeah, I don't like her.

Axel laced his fingers between mine, jolting me back from my thoughts. He slung my duffle bag over his shoulder. "Ready?"

I sighed with a nod and walked outside to my old, beat-up Beemer, the last of my parents' gifts before they—no, I wasn't going to think about that, not now. I wasn't ready. Would I ever be?

"How come you're training them?" I asked once we stood next to my car.

He hesitated, shifting his weight, his fingers running through his hair—all tells that he wasn't comfortable answering my question. "I've been at it a lot longer."

"How does it feel?" I changed the subject, drawing circles over his dagger tattoo. "I mean, having magic. Have you always had it?"

"Somewhat." Axel pitched my duffle into the backseat. "The dormant gene is awakened when a Dracian turns seventeen. We're stronger, faster, and have a stronger sense of hearing before then. But once the gene's activated, everything is amplified. It feels like a blood rush, like everything inside is bursting to come alive and anything is possible. Everything's clearer."

"So, you've been awakened for . . ."

"Eight years."

"But you're only nineteen."

He shrugged. "I'm a freak of nature. Five months after I turned eleven, I found the mark, indicating my magic had been awakened."

"Mark?"

"Yes, every Dracian is marked when their magic awakens."

"Oh. So . . . is this the mark?" I pointed to the daggers on his arm.

"No. These are the tokens of my Legion pledge. Each dagger represents a rank. Six daggers is the highest you can reach."

"Oh!" He had five; he was high in the chain of command, higher than Joshua, but same as John.

I held his pale-blue gaze, grasping his hand.

His eyes seemed to change color based on his mood. I could tell when he was overpowered by strong emotion because his irises started to glow. Pale blue usually meant something was bothering him.

"I'm patrolling for the next week," he said, his lips pressed into a thin line. "Time to pay up."

"Pay up?"

"Yeah." He drew my hand to his lips and kissed each finger softly, sending tingles straight to my heart. "The trade off I had to do with Tyler to get your number. I'm covering for him this week. But it's worth it."

"Oh!" Guilt gnawed at the walls of my heart. "I'm sorry."

He put his finger under my chin, lifting my face to his. His eyes emitted so much emotion that my heart ached in a whole other way. And God, he smelled so good, even after the workout.

So freaking not fair.

"Don't be." Standing at five-five without heels, I was quite a bit shorter than his six-two. He bent down, pressing his lips to mine. We both sighed in satisfaction. "You are"—he kissed my palm and wrist—"my favorite kind of hell."

My heart fluttered as I drank in his intense stare. I knew exactly what he meant. It hurt to be away from him, but knowing I'd see him again made the pain bearable.

"Hey, lover boy, if you're done sucking face, E wants to see you."

"How are you guys related again?" I asked, shaking my head at Tyler. "I better get home." Despair coiled itself around my chest, making it hard to breathe.

"I'm really proud of how well you're doing, Ren." He kissed my forehead. "When I get back, we'll start with offensive training."

"Yay." I squealed in delight.

Axel chuckled, opening the car door for me.

CHAPTER TWENTY-THREE

IT WAS SATURDAY NIGHT, AND AXEL AND I HAD DECIDED TO GO to Christian's Before Finals party. By the time we arrived, his place was packed. Music blared, drinks sloshed freely, and couples snuck upstairs and behind closed doors to swap bodily fluids. A couple of guys had gathered in the corner den to play video games, engrossed in a virtual death-match, accompanied by colorful, profane encouragement from their audience. A few paces to the left of that room, half-dressed couples found an alternative use for the granite countertops, while the wrestling team manned the kegs.

I waved to Pey from across the living room, and she smiled back with drunken eyes.

"Hey, look who finally showed up!" Christian said, his words slurred from alcohol. He pulled me into a tight hug, almost knocking us over—probably would have if Axel hadn't been supporting me.

"Easy, there." Axel put his hand on Christian's shoulder, his grip obviously bordering on bone crushing.

"Hands off." Christian shrugged free of Axel's grip and gave me the once-over, pausing at my chest as he licked his lips and walked away.

Axel let out a furious snarl.

"Let him go, Axel. He's drunk," I said through our connection.

He relaxed after a beat. He sighed, a grin spreading across his features. *"The things I agree to do for you."*

I smiled back sheepishly.

"Ree-Ree." Pey came over and hugged me. I could smell the alcohol on her breath. She let go of me and gave Axel a hug, grabbing his butt.

Ohmigod. My best friend just grabbed my boyfriend's butt!

"Uh, hey," Axel said, laughing nervously and looking to me for support.

I shook my head, chuckling. I caught Dean staring at my hand in Axel's.

He pulled Faith Lorrisk onto his lap and kissed her—French kissed her. Hoots and whistles rose, encouraging them. I saw an empty bottle on the floor pointed toward Dean and suddenly remembered the kiss he and I had shared not too long ago. I started to look away, but he opened his eyes, daring me while he continued kissing Faith. When time was called, Faith panted as her red, swollen lips trembled. Dean laughed like it was the best joke ever.

"So, you guys joining in, or what?" Hunter asked.

"No way!" I responded far too quickly.

"What she said. Besides, she's the only one I want, and I don't need a bottle to tell me when to kiss her." Axel pulled me to his chest and nuzzled my neck, kissing me gently. I was shrouded in his arms and looked up to find him grinning.

He's so beautiful. And he's mine. My heart swelled with pride.

Pey tugged on my hand. "Let's dance."

She swayed back and forth with her hands in the air as we walked toward the makeshift dance floor. Pey and I had our own version of the *Napoleon Dynamite, Roger Rabbit,* and other self-invented moves. Soon, Landon joined, making our duo a trio. The pulsing beat of a dance track with a country overlay played, and Pey and I got into it, jumping, twirling each other, bumping our hips and butts, laughing hard.

"*I'll be back in a few. Don't leave.*" Axel's voice came through our connection.

"*Is everything okay?*" I asked, searching for him.

"*Don't worry, baby. Have fun. I'll be back.*"

I sighed. I *felt* his lips against mine. Did I just imagine that? Heat coursed through me and my head felt strangely light.

"Ohmigod!" Pey said, pointing to the stereo. A song I hadn't heard in years rang from the speakers. "This is our song from eighth grade spirit week. We so gotta do it."

"Now? In front of everyone?" Having to dance with Dean in the vicinity of Axel could be catastrophic. "It's been four years. I don't think I remember."

"Oh, I remember," Dean said with a mischievous smile, walking toward me.

"I don't know about this . . ."

"Just like riding a bicycle, Nellie." He grabbed my waist and pulled me to him. Our faces were inches apart.

"I don't remember us having to be this close," I said, earning an impish smile from him.

A crowd gathered around us, chanting and clapping to the rhythm. I sighed. I put all other thoughts aside and let my mind fill with memories from the rehearsals. Dean was right; it was like riding a bike. After a few missteps, everything became a piece of cake. And by the time the song ended, I was laughing and having fun.

Memories were a blessing.

Tingles at the back of my head, followed by a growl in my mind, confirmed that Axel had seen us. He stood by the entryway door. I jumped off Dean and headed toward him, removing my black cardigan in the process.

I grabbed a fistful of his shirt and pulled him into the crowd, walking backward, wearing a lascivious grin.

"*What are you doing, angel?*" He chuckled.

I placed his hands on my waist where the hem of my halter top was slightly raised and moved my hips against him. I ran my hand down his arm, swinging my other arm over my head while I continued to roll my hips. I had never expressed myself so freely in public. But feeling Axel's hands on my skin was quite possibly my favorite thing in the universe. I let myself go, and he responded with equal enthusiasm.

"*Proving to you that I belong to you. Only you.*"

"*You don't have to prove anything.*"

I placed one hand at the nape of his neck and brought his lips to mine. My other hand caressed his cheek and the corner of his mouth as I kissed him until he groaned, tightening his grip on my waist. The whole world dissolved into nothingness. My heart raced against his chest and my knees weakened. He nipped at my lower lip. When I pulled away, he groaned in protest. I smiled at him through my lashes.

"*Angel.*" He sounded strained and breathless. "*That wasn't very nice.*"

His hands trembled as he moved them up and down the curve of my waist. I let out a shaky breath. I loved the fact I could affect him like this. I turned around and brought my hands back to him. He gripped my hips and pulled my back closer to his front as I swayed to the music.

I closed my eyes, laying my head against his chest, moving against him. Axel inched his hand toward my exposed waist, then slowly slid it across my stomach and up and down my hip. My breath grew shallow and my body trembled. Axel froze, gripping my waist harder as my body responded with another round of trembling.

"Angel." His warm voice danced across my sweaty neck. "We need to stop. Now."

I didn't know what had caused the sudden change of heart, but I nodded and let him lead me off the dance floor.

Pey met us halfway to the kitchen.

"Bathroom break. Come with." She didn't wait for my response, grabbing my hand and pulling me away. I sent an apologetic half-smile to Axel as she dragged me down the hall to the half-bath.

"Holy hotness," Pey squealed.

My thoughts were still on Axel, wondering if I'd upset him somehow.

"What the hell were you two doing on that dance floor?" Her eyes were full of excitement.

"Dancing."

"Not like that," she said.

"What do you mean?"

"You guys were . . . I don't know . . . it was something more."

I rolled my eyes and turned to look in the mirror. I was sweating and my cheeks were flushed. As I splashed cold water on my face, Pey smacked my butt, making me squeal in surprise.

"What the hell, Pey?" I said, rubbing my butt.

She raised her eyebrow. Right, she was waiting for my response.

"We were just dancing."

Someone banged on the door.

"No, you weren't. You guys were . . . I don't know . . . it was like . . ."

The knocking started again.

"Occupied!" Pey yelled.

"See? You can't even describe it." I tried to convince myself.

"Because you guys were throwing such intense sexual vibes, it was like watching you make love."

"You're being ridiculous."

This time, when the knocking came, Pey threw the door open, ready to unleash her wrath on whoever waited on the other side.

"What?" she snapped. Christian looked around her, staring at me with a roguish smile.

"Fine, it's all yours." She shoved him aside and walked out.

Before I could follow, he blocked my way, taking a step forward. I automatically took one back, hoping to pivot around him. Something didn't feel right. He closed the door and locked it. The knob jiggled, and then banging reverberated through the bathroom. Pey's voice followed. I couldn't figure out what she was saying, everything sounded muffled. Blood rushed to my ears. My sense of sight heightened; I could see the dust swirling around the room. I could hear threats outside the door.

"Christian, open the damn door before I beat the shit out of you," Pey yelled.

He didn't respond, and I was too shocked to speak. He advanced, matching my retreat until I was cornered against the wall.

"If I'd known you could dance like that . . ." He pressed himself against me, placing his hands on my hips. Disgust filled my stomach as I felt *him* against me.

"Christian, get off me." I turned my head away from him. "You're drunk, and I really don't want to hurt you."

"Oh, baby." His eyes widened and his pupils dilated, showing all black for an instant. His hands shook, like he was fighting for control. "If you want to hurt me, I'm game . . ." He leaned in and kissed my neck. Bile rose in my mouth. "No wonder you have those two wrapped around your f-finger."

I pushed him, but he wouldn't budge. A swirl of red ribbons glistened in his irises. *What the . . . ?*

"Oh, don't act so innocent. Although, a sexy schoolgirl outfit might go well with that a-act." He squeezed his eyes shut. "Shut up, shut up."

When his reopened them, they were no longer his. The whites had turned red, and lust gleamed from them. He gave me another once-over, undressing me with his eyes. He leaned down and kissed me across my collarbone. I shuddered in repulsion. Nausea rattled inside me.

Why is he so strong?

"The way Dean's been looking at you . . . and that dance. You, baby . . ."

He grabbed the nape of my neck, pulling me with force toward his face. His fingers dug into my flesh. His eyes widened again, the red swirls churning in them, and a plea-like sound escaped his lips.

"Christian, stop!" I screamed. My heart raced. "Please, Christian."

"*Ren?*" Axel's fear hit me like a tsunami. He pushed through my mind, almost like he wanted access to my sight. I didn't know if he could do that.

"*Bathroom,*" I responded and squeezed my eyes shut.

If Axel found him like this . . . the consequences would be horrid. I made a quick decision just as Christian was about to plant another kiss. Either he lived in pain for a couple of hours or he'd be permanently castrated.

I thrust my knee into his groin. He fell to the ground and cupped the area of impact, crying like a little girl. I tore open the door and ran into Axel. Pey stood behind him, her eyes teary. Axel searched my eyes for two seconds before his unmistakable fury turned to the lump behind me.

"I'm going to kill him." Axel stepped around me. His magic tingled like fire, hammering against my skin. This was going to end badly.

"No. Axel," I called to him, hoping to stop him from making a mistake he'd regret.

"*Alexander!*" He froze and I knew he'd heard me. I let out a sigh. "I need you," I said out loud. He turned around, his anger still flaring like a volcano ready to burst. I placed my hand on his cheek. "*Please take me home.*"

Taking a long, deep breath, he threw his arm over my shoulder and pulled me gently against him. Instantly, I felt him calm down, relaxing me in turn.

"Okay," he said. "Pey, do you need a ride home?"

Landon and Dean rounded the corner.

"I got her, man," Landon said. He looked behind us and his face drained of color. "Did he . . . ?"

Landon didn't even finish the sentence before Dean had put two and two together. Before any of us could stop him, he walked straight into the bathroom, ramming his fist repeatedly into Christian's face.

I screamed.

Tyler and Marcus grabbed him by the arms, pulling him off the bloodied, limp Christian.

"Stop this shit," Tyler yelled. "You're gonna kill him."

"Then he deserved it," Dean stated, like it was factual, like winters are supposed to be cold. "Let go of me, Froot Loops."

"Not until you're done acting like a maniac," Tyler countered, keeping his grip around Dean's arm.

"Fine." Dean shrugged. When neither Tyler nor Marcus let go, he yelled, "I said I was fine."

After a second, Tyler and Marcus released, hesitantly.

"Tyler, let him beat the shit out of Christian," Pey said. "It's not okay for him to force himself on Ren like an animal."

I flinched. "Nothing happened. I took care of it. He wasn't *himself*," I said, looking at Axel and then Dean, hoping they got my drift.

"*What do you mean?*" Axel asked through our connection.

"*I think I saw red in his eyes. But not like the Goarders. Can humans be possessed?*"

"*Not that I'm aware of,*" he responded. "We'll see you guys later. I would suggest you leave soon." Axel looked pointedly at Pey and Landon, his tone leaving no room for argument.

They nodded in agreement.

Axel put his arm around my waist as he guided me toward the door, Dean and the rest of the Dracians in pursuit.

†

"How could we miss something this important?" Axel shoved the door to the study open. Elijah was already inside, engrossed in a book that looked older than a dinosaur. I jogged behind him to catch up.

Damn his long legs.

Elijah looked up as we entered and placed the book on the desk with a thud. He leaned back in his chair, crossing his arms over his chest. The chair creaked in protest.

"It doesn't make sense." Axel paced back and forth, rubbing his hand over his forehead.

Elijah looked to me, his brows raised. I opened my mouth to explain.

Tyler entered the room, flanked by Dean, Marcus, and Trinity. "Ren found a crucial piece of evidence," Tyler supplied.

"And I'm absolutely appalled we never caught it. No wonder we keep getting our asses handed to us." Axel's voice vibrated against the walls of the study.

No one responded as an uncomfortable hush settled in the room.

A thunderous sound tore through the silence, making me jump. I turned toward it, only to find Axel shaking his right hand and wincing, flexing his fingers gingerly. Behind him was a hole the size of his fist. I ran to him, panic on the verge of exploding. I took his hand into mine to inspect the damage. Red, nasty scrapes oozed with blood.

"Well, there goes our security deposit." Tyler pinned us with a comical stare.

"*Alexander, it's not a big deal.*" I ran my fingers over his bloodied knuckles.

"I'm so sorry. The only reason he got close to you . . ." Axel grasped the nape of my neck, pressing his forehead against mine, letting out a sigh of frustration. It almost seemed like he needed my touch to help him calm down.

"Shh . . . I'm okay . . . really . . ."

I held his face between my hands and placed a gentle kiss on the tip of his nose, smiling. He let out a shaky breath, overwhelming me with his scent—earth and a hint of cloves.

"We'll be okay," I said. *"We will."*

"If you two are done groping each other like wildcats . . ." Dean started, jealousy lurking under the peak of his voice.

I let go of Axel and turned to our audience. "We aren't groping, you perv."

"What's going on?" Katina, Elijah's better half, walked into the room, sliding across the hardwood floor in her fluffy purple slippers, tugging at the pink robe covering her nightclothes. I'd only met her once before, when she'd brought over *"much-needed nutrition for growing kids."* But during that meeting, I'd been as completely taken with her as she'd been with me.

Marcus shrieked like he'd seen a ghost. "What's that on your face?" He chuckled, holding on to his stomach, pointing at her.

"If you like having your limbs intact, Marcus, you'll not point that finger at me," she said, swatting him across the chest.

Katina had huge, pink plastic hair curlers covering every inch of her head and white goo masking her face. She slowly chewed on the cucumber slice she held in her right hand.

"Sweetheart." Katina hugged me, rubbing my back. Then she turned to face the edgy group of Dracians and asked, "What in the ruckus is going on here?"

"We learned that Telalians can possess humans," Trinity said.

"Interesting," Elijah commented, his voice heavy with thought.

"Interesting? *Interesting*?" Axel trembled with vehemence.

"Calm down, Axel. Show some respect," Katina said in a cautious, motherly tone. "We understand you're worried about Ren, but we're still your guardians. Your elders."

Axel lowered his gaze. "Sorry, ma'am."

I took his hand in mine, giving it a quick squeeze. Katina might be a petite woman, but she presented a force of her own when disciplining her cubs, so to speak.

"Ren, please brief us on the events that led to that conclusion," Elijah requested.

"It was more like an assault," Dean scoffed, anger lacing his sarcasm.

Tyler sat in a rolling chair, pushing back and swirling in the process. Marcus and Trinity took a seat on the red leather sofa across the room. Dean flopped next to Trinity, shoving her aside, and then turned to place his feet in their laps, earning a shove onto the floor. The room erupted in chuckles.

Axel refused to relax, so I stood next to him and slid my arm through his. "Christian cornered me in the bathroom."

Axel and Dean growled in sync.

Seriously? Growling?

I squeezed Axel's hand quickly before continuing. "He was strong. Like, supernaturally strong. I could barely push him away. I saw red ribbons swirl around in his eyes . . ." I thought back to how intense Christian had been. "H-he . . . it was like he wasn't in control, but he was fighting for it. At the time, I couldn't think straight, but, now that I'm thinking back—"

"I've never heard of Goarders fighting for control," a deep voice interrupted, and I looked toward the sound. Dimitri, Axel's best friend and my sparring partner on occasion, leaned against the doorway, his legs crossed lazily. "Sorry I'm late to the party. But I wouldn't mind tearing the dic—"

"Dimitri," Katina warned.

"—off the guy that laid his hands on you. Just say the word, princess," he added, winking at me.

"Get in line." Axel gritted his teeth.

I nudged Axel playfully. "I took care of it when my knee connected with his groin."

"Good girl," Dimitri said with pride in his eyes.

"What do you mean Christian fought for control?" Elijah asked.

I cleared my throat.

"Um, when he gra . . . ah, reached for me, his hand trembled like he'd had too much caffeine. His eyes were glazed, like he was on drugs or something. He spoke the words, but they were off. He talked to himself . . . I think."

"Did you notice that when you first saw him at the party?" Dean asked.

"What do you mean?" I asked, confused.

"When he pulled you into a hug . . ."

"Oh . . . I didn't notice." I looked to Axel.

"I didn't either," Axel said, shaking his head.

"I've seen Christian drunk before. It didn't strike me as odd that he would grab you in front of m . . . everyone," Dean said, fidgeting uncomfortably in his seat.

I jolted in surprise.

"What is it?" Axel asked, as Dean jumped to his feet.

My face heated with embarrassment.

"N-nothing." My hand reached into my back pocket, pulling out the culprit. "Phone," I said lamely.

"Carrying a vibrator around for those not-so-pleasurable moments?" Tyler asked, earning a smack in his gut from Trinity. "Hey, ow . . . aren't we touchy today?"

Pey: How u doin?

Me: I'm in the middle of a war zone.

Pey: That bad? Let me know if u need me 2 play ball. *wink*

I chuckled, shaking my head. She'd unleashed operation "play ball" when Wade Newman had conveniently forgotten the meaning of "*no*." It was some weird combo of kick, pull, and whack.

When word had gotten out about how well "fragile" Pey's defense mechanism worked, it became the new "it" thing for girls. As time went on, it became a sexual reference and an excuse to touch forbidden places.

I wondered when Axel and I would get there again, not "play ball" of course, but . . . other activities involving the forbidden zones.

"*You're not helping, angel,*" Axel said through our connection.

He pulled me to his chest, his hot breath brushing against the sensitive skin under my ear. A visible shiver rolled through me as goosebumps covered my body, top to bottom.

"*It's nothing to be embarrassed about. You're just making it hard for me not to throw you over my shoulder and get us out of here.*"

"*Are you prying into my thoughts, Mr. Knight?*"

"*It's hard not to pry when you're practically screaming them into my mind. Remember, when you're overly emotional . . .*"

"Oh!" I said, quiet as a wisp, but the whole room heard me. I smacked my head with my palm and groaned.

Axel chuckled.

"I swear, half the time, you two look like you're having mind-blowing sex talk," Tyler said. When neither Axel nor I responded, Tyler jumped to his feet. "You guys are having sex *up there?*"

"No," Axel and I blurted at the same time. I averted my eyes, nibbling at my cheek. Axel shifted uncomfortably, a cat's-outta-the-bag response.

"But you can talk to each other?" Elijah asked, observing our reaction.

Axel responded after a momentary pause, "Yes."

"Care to elaborate, your high-ass?" Dean asked.

Can he be any more of a jerk?

"It's been a few weeks, I guess. And our connection has gotten stronger." He pivoted me to face him, looking at me with adoration. "I can feel her emotions and thoughts as if they were my own. It works just like the Legion connection . . . only better . . . stronger."

"But that's impossible," Katina said. We turned to her. "What you're describing is for the bonded *and* consummated. The only reason Legions can talk to each other is because of the ritual."

"Busted! You guys made whoopie!" Tyler said, his balled-up fist covering his mouth. I was certain my face turned a hundred shades of red. This time, it was Dimitri that smacked him in the head. "Hey . . . I'm not liking this moody thing you all have going on here." He rubbed the back of his head.

I caught Dean's scowl and right about then, I would've done anything to be six feet under.

"We didn't consummate, nor did we bond," Axel said, understanding my discomfort.

"How . . . ?" Katina said, almost in awe.

"She's special," Dean answered, his voice laced with anger, disappointment, and something much more heartbreaking.

He looked at me with clear hurt. Was he jealous I was special? If I even was. I mean, it was more plausible that I was a freak of nature or something. I shook my head, remembering something else from when I'd first met Axel.

"I-I'm not sure if this will help, but . . . um . . . I've always been able to feel Axel . . . if he was pretty close to me."

"Feel me how?" Axel asked, lifting my chin toward him.

"*Every time you were around, before I saw you, I felt tingles . . . like my skin vibrated or something.*" I blushed. "Some kind of sixth sense or something."

Axel held my face between his hands and looked into my eyes, searching. The way he looked at me, it was like I was the only beautiful thing in the world. Axel's lips collided hungrily with mine and I forgot the audience. I threw my arms around him, pulling him closer.

"*You are absolutely amazing,*" he said as he pulled back, hope filling his eyes. Turning toward Elijah, he asked, "Does this mean . . . ?" There was a hint of joy in his voice.

"It could. Or it could be because she's the Echo," Elijah said reproachfully. His expression grew clouded, his gaze distant, like he was suddenly consumed by thought. My gaze shifted to Axel and he had the same expression. Were they talking to each other? *Oh, what I would give to hear them talk.* So I tried just that. I concentrated on Axel, trying to breach his mind, and heard a fraction of the conversation before he closed it.

" . . . *hide our relationship. The law can't separate us if we're*—" Axel looked at me with his eyebrows raised. "Did you hear what I just said?"

I looked down at my fingernails, ashamed. The black and gold polish I'd applied earlier in the week was cracked in odd places. It gave my nails an eerie look, like spider veins.

"I'm sorry. I didn't know . . . I'm sorry . . ."

"No, it's okay." He chuckled, pulling me into a hug. "I'm . . . absurdly surprised you could get into my head." He paused. "As a Legion, we're all privileged with a direct connection to other Legions' minds, but it works like a phone. You only get access to our thoughts if we speak to you directly. What you just did, even the bonded *and* the consummated can't do. You defy all the rules of our magic."

"Can you read my mind?" Elijah asked with curiosity.

"I'm not sure."

He gave a simple nod of encouragement. I blew out a deep breath and concentrated on him, imagining the connection between us. I visualized his thoughts flowing into my mind.

"*You can do this, Ren. I believe in you.*" I sucked in a breath.

"I heard you!" I said. Then I looked at Katina, repeating the process. It was blank. I couldn't hear anything. I felt disappointed but tried again.

"*I wish Elijah would cut back on his work and spend more time . . .*" I blushed, pulling out of her mind immediately, not wanting to hear the end of that thought.

". . . *Indian knife fight. Prince Alastair wanted an update. I can't betray Axel, but . . .*" Trinity looked up and glared at me, like I was the cause behind the world's hunger problem. Her thoughts shifted to another language, a Chameleon caught in a bag of skittles. When I pushed back into her mind, her thoughts were in a language I couldn't comprehend, so I turned to Dimitri.

"*That's right, princess. I'm ready for you.*" He smiled at me.

"*You're no fun.*" I pouted.

". . . *wait to go back home to my Mikaela. I hope we get bonded. But not everyone gets what they want . . .*" I pulled back from Marcus's personal thoughts, and my heart ached for him. Why wouldn't they be bonded?

I turned my attention to Tyler, who was picturing me in my undergarments. I pulled back with a gasp. He gave me a wicked smile and a wink. "*Stay out of my head, woman.*"

"You horrible little . . ."

"Hey, it's not my fault you wanted in," he said. "*Maybe next time you'll think twice.*"

I flipped him off in my head and knew he got the message when he chuckled.

"Naughty, naughty . . ." He gave me a flirty smile.

"You're a mystery, Ren." Elijah patted my shoulder proudly. "We have much to learn about you—from you." He turned to the group, his voice commanding. "I'll report the findings about possession to the council. From here on, let's ensure Ren is always escorted."

"I call shower duty," Tyler said.

Dean snarled.

"Not if you want to continue breathing," Axel threatened.

"All the better, I could haunt her twenty-four seven." He laughed. "No rules." He wiggled his eyebrows at me.

Objects from Elijah's desk flew at Tyler from four different directions. "You guys have no sense of humor!"

I looked up to Axel, who had a small, subtle smile on his lips. Things were going to be okay. I just knew it.

CHAPTER TWENTY-FOUR

IT HAD BEEN FIVE LONG DAYS AND AN IMPOSSIBLY NEVER-ENDING Saturday. It hadn't dawned on me until this week just how much I needed Axel. I thought between shopping for the wedding, finals, and spending time with friends, it would get easier. But that proved to be a total sham.

I stared at Betsy, the training dummy extraordinaire. I'd even thought training would help keep Axel out of my mind. I practiced the moves he'd taught me; I kicked, jabbed, and punched Betsy at the marked sites. I wasn't sure how much time I spent beating the crap out of her, but when I was near exhaustion, I decided to take a break. I was covered in sweat, breathing hard, and more than a little proud of myself.

"Did Betsy do something to offend you?" I groaned at the feminine voice that greeted me. "Because you look like you're about to get into a catfight, and it'd be embarrassing if you lost to an inanimate object."

I fought the urge to smack Trinity. Instead, like a *mature* adult, I shouldered past her toward my gym bag. Since the first time she'd laid eyes on me, and every opportunity thereafter, I'd received nothing less than pure hostility from her. You'd think I'd kidnapped her children and sold them on the black market or something. I didn't understand what I'd done to get on her shit list.

"Don't you have some sick puppies to skin, or elderly folks to give wedgies to?" I picked up my duffle bag and headed for the door.

"You don't belong with us. You're weak and pathetic," she said, venom dripping from every word.

"What?" The strap of the duffle bag rolled down my arm.

"You think you can fight me?"

I caught the challenge in her threat. She wanted a fight? She was going to get one. Yeah, I might get my ass whooped in the process, but I was done with her bullshit. I'd never been one to be intimidated by a bully. And I wasn't going to start now.

She threw a staff at me and I stumbled to catch it. Axel hadn't prepared me to fight with weapons.

Ah, crap! Okay, maybe I'm a little scared now.

Already tired from my earlier beat-the-crap-out-of-Bet-sy training, I barely had energy to move. But I wanted—needed—to prove to her that I belonged here . . . with Axel.

Trinity was beautiful, graceful, and deadly, all wrapped in a nice pretty bundle. When she wasn't directing her murderous tendencies toward me, that is.

"What the hell, Trin—"

I jumped, barely avoiding the staff aimed at my feet. I spun around her, but she was too fast. She whacked me between my shoulder blades. I yelped, losing my balance and falling forward, face first. I rolled onto my back and blocked her attack, kicking her in the stomach.

"Not bad, princess. You actually learned a few things other than how to shove your tongue down his throat."

"What's your problem?"

"He thinks you're special, but you're nothing more than another bimbo."

Her quick swipe caught me off guard, hitting me right on the forehead. Warmth trickled down my face. I touched the blood with the tips of my fingers and stared, shocked. She was actually *trying* to kill me.

Hatred filled her eyes. "You're like all the girls he's ever come across. Pathetic," she spat. "Have you no shame? No self-respect?"

Black swirls of humiliation and frustration uncoiled inside me. I fought to control the fury boiling my blood. My heart rate picked up and I struggled to breathe. In that moment, it felt like everything around me moved at a snail's pace. The ground below me trembled, or, at least, I thought it did.

Trinity advanced.

"Stop!"

She froze, her staff perfectly aimed for the middle of my head.

Elijah stood in the doorway. Thank God he'd intervened. Trinity would've split my skull open and *then* beaten me to a bloody pulp.

Marcus followed behind him. I worked to slow my hammering pulse. *One, two, three, inhale. One, two, three, exhale. Rinse and repeat.*

"Leave. Don't come back until you learn to control your anger," Elijah ordered Trinity.

"Mark my words, princess—you'll be the reason he dies," she said before storming out of the room.

Once she'd left, Elijah took slow, deliberate steps toward me. He crouched in front of me, smiled, and reached for my bleeding head. "Let me . . ."

I jerked back automatically. "Sorry. I . . ." I winced at the stinging pain across my forehead. "I'd rather you not use any magic."

"Understandable." He snapped his fingers and Marcus brought over the first aid kit.

"May I?" Elijah asked.

I nodded.

He worked methodically, cleaning, applying antibiotic ointment, and sealing the wound. He then handed the kit back to Marcus. Without saying a word, Marcus turned and exited the room, leaving us alone.

"Let's take a walk." He stood and held out his hand.

"Thank you," I said as he pulled me to my feet.

I hooked my hand through his looped arm. He patted it, leading us out to the front of the training room. The crisp December air streamed over us. I inhaled deeply, taking in the smell of winter and dried grass. A beautiful, bronze sculpture of a running woman with two kids stood before us.

"Axel is like a son to me. Katina and I watched him grow and become the person he is today." His voice filled with pride. "But he has a lot of responsibility on his shoulders." He paused, his eyes trained on my stoic gaze. I wondered why he was telling me this. "He's terrified about you being part of this world, about introducing you to the dangers that entails."

"I don't wish for anything different. Axel is the best, un-invited miracle in my life. He saved me." And that was the truth. Before him, I'd felt so lifeless, taking it day by day, simply going through the motions.

He smiled like he understood. "And you, him. I couldn't imagine a better person for him to fall in love with."

"H-he's in love with me?" I stammered.

"As, I know, you are with him." I couldn't deny that accusation. The more time we spent together, the deeper our connection went. I could read him, feel him and his magic, from across the city. I couldn't do that with anyone else. Not even Dean.

Elijah smiled, his forehead and the corners of his eyes crinkling. "You're as much his strength as his weakness. Trinity's frightened by that. She's known Axel her whole life, and she's afraid he might—"

"Is she in love with him?"

Please say no. Please say no.

"Her loyalty might come across that way." That wasn't an answer. "She's afraid he'll give up everything he's ever worked for, everything he's ever dreamed. That he'll abandon his mission . . . for you."

The depth of that statement sank in slowly.

"Elijah, I would never—"

"I know, sweetheart." He placed his hand on my cheek, the way my father used to. "You're something special to him . . . to us." He sighed and dropped his hand. We turned, walking back toward the training center. We were almost at the top of the stairs before he said anything else. "We're happy to have you as part of our family, Ren. No matter what anyone says, you're the best thing that's happened to that boy. I've never seen him so alive. You need to know that."

"Thank you, Elijah." I could see how much he cared and loved each and every one of them. Even Trinity. "Can I ask you a favor?"

He nodded.

"I would appreciate it if you didn't mention . . . the conflict between Trinity and me to—"

"I think that would be best," he agreed.

CHAPTER TWENTY-FIVE

"You're on, dude. I'm going to wipe this dirty floor with your bare ass," Landon challenged.

"Keep talking, pretty boy, because you'll be kissing this sexy white ass before you know it." Dean towered over Landon.

"What the hell, guys? We're trying to eat here." Pey eyed them before throwing curly fries at Dean. "Keep the ass talk to a minimum."

"That's a waste of curly fries, Pey," I scolded her playfully.

"Whatevs." She wrinkled her nose, shaking her head.

"Your boy, here, thinks he can beat my team in Ghost Recon—" Dean started, sliding into the booth, next to me.

"That's interesting. Really. But *we*"—I pointed to Pey and I—"don't really care."

Pey and I both giggled.

"What'd I miss?" a soothing voice asked. Tiny flutters burst in my stomach.

"Axel!" I squealed, delighted. He was dressed in black from top to bottom and looked super hot.

"Whoa. What bank are you planning to rob?" Pey took a bite of her sandwich, eyeing Axel suspiciously.

He chuckled.

I tried to get Dean to move, but he wasn't budging. I shoved him harder and he scowled before finally scooting out of the way. Axel gave a fist-bump to Landon and a nod to Dean. I got out of the booth and gave Axel a sideways hug. He slipped his hand around my waist, pulling me closer.

"Do you have a minute?" he whispered, lacing my fingers in his with a squeeze.

I nodded enthusiastically, following him as he led the way outside. Once we were safely out of hearing range, he pulled me into a hug. My legs nestled between his and I heard him inhale deeply.

"I've missed you so much," he said, his voice strained.

He pulled away a little, looking into my eyes. I rose on my tiptoes and pressed my lips against his. He groaned into my mouth, pulling my bottom lip between his teeth. His hands traveled up and down my lower back, under my shirt, his fingers greedily memorizing the contours of my skin. When he pulled back, we were both breathing hard. He wobbled, his eyes clouded with desire.

"I don't ever want to get used to feeling so powerless."

He tucked a loose strand of hair behind my ear and kissed my forehead. His brows fused together as he traced his finger over my scar from earlier. Surprisingly, the skin had healed quickly around the open wound.

His lips touched the scar carefully. "I don't remember seeing this before."

My eyes locked with his. "Um, it's nothing. I . . . um . . . hit my head."

I ran my hand over his cheek and jawline. He was as beautiful and radiant as his heart.

A smile crossed my face. Then, reality came crashing into perspective, leaving a bad taste in my mouth. I wasn't supposed to see him until tomorrow.

"Hey, is everything okay? I mean, you were supposed to be on patrol tonight and you're here . . ."

"I was in the vicinity, and wanted to see you before we went . . ." His eyes churned dark blue, like muddy water.

"Alexander, you know you can tell me anything, right?"

I searched his eyes, hoping he would confide in me. His silence only tortured me further, telling me that something had changed, the stakes were now higher.

"Is it going to be dangerous?"

Even if it was, I couldn't ask him not to go. This was his job; this was Axel.

He nodded. "We have a strong lead on the missing people, and how Christian might have been possessed." He must've seen the panic in my eyes. "But we have the element of surprise. And *all* of us are going as a precaution."

"All of you?" My voice cracked. Blood rushed to my ears.

He nodded silently.

What would require that level of involvement? He looked at me like the first time we'd met, with awe and longing. I didn't trust myself to say anything. I didn't want to be one of those girlfriends who would make him choose between his responsibility and me. I couldn't . . . I wouldn't do that to him. I needed to be stronger. I took a deep breath and placed my head against his chest.

A deep voice interrupted us. "We need to get going."

I opened my eyes and peeked around Axel.

Dimitri gave a sheepish smile. "Hello, Ren."

"Give us a minute," Axel replied, without taking his eyes from mine.

"Be safe. Call me when you get home?" I asked.

He nodded and gave me a gentle kiss on my forehead. He pulled away, disappearing into the night. I called out to him, "Call me."

"You okay?"

I turned around, startled. Dean leaned against the doorway, concern filling his eyes.

"What are you doing here? Shouldn't you be going with them?"

"I came to check on you, first," he said, as if it was the most natural thing to do.

My voice softened. "I don't need a babysitter."

Big, warm arms wrapped around me. My initial reaction was to push him away. I wanted to run after Axel. Tell him to come back, to stay. But I caved in to the sense of security that wrapped around me. It had been a long time since Dean had tried to comfort me, and I'd missed it. It was . . . nice, so I let him. My eyes burned. I squeezed them shut, taking a deep breath as tears rolled down my cheeks.

Dean tightened his hold in response.

†

It was around eight thirty when I got home that night. Dean had dropped me off, making sure I was okay before he left. I took a long, hot shower, worry gnawing at my insides.

Something just didn't feel right.

I could sense a hum against my skin, vibrations that traveled from the core of my heart to my nerves, telling me something horrible was about to happen. I wanted to pick up the phone and call Axel, but I was afraid to, in case he was in the middle of his mission.

Instead, I found myself TV surfing. Eventually, though, the mindless entertainment lulled me to sleep and I passed out.

†

I walked through a narrow, dimly lit hallway that led to a flight of creaky stairs. Loud music pulsated through the walls. Someone walked right through me and I gasped in horror, spinning around. Two more followed before I stepped away, pressing myself against the wall of the already tight walkway. Was I dead? What was going on? My breath came in gasps as claustrophobia kicked in.

Then I saw him. Axel. He signaled Dimitri, Dean, Tyler, Trinity, and three others I'd never met to go around. The rest continued forward, taking the first door on the right.

Two Goarders looked up as Axel's team burst into the room, surprise written all over their faces. A kidney punch and a left ear cuff brought the first one to the ground. An uppercut and a roundhouse kick sent the second to the floor with a thud. Without a moment's hesitation, a dagger plunged once, twice. Axel signaled Elijah, Joshua, and his two other allies to watch and go around as he continued forward. I followed Axel.

He placed blue, star-shaped metal pieces on the walls, clicking his watch each time like he was setting a timer. Silhouettes approached us as we reached the end of the hallway.

"Axel, behind you," I whisper-yelled when I realized they weren't Dracian. But it was too late.

He was caught off guard as a knife slashed toward his face. He ducked, dancing out of range, quickly got his bearings, and attacked.

Four more advanced his way, weapons drawn. Why wasn't he using his magic? My mind raced. He was going to be outnumbered in no time. He needed help. He needed *my* help. Without thinking, I ran toward him.

I approached the Goarder in Axel's blind spot, throwing a punch. It sailed right through the side of its head and I fell, face first, to the floor, knocking the wind out of myself in the process. Wheezing, I got up and tried again. Another punch, kick, pull. Nothing worked! I was a ghost in a dream. I screamed in fury and frustration as red dust sprinkled me like confetti.

I whirled around to see Axel kick up with his feet, coming to a standing position. He sank into a fighting stance, balancing lightly on the balls of his feet. He faced his opponents, his hands in front of his face, ready for the oncoming fight. Axel's fingers dug into the sleeves of his black Legion gear. The first two Goarders reached him and he drove forward like a spring, pushing off the narrow walls and becoming airborne. Blue streaks wrapped around his forearm, extending from his hand as he sliced into the first Goarder, landing gracefully behind the dismembered body.

The music pumped louder and more bodies joined the chaos. I bit my lip so hard a metallic taste filled my mouth. I was helpless. All I could do was watch the horrid scene unfolding before me.

A Goarder lunged, slashing its weapon. Axel grabbed its arm, pushing it into the wall as his elbow connected with a second Goarder's face before he plunged his dagger into the first one's back. He then did an axe kick, full sweep, and elbow combo at the unsuspecting third Goarder.

The second one was on its feet again, black ooze dripping from its mouth and eyes, its knife swaying back and forth. Axel blocked its reverse stab at his face, grabbing it by the wrist and striking its locked elbow with his free hand. The sickening snap of breaking bone echoed off the walls as the Goarder screamed, dropping the knife. Snaking his hand under the Goarder's arm, he wrapped his fingers behind its neck and pushed. The Goarder flipped forward, landing with a thud on its back. Axel quickly knelt beside its writhing form and plunged the blue weapon into its chest. It disintegrated as he stood, watching the remaining Goarders close ranks around him.

My heart rate spiked and I let out a helpless cry. He blocked the first punch to his jaw, but missed the second that caught him square in the kidney. He blocked two more advances before a blow to the head dropped him flat on his back. I screamed, fear coursing along every nerve.

Lying on his back, Axel struggled to defend himself, blocking the Goarders' sharp weapons from slicing him to pieces. A streak of blood ran down his bicep. He was hurt, and there was nothing I could do.

Nothing!

Something whizzed past my ear and I turned to find Dean and the other allies joining the fight, adding throwing stars and magic to the chaos of the hallway. Relief flooded through me as the odds shifted. Dean and Joshua tag teamed, taking on the Goarders in front of Axel, while Elijah and Skye took care of the ones behind, leaving Axel to defend against the one pinning him down.

Dean turned as his opponent disintegrated and sent a fireball toward the Goarder that still had the upper hand on Axel. It reared back as flames rippled across its shoulder, trying frantically to pat them out and allowing Axel to bury his blue weapon in its abdomen.

"*Thanks*," Axel mouthed. Dean eyed him with a cocky grin.

Joshua, Elijah, and Skye wiped their weapons clean, panting and swiping sweat off their foreheads. After a moment to regroup, they all continued forward, clearing one room at a time, getting rid of any Goarders they came across, until finally, Axel signaled a halt.

He held up two fingers, pointing to the wall, then his wrist, indicating that time was running out. He flicked his fingers toward the rear of the group and they each turned, disappearing back the way we'd come. I started to follow, but got distracted when I saw a quivering figure in the shadowed corner of the room. Axel stopped beside me, unaware of my presence.

"Hello, Alexander," she said weakly. She glanced in my direction with a smile.

I looked over my shoulder, only to realize there was no one behind me. Could she see me? Who was she?

Axel's watch beeped. He tucked away the blue weapons, folding them back into his sleeves, and grabbed her limp body in both arms. Securing her safely, he ran toward the window. I heard the first blast echo not far behind me. I bolted, following him as he smashed through the window and plummeted into the darkness. I stopped, fear surging through me. But I didn't have time to process the fact that Axel had just jumped out a window. A deafening crash sounded behind me and heat surged through the room. Without thinking, I ran, jumping through the shattered glass. Fire roared through the broken window like an angry dragon, licking my skin as I fell toward the water waiting below.

†

I woke screaming, patting myself as if I were on fire. My breath came in labored gasps and my hands went to my throat as I coughed up smoke.

Thick. Black. Smoke.

I was drenched in sweat, and my skin sizzled with burn marks. Hot tears flowed easily from my stinging eyes. I gasped between each sob.

What the hell?

My chest constricted like I was about to have a heart attack. I placed my hand over my heart, feeling it hammer against my ribs, and shot out of bed. *That felt too real, too intimate to be a dream.* I took a deep breath, and before I let it out . . .

Joshua! I ran to his room. I pounded on the door, but he didn't answer. A pang of panic surged through me. *Is it possible it wasn't a dream? No, it couldn't be. I wasn't . . .*

But I knew. I just knew something bad had happened. Every fiber in my body told me so.

I ran back to my room and picked up my phone, hoping to see a missed call or text from Axel. Nothing. The clock read three a.m.

Oh. God. Nonononono. He was supposed to call me. I tried to dial his number, only to select the wrong person several times. I threw the phone on my bed and wrapped my arms around my trembling body. I needed to calm down.

One, two, inhale. One, two, exhale.

After several minutes, I tried again.

Ring. Ring. Ring.

No answer.

I tried again.

And then again.

My breathing became shallower with each try. I ran down the stairs, tripping over the last step. I didn't know what I was doing or where I was going. My body still itched like it had been burned. I needed something to cool me off . . .

I yanked open the front door and ran out into the yard. Everything around me was blurry, like I was still dreaming. I screamed, falling to my knees, placing my hands on either side of my head as I cried, unable to control my sobs.

My heart felt like it was being ripped out, like someone had punched a hole in my chest and grabbed ahold of the beating muscle, twisting and pulling it out. I wanted to die. *Please, let me die.* Then, two strong arms engulfed me in an embrace.

"I'm sorry. I got here as fast as I could." I knew that voice. Who was it?

I didn't care. All I knew was that I was safe. Safe in his arms.

"I'm sorry, babe." He lifted me, and before I knew it, I was lying in the warmth of my bed. I panicked, shooting up, grabbing his arm, urging him not to leave me alone.

"Please . . ." was all I said before he was beside me, wrapping his arms around my shuddering form, tucking me safely against his chest. Smooth, comforting coolness wrapped around me like ribbons and the irritation on my skin began to calm.

"I'm here . . . I'm here . . ."

I sighed as blackness consumed me.

†

I shot up from my pillow. The vehement sound of my alarm filled the room at a deafening volume. Annoyed, I rolled over and hit the snooze button. I almost shrieked when I realized I'd rolled back on top of someone. The next second, strong arms pushed me and my butt connected to the floor with a thud.

"Ouch." I grimaced.

I crawled to my knees, rubbing my hand over my sore butt, and peeked at the bed.

Figures!

"Dean Tristan Jensen." Anger built inside me, the throbbing pain in my butt forgotten.

It'd been ages since I'd called Dean by his full name. Back in sixth grade, he'd provoked me to prove my bravery by placing an apple in the middle of my then bushy hair while he threw knives at it—*blindfolded.* The first time he'd thrown a knife, he'd purposefully nipped my ear. When I'd teased him for lack of talent, he'd pierced the apple dead on. I'd known then that he was going to be a pain in my ass for the rest of my life.

Throwing pillows at him didn't work. He simply towed them along his body and went back to sleep.

When I tugged at those pillows, an irritated groan rumbled from his chest, along with some incoherent words. *He sleeps like there's no tomorrow.* I stomped off and returned with half a glass of water.

"Last chance, buckaroo," I said with a sly smile. He mumbled something. "Your funeral. One . . . three." I dumped the glass of water on his face.

He shot up, growling and pulling me on top of him, earning a knuckle-punch to the chest. I squealed, trying to free myself, only to have him pull me closer. I jabbed him in the chest with my elbow.

"Ugh . . . let me go, jackass," I snarled.

"What the hell, Pernell?" He loosened his grip and opened his eyes into thin slits. "I'm trying to get some sleep here."

"What are you doing in my room? In my *bed*?" I smacked him.

"Hey!" He rubbed his head and gave me a look.

I didn't know what to make of it.

"You asked me to stay."

"Are you freaking kidding me? I would never—"

"Before you go ape-shit . . ." He pulled up to a sitting position, facing away from me. "I came home last night and found you on the front lawn. So I brought you back here, and you asked me to stay. I never meant to fall asleep." He faced me with a lascivious smile. "I gotta say, even with no action and you snoring like a pug, it was the best night of my life . . ."

"Ha. Ha!" I threw a pillow at him. "Get out."

Dean chuckled, rolling off the bed. "You should probably put some clothes on, though. It was *hard* to be a gentleman last night."

"You aren't the boss of—"

"I've barely slept, and I don't have time to argue." He sounded half angry, half amused. *Moody much?* "One way or another, you're getting out of that bed. You have thirty minutes, and then I'm dragging your cute little ass out there, even if you're wearing *that*." He gave me the once-over, top to bottom. I swear his cheeks turned pink before he shut the door behind him.

I looked down to find myself in my nightclothes—pink cami, white boyfriend shorts, and no bra. Good God. I may as well have been naked. *Utter mortification of the century.* I flopped back onto my pillow with a groan, rubbing my eyes with the heels of my hands.

The events of last night slowly crept into my mind, along with the pain that prickled deep in my core. I untangled my legs from my tousled comforter and got ready for school.

I checked my phone. It was almost eleven a.m.—on a Monday. Ah hell, I'd just missed half a day of school. Good thing finals were last week. I went down the stairs to find Dean in the middle of a family feud with his parents.

"Don't know . . ." he said between bites of food. "She was hysterical. She freaked out, Dad. I've never seen her like that."

"She doesn't remember what happened?" John sighed. "How . . . ?" He noticed me coming down the stairs and halted the conversation. "Ren. How are you?"

"Come join us for brunch, sweetheart." Sandy gestured for me to sit on the barstool by the island.

It was no surprise that the Jensen family was in our kitchen after the kind of night I'd had. Since my parents' death, the Jensens had always stepped up to take care of me. I'd had dinners made, impromptu game nights, and even an occasional sleepover. They'd never listened to my protests that I could take care of myself.

"I'm fine. Thank you." I looked around for Joshua. A pang of worry coated my voice when I asked, "Where's Muskles?"

"He's with Cassie," John responded.

"Oh, good. *Good.*" Joshua was okay. So maybe it had been a dream.

I took a deep breath, feeling a weight lifting off my chest. It must have been my overactive imagination. But there was still something that didn't feel right. *Axel.*

"I need to go check on something. Can you tell Muskles that I'll be back later?" I asked John.

He nodded. I sauntered out of the house without another thought. I needed to do something before I could even think about going to school.

Find. Axel.

"Wait up." Dean followed me to my car.

"I'm driving."

He let out a disheartened grunt and got in the passenger side. "You're so infuriating."

"Well, no one's asking you to tag along," I snapped back. I felt like a complete tool. Dean had been nothing but nice to me. He could've left me out in the cold or taken advantage of my situation. But he'd done neither. I looked straight ahead, my hands on the wheel in a death grip. "Dean."

"Yeah?" From the corner of my eye, I saw his eyebrows shoot up, possibly wondering what else I could blame him for.

My chest tightened at the thought. I had been such a horrible friend to him when all he'd done was be there for me. He deserved better. So I said the one thing I rarely ever told him:

"Thank you."

†

It was the longest six miles I'd ever driven. When I got there, I heard loud grunts and the clanging of metal on metal and panicked. I didn't even bother to close my car door before I ran into the building, ignoring Dean's calls to slow down. My heart pounded in my chest and my head spewed horrible images of what lay inside. I came to a halt just inside the door, panting like I needed every breath to save my dying body, and swept my gaze across the training room.

No Goarders or evildoers about to annihilate the universe. Just Axel and Dimitri, locked in an intense sparring match, surrounded by Tyler, Marcus, and Trinity. This is why he wasn't returning my calls? Seriously?

Axel moved with such speed, it was hard to see the sword in his hand. His toned, lean arms moved with control, each motion executed with the grace of a dancer. Dimitri backed him into a corner and Axel bobbed under his massive arm. He ran across the mats, leading Dimitri toward the opposite wall. Dimitri chased after him at full speed. Axel dodged, spun, and pushed off the wall into a backflip, just as Dimitri dove in with his sword.

Dimitri shouted and swung at Axel, but Axel blocked, dancing away again. He slashed at Dimitri as they moved back across the room, but Dimitri deflected his blows easily, moving faster than I could follow. Dimitri kicked Axel in the gut with a triumphant grin. Axel smiled slyly, holding on to his stomach, and sliced Dimitri's leg with the tip of his sword, grazing the skin just below his outfit.

A string of impressive curse words echoed around the training room. Axel responded with an equally impressive torrent involving Dimitri's lack of skill and bruised ego. Everyone in the room was laughing.

My lips twitched up at the image of me kissing that dirty, *dirty* mouth.

Axel finished off the demonstration with a simple spinning back kick, disarming Dimitri. He stood over his fallen opponent, his sword hovering above Dimitri's throat. A crooked smile spread across Dimitri's lips as he tapped the mat three times with an open palm.

"You're excelling." He chuckled, taking Axel's waiting hand. "Maybe it's time you got a new bodyguard?"

Bodyguard? What is he talking about?

"Not a chance, my friend. Not a chance." Axel patted Dimitri's shoulder and walked back to the group of eagerly waiting students.

All eyes—filled with admiration and respect—followed him. He stood in front of them, his shoulders back, his voice commanding as he laid out his instructions. The group paid close attention, like his words were the Holy Grail.

A slight thrill passed through me, almost making me forget the reason I was here.

Almost.

Tyler's eyes flickered in my direction, but I stormed out of the place without a second thought, letting the door close behind me.

CHAPTER TWENTY-SIX

AFTER WHAT SEEMED LIKE HOURS COOPED UP IN MY ROOM, I was nearly done packing for my trip to Chicago. A few more boots and jeans should just about do it. The clunk of metal hitting the floor caught my attention as I pulled out the box with my favorite boots.

A blue dagger lay by my feet. Squatting down, I picked it up, remembering why I had it. Axel had sent the Tibt as a surprise when he'd found out that he couldn't accompany me to Chicago. Something about the *Throne* summoning him on official Dracian business. I shoved the weapon into the closet, sighing.

Grabbing my favorite book from the nightstand, I settled onto the floor in front of my bed and got lost in Anne Frank's story. Moments later, I heard a knock. I ignored it, increasing the volume of my stereo, leaving very little ambiguity as to my present mood. The door opened slightly and I threw the closest thing I could get my hands on. Joshua caught it without hesitation.

He turned down the volume before he looked at me, his features amused. "Boy, am I glad you hate playing darts."

"Who says I do?" I ground out.

I knew my anger was directed at the wrong target, but I couldn't help myself. I'd always been a grounded person . . . okay, who was I kidding. *Emotion* was my middle name.

"What is it, Joshua?" I sighed in a lame attempt to calm myself.

"Well, I thought I'd bring you some dessert."

He handed me a slice of cheesecake. Oh, how my brother knew the way to my heart. He sat beside me on the floor, next to my worn-out book.

"Do you want to talk about it?"

"No." I didn't want to, but the words came tumbling out anyway. "I mean, if he's able to sword fight, you'd think he'd be able to pick up the damn phone and call me. But *nooo!* Why would he care if I've been worried sick for the past twenty-four hours? I saw him almost die, Joshua. I saw you there, too."

His eyebrows shot sky-high. I took a small breath, willing my heart to pace itself.

This wasn't the time to freak out about a stupid dream.

"It was just a dream, but it felt so damn real." My heart hurt. I sighed heavily, rubbing my eyes with the heels of my hands. Joshua placed a hand on my shoulder and squeezed. "I was stupid to think I was important to him. Well, guess what? He's not that important to me, either."

Somewhere, deep down, I knew I was being unfair and irrational. But damn, after everything I'd been through, I had every right to be pissed.

"Why do you think you're not important . . . to him?"

Was he even listening to what I'd just said? Comical laughter erupted. Joshua put his hand on mine.

"Why don't you get ready and come downstairs? We'll go out for dinner." When I pulled away, he was insistent. "I won't let you starve yourself because you have an *ungrateful* boyfriend." He winked at me.

An unexpected smile pulled at the corners of my mouth. "Okay. But only because you called him an ungrateful boyfriend."

"Listen, kiddo." He let out a deep breath. "God only knows that I haven't been the greatest big brother in the world. Hell, no matter how much I try, I can't seem to be able to spend more time with you. But you've always been my number one priority."

"What are you getting at, Muskles?"

He shot to his feet and shoved his hands into the front pockets of his jeans.

"I hate admitting this." He looked uncomfortable, shifting his weight from one leg to the other. "But Axel . . ."

"Don't go there." I finally understood.

"He loves you, Killer. He'd do anything to make you happy, die to keep you safe. Just as I would. His love toward you is unconditional."

I knew Axel loved me. Elijah had told me that much not too long ago.

"I've never seen anyone bust their ass like he did today, just to get a girl to forgive him." He smiled at me. "That's not a store-bought cheesecake."

I admit, my heart swooned a bit with the mention of homemade cheesecake. But that still didn't excuse the fact he hadn't had the decency to let me know he was okay. Or to apologize in person.

"Well, he isn't getting off the hook just because my stomach's satisfied."

"I could ban him from the face of the earth if you want me to," he offered, locking eyes with me.

"No," I shouted, too quickly.

Joshua gave me a knowing smile.

"I'll let him suffer for a few days."

"If he lasts that long." He chuckled. "Cut him some slack, okay, kiddo? We're all flawed in some way. Do what you feel in here," he said, pointing to his own chest. "And wherever you go, whatever choice you make, dive in without holding back." He turned toward the door, but paused as he reached for the knob. "At least his flaws are tied to his *responsibilities*."

I raised my eyebrows. "When did you jump on the Axel's-awesome bandwagon?"

He chuckled and rumpled my hair. "When wasn't I?"

Should I answer that?

"You have two hours to get ready. So hurry up, will ya?" he called, closing the door behind him.

Joshua's words echoed through my mind as I stood and fell back onto my bed. "*Wherever you go, whatever choice you make, dive in without holding back.*"

I felt like I'd done just that. I'd fallen hard for Axel—truly, madly, unexpectedly.

†

"You'd be doing me one hell of a favor if you'd tell me where we're going," I whined.

"Just wear something casual, preferably something that covers you head to toe," Joshua yelled up the stairs. "And leave Grumpy behind."

"Well, I wouldn't be *grumpy* if you'd left the rest of *my* cheesecake alone, douche!"

He chuckled. "Just get down here. For God's sake, I'm about to turn into dust. You're worse than Cassie . . . ouch!"

My phone buzzed.

Axel: THIS REMINDED ME OF YOU.

When I clicked on the attached link, my cell blasted with "The Gummy Bear Song." I started laughing.

"Stop laughing and get your ass down here," Joshua said. "Ow!"

Me: IT MUST BE THE BUBBLY PERSONALITY.

Axel: NOPE.

Me: THE INCREDIBLY SEXY VOICE?

Axel: HMM . . .

My heart fluttered and I grinned.

Axel: NOPE

Me: THEN IT'S DEFINITELY BECAUSE THE GUMMY BEAR IS SO EDIBLE.

Axel: BINGO!

I nearly dropped my phone reading that reply. Heat flooded through me and my heart raced. Be still my heart.

Axel: I HAVE A SURPRISE FOR YOU.

Me: YEAH?

Axel: YUP.

Me: WHAT IS IT?

Axel: IT'S BEEN DELIVERED TO YOUR HOUSE.

"Would you get your ass down here already?" Joshua interrupted my thoughts.

"Say that one more time and I swear to God, I'll turn you to dust myself," I muttered, knowing all too well that he couldn't hear me.

I cleared my head and looked into the mirror, giving one final assessment. I wore a floor-length, white silk skirt that sat below my hipbone and an off-the-shoulder, orange silk top that sat above my hipbone, leaving a strip of bare skin showing. I complemented my attire with sizzling, orange, T-strap heels. Mom's amulet, as always, hung low around my neck. My hair was pulled into a high ponytail, but I'd left two strands shaping my face.

With newfound confidence, I stepped out of my room and walked down the stairs. My skirt flowed around me like waves of soothing water. I checked my phone one last time in hopes of another text from Axel.

"Beauty takes time, my dear brother," I said roguishly. "Will you—"

I almost fell flat on my face, missing the last step. I stared at *him* waiting at the end of hallway, rocking nervously on his heels. Axel always looked breathtaking, but even more so tonight. He wore a black, designer suit with a white shirt that peeked between his jacket lapels.

"I beg to differ." His eyes glowed bright blue.

I gawked at him like a hungry baboon.

Not a monkey.

Not an ape.

A. Baboon.

Heat rushed into my cheeks and I looked down at my feet, embarrassed.

Joshua walked into the room, his hands shoved into his front pockets again. "She's surprised, all right."

Cassie smirked. I took a few deliberate steps toward Axel, still unsure if he was really here.

"*I have a surprise for you,*" he'd texted, not five minutes ago. "*It's been delivered to your house.*"

"I'm here to ask you out on a formal apology date." He took a few steps toward me.

"I . . ." Ah, hell, why was it so hard to talk when he was around?

He smiled. "It's the least I can do for being an inconsiderate boyfriend."

I looked at Joshua for support and he shrugged.

"Okay." I didn't need to be asked twice.

Cassie handed me a jacket, giggling. "Have fun, kiddo."

"Behave," Joshua warned.

I waved quickly to both of them. Axel nodded and held his hand out. I took it with a little hesitation. He led me down the driveway to his parked car.

He held the door open and waited until I took a seat before letting go of my hand. This was going to be a night to remember. I could feel it.

†

"You look beautiful tonight," Axel whispered in my ear.

I pressed my lips together, pushing back an involuntary shiver.

"Are you cold?"

"No. If anything, it's getting a bit warm out here." I sucked in a deep breath, puffing up my cheeks, and blew the air back out in a nervous huff.

An awe-inspiring scene came into view. The path we were on led down a cobbled walkway to a gazebo. It stood in the middle of a tiny pond bordered by a beautiful garden.

Axel pulled my hand into his, intertwining our fingers. The familiar sensation I'd missed over the past few days spread from the tips of my fingers all the way to my toes. His hand quivered in mine, like he was nervous. He pulled me closer, leading us to the middle of the gazebo. Moonlight reflected off the calm water that surrounded us.

Flickering candlelight bounced off the red and white chiffon fabric draped around the horizontal columns. A table for two sat in the corner, adorned with beautiful daisies, roses, and gardenias. Soft, soothing music filled the air like an afterthought. My heart hammered against my chest as my eyes drank in the magnificent sight. Was it getting warmer in the middle of December or was it just me?

The whole setup was remarkably romantic. It was perfect. Simply perfect.

He'd done all this for me? Maybe he thought he could get back in my good graces by charming his way back. It wasn't going to work, though. Nope. Not with me.

When I finally had the courage to look up, I found Axel's bright blue eyes staring at me. They looked radiant, like the brightest stars in the darkest night.

"Why?" I knew why, but I wanted to hear the words from him.

"Because you deserve everything that is beautiful," he said, matter-of-fact.

I blushed, biting my lip.

He beamed. "I hope you're hungry."

Right on cue, my stomach growled and a nervous chuckle escaped my throat. Déjà vu. I placed my hand over my stomach. "Famished."

He helped me out of my jacket. "It won't be cold, I promise."

"Heaters?" I asked. That would explain why it was feeling so hot. But maybe it was just me and my body's reaction to him.

"Magic," he responded, wiggling his fingers.

His magic.

The chair groaned against the wooden floor of the gazebo as Axel pulled it out for me. I didn't know what to expect, but I intended to live like it was my last night on earth.

"This is amazing. I should personally thank the chef," I said, chewing a tender piece of chicken drenched in apricot sauce.

"That could be arranged."

I bit the inside of my cheek to stop myself from smiling, knowing full well this food had *Axel* written all over it. "This deserves a kiss, at least."

A boyish smile appeared on his face. "Now, that's a great idea. I'm certain *he'd* appreciate it."

I sucked in a deep breath, heat radiating from every nerve. He was in a full-on swoon mode, apparently. I had a feeling there would be an ongoing cartwheel circus in the hollow of my stomach tonight.

"So, Ren . . ." he said after dinner, getting up from his chair. He slowly walked toward me and got on his knee, opening his arms. My heart flipped tenfold before I got the nerve to ask him what he was doing.

Still on his knee, he smiled, swaying his arms, gesturing for me to dance with him. I placed my napkin on my empty plate and stood, reaching for his open palm. With my hand in his, he pushed to a standing position, pulling me toward him as our song, the one that had played that day in the diner, started.

My heart hummed with desire as he held me close, swaying to the music. My mind emptied as thoughts evaporated. Thinking was overrated, anyway.

"This song . . ." I whispered.

"Hmm?" He seemed lost in his own world.

He pulled me another inch closer to him. I tilted my head up and my breath caught in my throat. His eyes were dangerously intense. My chest squeezed tight with desire, needing to kiss him.

He placed one hand on the small of my back. He traced my arm with his other hand, all the way to my fingers, before placing my hand over the erratic beating of his heart. My head swam with emotions I couldn't describe. His fingers gently caressed my back as he slid his hand up and down my spine, producing a deep, familiar feeling of bliss that made me oblivious to my surroundings.

"Did I tell you how beautiful you look tonight?" he whispered in my ear.

I shivered, my feet faltering. What was he trying to do to me?

"Yes, but I wouldn't mind hearing it again." *What the hell?* Really, did I have to be so needy and insecure, after everything he'd already done?

He laughed. "Temperance Marie Pernell, you're the most beautiful, exotic woman I've ever seen." He took a deep breath as he placed his forehead against mine.

My heart worked hard, sending a rush of blood to my ears.

"I'm so sorry, Ren. You have no idea how sorry I am for letting you down." He laced his fingers through mine, drawing circles on my palm with his thumb. "I'm probably going to mess up a lot. I've never been with anyone, and this is all new to me. You're the first girl I've kissed. I've never felt this . . . these feelings I can't even put into words because they wouldn't do them justice. You're my number one priority. It's just, sometimes I get swallowed up by my responsibilities, and I need a reminder." I opened my mouth to say something, but his finger on my lips stopped me. "Let me finish please," he pleaded. "You deserve a person that can devote themselves to you—"

"Are you breaking up with me?" My voice cracked as the words left my mouth.

"Always the patient one." He chuckled, softly.

I pouted.

He sighed. "You deserve a person that can devote themselves to you, and *I* intend to be that person. I'm sorry I didn't call. I'm not asking you to forgive me, but I want you to know I'll do my damnedest to be the man you deserve, even if it takes me my entire existence to make it happen. There's nothing in the world I value more than you," he said with a sad smile. "This . . . having this with you . . . I . . ."

I placed a finger on his lips, which he kissed immediately. Such a simple gesture, but it told me just how much he cared. It wasn't exactly what I felt for him, but it was enough to make me feel warm and fuzzy.

"I know . . . thank you." A smile curved his lips against my finger.

"I'll always fight for us. No matter what."

Is that his way of saying "I love you"? I shook my head.

"How about a truce?" I smiled at him. "We're both flawed in more than one way. We aren't perfect, but together, we're cosmic, and I intend to see it through if you do."

He placed his hands on my face, tugging me to him, and kissed me. When he pulled away, his eyes were still closed.

"Always," he murmured onto my lips before he kissed me again.

A new track played. Axel picked up the pace, still holding me close to him. I placed my head on his chest. His heart *thump, thump, thumped* against my ear. I felt small but secure in his embrace.

I closed my eyes, enjoying his touch, his closeness. His hands slowly dropped from my arms, tracing a path down to my waist. We were barely moving. But it was perfect.

Being here felt comfortable, right, like home. I didn't want to lose this. Ever.

"Alexander, where do we go from here?" I whispered, not daring to see his reaction. We had crossed some sort of line. We'd declared our intentions to be with each other, and yet, not really. My insecurities were in overdrive tonight.

Axel stilled, holding his ground, and gently tilted my chin. My eyes flickered open, and it was like we stared into each other's souls.

"Wherever *you* want to, *Meus Aeternus.*" He closed his eyes, as if to determine what he wanted to say next. He dropped his finger from under my chin.

My heart fluttered like hummingbird wings.

"But . . . *I* want you. I want us." He took a deep breath, like he was about to cut his heart out and lay it before me, ready to be pulverized into countless pieces.

"From the first time I saw you, my world has taken a different orbit. And when you glanced my way *that* very first time, I knew you'd be . . ." His Adam's apple bobbed, like he was struggling to find words . . . or maybe emotions. "You're my savior, my angel, my own personal demon."

His eyes bored into mine, vulnerable and scared. I had a feeling this was a side not many got to see.

Pride swelled in my chest, and I smiled saucily. "That's a good thing, right? Me being your *personal demon*?"

"Most definitely." He smiled back, then chewed on his lower lip. "If you'll have me, this" —he pointed between us— "*this* will be what you want it to be, nothing more, nothing less."

I nodded and let silence fall between us. Then, slowly, I closed my eyes, laying my ear on his chest, listening to his fast-beating heart. His words were overwhelming. I needed to breathe.

The air around us flowed in rhythm. I felt the slightest touch tickling my face, my arms, all the exposed skin on my body. I opened my eyes to raining rose petals of all colors. For the third time tonight, I was in awe.

"Are you doing this?" I looked at him, enthralled.

He gazed at me from under his eyelashes and nodded. "You like it?"

"No," I said, pausing. He frowned. "I love it! I don't think even Heaven could compete with the world you create for me."

Axel's chuckle skipped every organ in my body, hitting me directly where it mattered most—my heart. "You know, I never thought I'd be this lucky."

I looked up at him, confused.

"I first saw you a year and a half ago, so beautiful, so confident, so unbelievably compassionate." The corners of his lips curved into my favorite smile—the one that reached all the way to his eyes.

"So you *have* been stalking me," I teased.

He chuckled so softly the vibrations tingled playfully against my skin. "I wish." He frowned, deep lines etching his beautiful face.

"What is it?" I ran my hand across his forehead.

"Ren, there's something I need to tell you. But . . ." He chewed on his lip.

"Tell me," I said, taking his hand into mine.

He led me back to my chair. "I think you should sit."

I did what he asked, but didn't think anything good ever came when talking and "*I think you should sit*" were in the same vicinity.

He knelt before me, like a sinner asking for forgiveness, his hands holding both of mine. When I looked into his eyes, they turned pale blue. This was terrible. My heart sank. "The first night I saw you, you were in deep conversation with a homeless woman, offering her your shoulder and food. I wanted to come and talk to you right then."

Which night was he referring to? I racked my brain for when I'd last talked to a homeless woman. It had been so long ago . . . not since . . . I gasped. Not since the night my parents died.

"Nala had told me I was going to find the Echo that night, which I guess I did"—his smile didn't reach his eyes— "and that I would be meeting people. Your parents, Ren. They were out there to meet me, and somehow . . ." He looked away from me, like he was ashamed of himself. But his grip on my hands tightened. Was he afraid I'd let go . . . leave him to his misery?

And I did. I pulled away and stood, not wanting to hear whatever it was he was about to say. He looked up, his eyes paler than I had ever seen them. "I-I-I don't understand." I trembled. "What are you saying? No, I can't . . ." I couldn't listen.

"You need to know." His voice was weak and shaky. His voice *never* shook. "You have the *right* to know. And I'm sorry I've kept this from you for as long as I have. I'm so sorry."

Axel swallowed hard, the tendons in his neck tightening, and I could practically taste his fear and disgust. He was scaring me, but words wouldn't leave my mouth.

"No," I said, shaking my head, taking a step back and almost tripping over the chair behind me. My hand went up when he tried to help. "Don't . . ."

"I was with your parents when they died." The words clawed their way out of his throat, scratchy and desperate. He looked into my eyes.

"No. Axel . . . no, I can't . . . don't . . ." I squeezed my eyes shut and pressed my palms to my ears, wishing I could turn back time as the next words slipped from his mouth:

"I'm the reason they're dead."

My lungs felt like they were collapsing, breathing was getting harder. Everything inside me hurt like some devil was having the time of its life. No noise penetrated my eardrums. My legs gave out and I collapsed into the chair I'd nearly tripped over moments ago.

What did he just say? Why the hell is it so damn cold?

"Ren . . . Ren . . . Ren." Axel's hand was on my shoulder, shaking me. Through the blurriness, his pale blue eyes stared back with shame, pain, and fear.

My throat burned. I didn't respond. I couldn't. Axel pulled his hand from my death grip. Where warmth had resided, cold took over. He took two steps back, putting distance between us, and turned his back to me.

Tears spilled down my cheeks.

"That night, when your parents were killed, they were trying to protect me. They gave their lives to protect *me*." He said the word like it was the most disgusting thing in the world.

That didn't sound right. Axel wasn't disgusting. From the moment I'd laid eyes on him, he was beautiful. Crappy at keeping his promises and good at making me cry, yes, but nonetheless, beautiful. I didn't understand. My brain couldn't comprehend what he was saying.

"I never meant for them to die. I was surrounded, and we didn't see Remus, the Proxy, until it was too late. He blasted me with fire, nearly taking my life. He would have . . . if your mom hadn't stepped in. But just when we thought we were free, Rolium appeared, and . . ." He stopped, unable to finish the sentence. "It should've been me. I failed them, *too*."

Axel turned on his heels and walked back to me. He fell to his knees again, holding my hands in his, begging for forgiveness. His entire person radiated grief and regret.

"I swear to you, Ren, I wish it was me that died that day. I tried, I fought back as much as I could. But I was . . . I swear to you, *Meus Aeternus*. Please, forgive me."

Something was off—my lungs burned and I had trouble breathing. Was he asking for my forgiveness because my parents were killed defending him and he'd hid that information, or worse . . . because he felt obligated to care for me out of guilt?

"*Amor Mei*," Axel said.

My eyes locked with his and suddenly, it made sense. Axel's guilt ate at him from the inside; the disappointment, the culpability, the need to gain clemency, it was all there for me to see.

He'd punished himself for too long, and even though pain poked inside my chest, I'd moved on from mourning my parents' deaths. I'd gotten the closure I needed. But Axel . . . he was still punishing himself.

"It wasn't your fault." My voice cracked as I whispered.

"It was. It was my responsibility, and I failed." His voice choked with regret, agony.

I placed my hand over his. "No, you didn't. Remember when I told you about how organized my parents were before they died? They knew what they were getting into. They knew the risks. If anything, their deaths would be on my shoulders. If it weren't for their love for me, their need to protect me, they wouldn't have been there."

"Ren. Don't—"

"All I'm saying is, we could blame their deaths on ourselves or we can move on from it, grateful that we did finally meet." I pushed forward, wanting to be face to face with him. He needed to hear what I wanted to say, because I realized his shame and guilt wasn't just about my parents' death, but his mom's too. "Forgiveness brings freedom. Freedom from being controlled by the past. Freedom from the emotional baggage. And freedom from the continuous battle with hate and bitterness. If you can let go, I promise you will be whole again and enjoy life the way I know your mom would want. You've already given back more than enough for something that wasn't your fault. Both times." I sighed. I moved my hands to cup his face and he leaned into my touch, closing his eyes. "You have to start with forgiving yourself. You've tormented yourself far too long, Alexander."

He trembled in my hands, looking more vulnerable than I'd ever seen him.

"You need to let go. You need . . . no, you *deserve* a life where love exists. Not hate, not vengeance. You deserve more—*we* deserve more. I want to be there to help you. Open your heart, and feel what life has to offer."

He opened his eyes and looked into mine in a way that left me breathless. He tenderly reached up and wiped the tears rolling down my cheek with his thumb.

"Finding you was the best thing that happened to me, Ren. I—"

I closed the remaining distance between us and crushed my lips to his. He stiffened, but I didn't want to talk anymore. I wanted to show him—us—just how much better life could be if we gave it a chance.

Axel's kisses were infectious, primeval, and soul deep. His kisses, his touch, his everything awakened me, inflaming my senses, my mind, my body, and my soul. I wanted more—*needed* more.

He tilted my head so I could open for him. I savored his every response. I kissed him more passionately as he pulled me off the ground, holding me flush against his body. Nothing else mattered. I heard his name slip through my lips over and over again, to which he responded in a way that made my world explode.

He fed the fire, deep in the core of my beating heart, that was constantly present and never satisfied.

He left my lips despite my protests, kissing my cheeks, ears, down the curve of my neck, and shoulders. He was in no hurry. He took his time, and I let my head fall back, closing my eyes. He kissed the hollow of my collarbone and then reversed direction, once again pulling my lips to his with force. Everything was magnified by infinity.

I kissed him. Tasted him. Breathed him. Devoured him.

I felt energized with every caress, as if kissing him fueled me with more vitality. My whole body responded to his desire. Needing more. Wanting more. A shiver traveled up my spine as he continued to explore my bare skin. Even the Earth's core couldn't compete with the temperature we emitted.

I pushed his jacket off his shoulders. It fell to the ground with a hushed thud. I tried to tug at his buttoned shirt, but it wouldn't budge.

I growled as I wiggled my way down without breaking contact. He smiled against my kisses, amused by my desire. *God, I want him.* As I undid the first three buttons, he stopped me, gently grabbing my wrists.

"Do you want to take your shirt off yourself?" I asked, confused.

"No . . ." He chuckled. "You're just making it very difficult for me to keep my promise to your brother."

"Sorry." *Not really. Okay, maybe just a tad for my lack of self-control.*

He placed his finger under my chin. "Don't be. You can't imagine how long I've waited for this moment. I want everything to be perfect for you, for us." His gaze dropped to my lips.

He looked a little flushed and his lips . . . *Oh, God.* His fully devourable lips were swollen from all the kissing, sucking, and biting. I smiled and kissed him again, gently this time. His lips curved against mine.

He put a hand at the nape of my neck while the other settled on my lower back. He kissed my temple and I nuzzled closer to the curve between his shoulder and neck.

"After a kiss like that, how do you expect me to leave you behind?" I asked.

"Then stay," he whispered.

I pushed back on his chest and looked up, glaring. "Maybe you should choose me over the Throne." I regretted saying it as soon as the words fell from my lips.

His eyebrows knitted together, pain etching in his pale blue eyes. "Ren, you know I'd always choose you . . ."

"I know." I sighed, pulling him back into a hug. "I'm sorry for being so . . ."

He kissed the crown of my head. "Don't ever be sorry, Ren. I always want you to speak what you're thinking."

I snuggled closer to his warmth in response.

Axel had said he couldn't put words to what he felt toward me. But even after knowing everything I did, I couldn't help feeling an intense draw to him. I knew there was only one emotion that would allow me to forgive. And it wasn't infatuation, or lust. It was something much more. Something more powerful than any other magic in the world:

Love.

CHAPTER TWENTY-SEVEN

"COME ON, REN. TOMORROW'S MY BIG DAY. IT'S NOT EVERY DAY a high schooler from nowhere gets an opportunity like this in the fashion world. Let's go celebrate," Pey said, walking toward the door. "Stop being all, 'I'm too good for this shit.'"

I fell face-first onto the makeshift sofa-bed, grunting into the pillow with frustration, my thoughts jumbled.

"I'm gonna sit this one out."

"What? She isn't coming?" Tyler remarked, feigning shock. "You know, for a girl that doesn't like attention, you seek it often."

"Yeah? How so, Tyler? Please, enlighten me."

"Enlightening you would take time, princess. Time I don't have. A lot of lonely Chicago ladies are dying to meet me and my little friend," he said, pointing downward and winking.

"Ew," Pey, Ella, and I said in unison.

I wrinkled my nose. "God, how are you even related to Axel?"

"I often ask myself that same question. He's so damn boring . . . such a stick in the mud."

"More like stick up his ass," Dean added, walking into the room.

I groaned. "You're both pompous asses. Leave me alone."

"You bailing on life again, Pernell?"

"Go find someone else to annoy." I waved my hand.

"And what? Miss a chance to infuriate you?" Dean smirked.

"You are—"

"Mere perfection," he interjected.

"You're full of—"

"Life." He wiggled his eyebrows, throwing himself on the bed and putting his arm around my shoulder.

I lurched away from his grasp. "Jerkwad."

"Geek."

"Wiseass."

"Know-it-all." His teeth made a world-premiere entrance as he grinned.

I glared. "Domeless wonderboy."

"Really?" He snorted, giving me a noogie. "Domeless wonderboy? What kinda insult is that?"

"Cheese fart." I shoved at his relentless hand, sorta proud of my insult.

"If you guys want to be alone, we could all leave," Pey interrupted, looking at her watch.

"Now, there's an idea. What say you, beautiful? You, me, alone." Dean looked suggestively at me.

I rolled my eyes. *As if.*

"Yeah. Okay. Have fun." Pey stopped just outside the door, her hand on the knob. "Don't do anything Joshua wouldn't." She gave me a sheepish grin and closed the door behind her.

I fell back on my pillow, exhausted from the day's travel. Flying was never my thing. Even as a child. My parents had always planned vacations by driving so I wouldn't freak. But I was here to support Pey.

"Looks like you have a lot of built-up frustration." Dean turned toward me, leaning on his elbow. "I have a few ideas how *we* could get rid of it. *Together.*"

"Screw the party. Can I watch?" Tyler said.

I jumped off the sofa bed with my hands in the air.

"Oh my freaking God! You guys are disgusting. Get out!" I screamed with such force that Tyler stopped mid-step, his smirk disappearing.

That was all it took for both Dean and Tyler to leave me alone. I didn't lose my temper often, so when I did, the point usually got across loud and clear.

Once I was alone in the ginormous suite, I crawled back on the bed and tried to sleep. But every time I closed my eyes, I saw hazy pictures, and heard people laughing, playing, and running around.

Counting backward, reciting formulas from math and chemistry, even tracing shapes on the sheets with my finger didn't do the trick.

Nothing worked.

I sighed, sitting up and staring out the window. Maybe some fresh air would clear my mind.

†

Faint music escaped from one of the ancient buildings nearby, drawing me toward it. A red and black brick wall and rustic double doors with blue lights welcomed me as I stepped inside Dimitriou's Jazz Alley.

The music was empowering and vibrations thrummed against my skin, caressing it. I took a seat at the bar and ordered a virgin passion fruit daiquiri, tapping my foot to the rhythm. People danced to the right of the stage, while others enjoyed the performance from their tables. Laughter and voices filled the air around me. The place felt so alive that I couldn't help but take part in clapping and hooting at the end of each performance.

Taking out my phone, I recorded a video to send to Axel.

A brunette woman with a dimpled smile caught my eye as she placed her hand over a man's shoulder. She threw her head back, laughing freely. My heart skipped a beat and my grip on my phone loosened. *It can't be.* The woman maneuvered through the crowd of happy patrons, leaving through the back door.

I texted Axel the video before my curiosity got the better of me.

Me: Wish you were here. XOXO

I shoved the phone into my back pocket as I moved toward the same back door. A gust of cold air whipped across my face, freezing me like a Popsicle in Antarctica. A layer of goosebumps rose under my clothing and my teeth chattered. I shoved my hands into my jacket pockets and moved forward in hurried pursuit.

I followed her through the back alley.

It can't be her.

Her hair looks exactly the same, though . . .

No. My mother is dead. We buried her. Didn't we? Thoughts mushed around in my head like a wave crashing against rocks.

The brunette woman came into view, and I closed the distance between us. A can hitting the asphalt made me spin, blood rushing to my ears, my heart pounding in my chest. *What was that?* My breathing became labored as I searched the dark alley.

But I didn't see anything. Taking a deep breath, I hesitantly turned back toward the woman. *No! Where did she go?*

I needed to be sure it wasn't my mom. I had to find her. I searched over a three-block radius, determined. Then, I heard her voice echo in the cold night. The same melodic voice that had driven monsters away, eased me into sleep, and soothed away every hurt, every fear.

"Mom?" I whispered.

I saw her turn as something hit the ground behind her. I put one foot in front of the other, cautiously approaching.

Curiosity killed the cat . . . or was that stupidity?

My skin prickled in warning and my heart worked faster, harder. Something didn't feel right. Mom would've come running to me, wouldn't she?

Run now. Leave. Not another step forward.

The warning bells became stronger, louder. I trembled with increased adrenaline.

Run!

I ignored my instincts and took another step forward, only to gasp in terror. A pair of black globe-eyes, so unlike a Goarder's, flickered toward me and my feet lost the ability to move.

A Proxy . . . like Rolium.

Shit!

It was stupidity, definitely stupidity that killed the cat.

In an instant, she was in front of me, her cold hand over my cheek and a warm smile on her face. She looked so much like my mom.

Only, I knew better.

When I fought back, she twisted my arm, pulling my head back by my hair. Her teeth in full view, she sneered. "Tsk. Tsk. Tsk. Didn't *I* ever teach you manners?" she said, mimicking my mother's voice.

I thrashed, hoping to find a way out of her grip. "Let go of me, you witch!" I pushed off the ground, grunting, but she didn't budge. I gave up, withering in her grasp. She was strong. Super strong. She leaned forward, bringing her lips to my neck. Her cold, wet tongue brushed across my skin, tasting me like a snake. I shivered.

"Mouthwatering," she purred. "Too bad I just had dinner." She inhaled my scent. "You smell divine . . ."

I laughed, hysteria overriding my sanity. *Only I would find a Proxy all the way in Chicago.*

She looked confused and loosened her grasp. Sweat started to form in ungodly places and my heart raced violently. The wheels in my head turned, thinking, planning my escape.

I need a distraction.

"I'm gonna have to politely decline your offer. You aren't my *type*. My *boyfriend* can attest to that," I said.

Good grief, I'm chatting now? Why don't I just invite her for a tea party and offer myself as a snack?

"Being a demon is a huge turnoff in my book."

Seriously. Shut up, Ren! Just shut the hell up.

A shiver shot up my spine. I knew I only had a few minutes left. She *would* kill me.

I can do this. I'm stronger.

A rush of courage and confidence formed inside me. I took a deep breath and stomped on her instep, elbowing her in the head with my free arm. She stumbled, letting go of me. I ran like Hell was after my soul.

"You're going to pay for that, you filthy little—"

I glanced back. An inhumanly-beautiful, blonde-haired woman had taken my mom's place. Shocked, I watched her jump, flying over me—vampire style. I instantly reacted with a powerful roundhouse kick that caught her in the ribs, sending her flying.

One for Ren. Zero for the she-devil.

She stumbled forward with a snarl.

"You're just like any other bully . . . overly confident." I slid into a fighting stance, ready for another attack.

Her fist flew in my direction, aimed at my jaw. I ducked, coming back up to retaliate, so focused on attacking that my guard dropped. Her palm connected with my chest and I flew backward, slamming into the wall several feet away. I pushed against the brick, trying to get back on my feet, groaning, struggling to stay strong. My legs buckled under me and I fell again, slumping against the building. My eyes started to close, but I forced them to stay open.

She strutted toward me with a wicked smile. I winced, wheezing, at the throbbing along my spine.

"I'm going to enjoy draining you." She crouched in front of me, her eyebrows lifted, amused. "I'll take your most profound desire and turn it into a nightmare while I feed."

I should have been pissing my pants, but sarcasm won.

"Get it over with, then, before you talk me to death."

Her features rounded and her skin shimmied as she shifted back into my mother. It was like watching a train wreck. I didn't want to look, but couldn't keep my eyes off her. In the blink of an eye, there she stood.

Mom. Her smile. Her hair. Her smell. My throat tightened and tears welled. I fought back a sob, closing my eyes to shut out her image.

No, this isn't real. She isn't Mom. She's a demon.

"Hmm . . . interesting. You're strong, but not enough to resist," she said in my mom's voice, churning the bile deep in my stomach.

I tried to block her, but she pushed through, entering my thoughts. I felt my mind ripple with each forceful intrusion. I screamed, attempting to push her out. My mind felt like Jell-O, vulnerable, easy to consume. But I wasn't giving up. No.

Images flashed, like the floodgates had opened.

Snakes writhed in Mom's hair, and over her body. They slithered their way up and down, wrapping themselves around her fragile frame. I heard the hissing and my heart plummeted in fear. She cried out, reaching for me, and I pulled back, unable to face her.

"Help me, baby. Help . . ." All I saw was snakes. Crawling into her open mouth, under her clothes. Biting her. Filling her with venom. I needed to help her. I had to be brave.

This isn't real. This isn't real. This isn't real.

"No!" I screamed.

The images stopped. My head throbbed and zinging pain tingled over my skin. Something warm trickled down my neck and arm.

"No!" I cried again. I opened my eyes and directed my hatred toward *her*. The Proxy. "Leave my mother alone, demon. Or so help me, God, I'll end you."

She laughed, crimson liquid dripping down the corners of her lips. Blood. *My* blood.

"You think you can kill me? As long as people have desires and nightmares, you can't kill me."

"You also thought I couldn't resist. You sure you want to test that theory?"

My body shuddered violently, ready to give up and throw in the white flag. But my mind wasn't going to revisit what I'd just experienced.

My skin buzzed like cold fire licked every cell.

Then, from the corner of my eye, I saw a silhouette at the other end of the alley, tracing a spot on the wall with an outstretched finger—a metal, claw-like finger that emitted red light.

Using the bricks as support, I pulled myself up, clutching my stomach.

I will *fight back. Mind over matter.*

"Pernell." My name echoed against the darkness.

"Ren," came another voice.

In the next moment, the demon's face scrunched and she screamed like a banshee in pain. The windows around me shattered as she disappeared.

Poof. No sound. No smoke. Just gone.

What the hell? I scanned the obsidian night and noticed the silhouette jumping onto the side of the building, pushing himself up to reach the top of the fence. He flew over it with a clean landing, throwing one final glance over his shoulder before disappearing into the night.

Who was that?

I fell to the ground and blacked out.

CHAPTER TWENTY-EIGHT

"**Wake up, sleeping beauty. We're going to be late.**"

I groaned in protest and winced, throwing one of my pillows toward the voice. I pulled the comforter over my head, snuggling deeper into my warm cocoon. "Leave me alone."

"No, you promised," Pey whined.

A pillow smacked me over the head. Twice.

"Hey. Ow . . . I'm up . . . I'm up . . ." I squinted from under the comforter.

"See you in fifteen." Pey blew me a kiss. "Ella, can you please grab the accessories? No . . . not that one . . . the one with the red ribbons. I'll have one of the boys pick up the heavier one."

I waited until the door had shut before getting out of bed. My head spun as soon as I stood, so I sat right back down. *Whoa.* Throbbing pain lanced through my arm and neck. I tried once again to stand and shuffled noisily to the mirror. I was bandaged. Slowly, I peeled back the gauze to assess the damage. It hadn't been a dream, after all.

Shit!

I ran my fingers gently over the swollen area and traced the thick red lines that had formed around the bite mark. I remembered my *friendly* encounter with the blood-sucking, psychotic Proxy. *But how did I get to my room?* I stepped into the shower, trying to revive the lost memories.

"Pernell, you in here?" Dean's voice reached my ears.

"Be out in a minute," I called back, shutting off the water as the pipes groaned.

I quickly dried off, and then pulled on my undergarments, a white, long-sleeve turtleneck, and washed-out skinny jeans. When I glanced in the mirror, I gasped. A hint of red swirled in my irises before quickly disappearing. Maybe I'd imagined it? Oh God, maybe I'd been infected the way Christian was. That would really put a damper on my relationship with Axel.

Hey, honey, I'm home. Guess what I did today? Drained another human.

I face-palmed and raked my hand down my face. My hands shook as I proceeded to examine my teeth and tongue. Everything was . . . normal . . . human. I shook off the paranoia. I was just exhausted.

When I walked out, both Tyler and Dean paced around the room, gathering the boxes Pey had mentioned earlier.

"Hey. Need any help?" I asked, shoving my feet into my boots.

My blood boiled as gooseflesh raised over my skin. What was going on with me?

Am I getting sick?

When I looked up, Dean and Tyler were observing me with concern.

"What?" Did they see the red in my irises, too? *Oh no, I'm gonna get staked before Pey's big day.*

They glanced at one another.

"How're you feeling?" Tyler asked.

"Better yet, what the hell were you thinking?" Dean asked, anger radiating from him. "Going out by yourself at night . . . in a new city."

"Sorry, warden. I didn't know I needed your permission to go out," I said, pushing my earlier . . . concerns away.

"What Dean meant to say was that something worse could've happened." Tyler approached me, trying to communicate something with his eyes. "You know?"

My hand automatically went to my neck. An itching burn prickled the infected area.

"I can take care of myself," I snarled.

"You don't look well." Dean placed his hand gently over my shoulder. "Have a se—"

I shrugged him off as rage bubbled through me. "Get your hands off me," I snapped.

I left the room abruptly, slamming the door behind me, shaking like I'd just escaped a life-threatening situation. I took deep breaths, making my way downstairs.

Pey immediately put me to work with the models. She wasn't joking when she'd said this was a big deal. People hustled, talking and stressing about little things. I smiled at them.

Amateurs! I rolled my eyes, then caught myself. *What the hell's wrong with me? I'm turning into Queen Bitch.*

I worked vigorously throughout the day, losing myself in the process.

Axel texted a handful of times, but I didn't bother to respond and didn't understand why. It was like I was being suffocated from the inside out. Everything was so damn bright, and my skin felt tight and constricting. Something was definitely wrong.

I was exhausted and annoyed, fighting against myself. One moment, I would smile and be polite; the next, I heard myself snap at people for no reason. My head hurt, and my body felt like it was being wrapped in a knot by a boa constrictor. Something was forcing me to let go of my control.

So, I did . . .

†

Getting into the club was a piece of cake. A bit of flirting and a wink was all it took for the idiot bouncer to let us in without checking our IDs. We stepped inside, swaying and dancing our way through the crowd.

Before I knew it, Pey was dancing with Landon, Ella was with some random dude, and I was gyrating with a sexy Latino. I wrapped myself around him and let him move me in ways I never had. I felt different. So unlike myself. I lost myself to the music, lust teasing my insides and soaking my surroundings.

"You wanna get outta here?" Latino guy shouted in my ear. "Somewhere more private?"

A lascivious smile crossed my lips and his eyes widened at my silent promise.

"The only one leaving this place is you," Dean growled from behind Latino.

"Who the hell are you?" Latino turned and locked eyes with Dean.

I pivoted around Latino guy, ignoring him, and placed one arm around Dean's neck.

"Jealously suits you, Mr. Jensen," I teased, drawing my finger down his chest.

"What're you . . . ?" Dean's pupils dilated with shock.

"Dance with me . . ." I fisted my hand in his collar and pulled him to the middle of the crowded floor.

I grabbed his hands, placing them on my hips. I swayed against him, encouraging. I turned around, putting my back to his chest. I teased my hair with my fingers and then held them above my head. I dipped down against him and snaked my body up the length of his.

"What are you doing?" Dean's voice trembled.

I smiled and pushed back against him, moving side to side. I heard him groan as he spun me to face him. His eyes were full of longing and desire. I smiled in satisfaction.

This, I can feed on. Far more filling than lust.

My fingers found their way to his jet-black hair and I pulled him down, his lips so close to mine.

"You're making it hard to be good, Nellie." He groaned with need as I pressed myself against him.

His grip tightened and he struggled to breathe. I felt his hunger slam into me. The way his hands tensed and fisted, fighting against everything he wanted.

"I. Want. You. Now." I brushed my lips against his. He stiffened, holding his breath. I nipped at his lower lip. "I'm sure you're the release this body needs."

Dean pulled away and his hand loosened its grip. His eyes looked wild, like a starved man. He glanced behind me.

I grabbed his chin, forcing him to look at me. I smirked. "I'll make it worth your time."

"You serious?"

Instead of answering him, I left a trail of kisses where the curve of his ear and jawline met. Then I slowly pressed my lips to his, parting them in no time. I devoured him. Oh, he wanted this, no doubt.

Like taking candy from a baby.

"Let's get out of here." Dean grabbed my hips, roughly dragging me out the back door.

Once we'd rounded the corner to a dark alley, he stopped and shoved me against the brick wall, hard.

"My, my, Mr. Jensen, what strength you have," I teased him, running my finger down his torso to the band of his jeans.

I looped my finger in his pants and pulled him against me with a quick tug. His neck tilted to the side and an animalistic grin took over, like a predator about to make a kill. I enjoyed every bit of it. He grabbed both my hands, pulling them above my head. I smiled.

"You've been a very bad girl." He sounded angry. "You need to be put back in your place." He reached for something behind him. I felt metal clamp around my wrists, burning my skin. I screamed.

I couldn't stop growling at him. I wanted to shred him piece by piece. But I couldn't move. I was trapped.

"You can't fool us, demon." Tyler stepped out of the shadows, along with two others. "Leave her body. Leave her, now."

"Dean, it's me, your Nellie," I begged him innocently. "Why are you doing this?" His eyebrows creased. A flicker of confusion crossed his features. This was my chance. "I thought you wanted me? If this is some sick joke to humiliate me again . . ." Tears welled in my eyes for added theatrics.

"Don't listen to her, Dean. You know Ren better than anyone else. She wouldn't degrade herself like this." Tyler gently placed his hand on Dean's shoulder and I wanted to snap it off. Suddenly, Dean's conflicted emotions cleared up. For the first time, I saw hate in his eyes, directed at me.

"We need to bind her and take her back," one of the voices remarked as he started to read text in a language I was all too familiar with. It was an ancient binding spell.

"Dean, please, don't let them hurt me." Fear struck deep in my core. I wanted to be free . . . *needed* to be free.

I felt Dean's cold hand on my cheek.

"No one will hurt you, babe," he promised in a soothing voice.

"You imbecile! This body could've been yours!"

The agony inside me spread. Something tugged at my soul, wanting to rip it apart. I felt a hand holding mine, never letting go. Screams came out of my mouth, but I didn't recognize them.

†

My eyes opened to a blurry image of James Dean. I closed them and tried again. A poster. It clung to a familiar mess of glow-in-the-dark stars. I glanced up and saw, as expected, a moon plastered to the ceiling.

I'm in my room?

My throat felt uncomfortable, like tiny needles had been jammed inside it. I rubbed my hand over my aching neck.

"You're awake." Tyler's voice startled me, and I shrieked like a little girl, wincing, jolting into a sitting position.

"Sorry. It's been almost two days, and we didn't know . . ."

"What happened?" I sounded like a scratchy record. Rubbing my throat, I scanned my surroundings. The wind chime Dean had made twinkled blue and white as sunlight reflected against it.

Instead of responding, he pulled out his phone and tapped on the screen. I wiggled into a more comfortable position, tucking my legs under my butt. Despite a few aches and pains, I felt strangely rejuvenated, like I'd just come back from a day at the spa.

Tyler sat on the edge of my bed, offering me a glass of water. "How you feeling?"

"Surprisingly great. I should black out more often."

"Here." He handed me a gummy bear. When I cocked my eyebrow, he shrugged.

I let the essence of strawberry flow across my taste buds, savoring the burst of flavor before swallowing it. Tyler left, mumbling something about informing the others of my change in status.

Feeling crusted in two days worth of grime, I heard the shower calling to me. I grabbed some clothes and headed toward the bathroom as memories began to prod through my consciousness. By the time I made it back to my room, I was mortified.

Oh. My. Freaking. God.

I'd cheated on Axel. I was a damn cheater. *Shit! Cheater! Cheater!*

Two knocks sounded against my door, startling away my depressing revelation.

"Come in." My strained voice sounded strange to my own ears.

Tyler entered, followed by Axel. My legs gave out, dropping me limply to my bed. He looked like he hadn't eaten or slept in days. Dark bags circled his eyes, and his cheeks were drained of color, making him look decades beyond his years. His eyes expressed pain and confusion.

He knew I'd cheated. Embarrassment and guilt consumed me.

How could I do this to him? To us? What the hell was I thinking?

I *wasn't* thinking. That's what.

Axel approached me with caution, unsure of his presence in my room.

He hates me.

And he has every right to, my conscience scolded.

He knelt before me so we were almost at eye level. His hand landed carefully on my knee.

I'm a horrible person! I'm worse than a Goarder.

He reached up warily and cupped my cheek. I leaned into his touch, knowing, without a doubt, that *we* were going to end . . . soon. I swallowed, hard.

Can you blame him? You cheated on him, for crying out loud.

His brilliant blue eyes locked with mine. I froze, lost in their depths. An uneven breath escaped my lips as I turned and kissed the inside of his palm. His eyes closed in response. Hope built in my chest.

Tyler cleared his throat. "I think I hear someone downstairs." Amusement colored his voice. I heard a click seconds later.

"Hi," I said and looked away, disgusted with myself.

"Hi." His hand still lingered on my face, gentle and evaluating.

He was hesitant, as if asking me permission to be here. I reached out to him, squeezing his hand.

"I'm sorry," I blurted out. "No one in their right mind would do what I did. There's no excuse. I'll understand if you hate me, and I disgust you, and you don't ever . . ." I couldn't finish that thought, because, truthfully, I'd fallen head over heels in love with Axel. I couldn't bear the thought of losing him, not even for this. I had messed up. Big time.

My throat constricted. I couldn't look at him. There was no way to explain what I'd done. No excusable reason. Yet, I could no longer imagine my life separate from his.

He interlaced our fingers, placed our hands on my knee and rested his forehead atop them, exhaling deeply. Then he stood, tilting my head so our eyes could meet. But I refused. I couldn't look at him. Not when . . .

"Look at me, *Amor*," he said. His voice was cautious and low. "Please."

I opened my eyes and tears coursed uncontrollably down my cheeks. I'd expected to see hatred or judgment. But all I saw was love. He ran his thumb across the salty river, wiping away my tears.

I'd cheated on him, and he was comforting me.

"It wasn't you. It was the Proxy." He held my gaze, his brow creased with worry. "*She* infected you, angel."

"But I knew what I was doing. I did all those—"

"When she infected you, she left a little of herself inside you somehow. We still don't understand it all, but it wasn't you, angel." He pulled me to him, wrapping his arms tightly around my body. His forehead leaned against mine. "Dean noticed it, too. You spoke in third person, like you were two separate souls. And your eyes glowed red." I opened my mouth to protest. "I know you think it's your fault, but please don't, okay?"

I let my tears—of melancholy, of anger, of relief—flow easily this time. He pulled me onto his lap and I straddled him, wrapping myself in his embrace. He stroked my hair, softly kissing the top of my head.

"I thought I'd lost you, that I'd never get another chance to hold you or tell you what you mean to me . . . what you are to me." He took a long, deep breath and exhaled roughly. "Screw caution."

Oh my.

I sat back, tilting my head down, and watched his eyes swim with devotion and desire. My heart raced unsteadily, ready to combust into a million pieces.

"I missed you, baby." With his strained and husky admission, something spiked inside me. Hearing him call me "baby" . . . if that wasn't sexy as hell, I didn't know what was. "I'll follow you even in death. I was ready to, when . . . I-I love you."

My lungs worked vigorously as my heart took flight in uncontrollable flutters. An unknown beast awakened inside me, sending tingles of excitement from my heart to every extremity. I was sure he could feel my heart pounding.

Axel loves me.

I pressed my forehead against his, still not entirely believing what he'd just confessed. I don't know why it surprised me, especially after Elijah and Joshua had flat-out told me he did. But hearing it from his lips, in this moment, officially made my wildest dreams a reality. I squeezed my eyes shut, then opened them, looking back into those brilliant blue irises that had held me captive since the first moment I'd caught their gaze.

"I'm lost in your touch, your magic. I think of you every waking moment and dream of you when I'm asleep. I love you in so many ways it's hard to breathe. I love you above everything— heaven, earth, body, and soul."

He absently played with my hair as he spoke.

I sat still and drank in every tiny detail, basking in the flood of his affection.

"If I could wish for one thing, it would be to keep you in my arms and love you until my last breath. I love you with everything I have. I will love you until I no longer exist."

I felt dizzy as his words struck me straight in the heart. His incredible declarations made me feel light, like I was floating amidst the star-filled sky.

Nothing could stop the tears that fled down my cheeks. I was completely out of sorts.

Axel looked at me, full of love and concern. The twinkle in his eyes spoke volumes, even though his lips had stopped moving. He wiped my tears with his thumb, his touch only intensifying my emotions and sending my heart into a fainting spell.

Concern clouded his eyes. I wanted to explain to him that these were tears of joy, but I was unable to speak.

"Angel, you don't have to say it back."

I collapsed, sobbing against his chest. How was it that he could tell me he loved me when I'd crushed his heart?

"Ah, baby, please don't cry."

It didn't matter what I'd done that night, or that I hurt him, he still worried about me, about my feelings. He never thought about himself. He didn't care about my mistakes, demon-possessed or not. He always put me first.

"Just shut up, Alexander. You're an idiot."

And he was. He was an idiot for loving me unconditionally, for thinking I didn't love him back. I'd have to be a heartless demon not to love a soul like his.

My Alexander.

I pulled myself up to a sitting position and placed my hand on his cheek, looking him in the eye. His brows furrowed in doubt and confusion, and he frowned.

"These are tears of happiness, silly." I ran my thumb between his brows, smoothing the crease. I leaned in. "I love you. I will love you until my last breath. Even in death. And, if there is such a thing as reincarnation, I want to be reborn so I can live to be yours over and over again. I will love you whenever, wherever, however. I *love* you, Alexander. Now, shut up and kiss me."

With lightning speed, his hands were around me and he hungrily pressed his lips against mine. Just like all the times we'd kissed, it was magical. Cosmic. He took his time with every peck, every nip, every kiss, like he was imprinting his lips on my very soul.

I felt an invisible bond wrapping around us, tying us together, linking us in mind, body, and spirit. He pulled back and smiled, knocking the breath out of me.

"You've made me the wealthiest man in all existence, *Meus Amor Aeternus*." He kissed my lips gently. "I'd like to give you something in return."

I nodded. He let go of me, allowing me space to move. When I raised my hips to get up, he held me in place and smiled.

"No need."

He removed a leather string from his neck and took off the pendant. He placed it in my palm and asked, "Will you accept this small token as a symbol of our love?"

I choked, unable to respond. It was a griffin, ancient and beautiful. Two cobalt diamonds represented its eyes; the rest was a smooth, antique gold. I took the pendant between my fingers, feeling effervescent as I admired its value—not in money or power, but as a token of our love.

Our love. I couldn't help but smile.

"It's beautiful." I said. "It looks old, and very much like your magical marking. Does it have magic? I—"

He traced my lower lip with his thumb, successfully shutting me up. He placed his forehead against mine, smiling.

"You're far too observant for your own good." He took the pendant from me.

"Yes, it's infused with *my* magic. And yes, it's ancient." He smiled, looking at me with an intense gaze that melted my heart into a puddle of goo. "I want you to keep this . . . I want to see it next to your heart."

My pulse thumped erratically and there was no stopping the idiotic grin about to form on my lips. I was sure if I looked in the mirror, I'd see a deep shade of crimson.

I removed the chain with my mother's amulet and gave it to Axel. He smiled, adding his pendant to the necklace. I pulled my hair up. He placed the chain around my neck, letting his fingers graze my skin. I shivered as he kissed my neck gently. I gasped. He continued to assault my skin with sweet, decadent kisses, blazing a path toward my collarbone.

He smiled, playing against my skin in ways that churned my heart and brought iniquitous thoughts to mind. I bit my lip, hoping he didn't notice the increase in my heart rate, my erratic breathing, or my scorching body.

Axel placed his hands on my hips, holding me in place, scrutinizing me. His eyes were glowing bright blue as they bored into my soul.

He groaned. "Don't bite your lip like that."

Feeling self-conscious, I ran my tongue across my lips, moistening them instead.

"Ah, hell." He smiled at me like he was starting to think the same iniquitous thoughts I had earlier. "Don't lick your lips, either, *Amor Mei.*"

I thought about tossing out some really snarky remarks, but before I could, I was on my back. He hovered above me, his hands on either side of my shoulders. His bicep muscles flexed through his t-shirt as he strained to stay in control.

"You're not helping, baby." His voice slipped into a las-civious, husky tone. His breath played around my lips, slowly moving toward my collarbone again.

I rolled my eyes, breathing heavily. "What do you want me to do, then?"

He tilted his head to the nape of my neck and sucked against the sensitive skin. "Don't speak, or think, or move, or . . ."

Of course, I didn't listen.

"What's gotten into you?" I chuckled, trying to wiggle out from under him.

When I looked into his eyes, I could see the fire blazing, ready to erupt. A longing for something more danced around his expression, so I did my best to encourage him. I pulled him down, kissing the bottom of his earlobe.

He groaned and let out a nervous chuckle.

"I . . . God. You're making this so hard. And resisting you has never been e-easy," he stammered. I continued teasing him with little nibbles that trailed all the way down his jaw.

"Don't you want me?" I asked shyly.

"How can I *not* want you?"

He put his weight on his elbow and used the other hand to lift my gaze to his. He groaned and kissed me with hunger, almost biting into my lip. This was a side of Axel I'd never seen. He was always so cautious, always the one to put on the brakes when things heated up.

"Being close to you . . ." He traced a finger all the way down to my hip. "Almost losing you, not knowing if I'd ever be able to hold you . . ." He shook his head as if to rid it of his thoughts. "There's nothing I'd rather do than . . . ravish you, taste you, love you . . ." His voice lowered with each word.

Warmth pooled low in my abdomen, making me weak all over. My heart plummeted and soared and hummed, all at the same time.

"I've missed you so much." He groaned as he nuzzled his face into my hair. "Your smell, your touch, your voice, every-thing . . . you make my existence worthwhile."

He kissed me like he was in a trance—strategically, slowly, devouring and indulging every sensation.

"Alexander." I tightened my grip on his shirt, then slowly pulled it over his head. I wrapped my legs around him and pulled him into another kiss as a moan slipped between my lips.

"Please tell me to stop," he begged.

"No," I replied as his lips went down my neck, his groans vibrating against my skin.

His hands found the hem of my shirt and pulled it over my head. He looked at me with love, adoration, and desire. His eyes turned dusky blue and his brow furrowed like he was in pain as he fought for control.

"So. Dangerously. Beautiful." He leaned down, kissing the length of my collarbone. My eyes rolled back in response. "And all mine." He left a trail of fierce heat with every kiss.

"God! My eyes . . ." I heard Tyler yell.

Axel threw himself over me, his back to my front, covering my body with his own.

"My godforsaken eyes. I think I'm blind . . . my eyes . . . my . . ." He stumbled around the room with a hand over his eyes.

"Get out," Axel growled, throwing a pillow at him.

"Okay. Okay. Don't get so testy . . . I'll leave you two back to your business." He shut the door behind him, making a point with his exit.

Axel turned back to me and relaxed. "Yes, definitely a distraction." He kissed the tip of my nose. "We should head downstairs."

I pouted.

A small, sad smile appeared on his face, his hand caressing my cheek. He kissed me gently. "Soon. I promise, *Amor Mei.*"

He handed me my shirt, waiting until I'd pulled it over my shoulders before he got up and retrieved his from the floor.

I heard Tyler's laugh echo along the walls. He wasn't even trying to hide his amusement.

Jerk!

Heat flushed my cheeks as reality crashed like a cascade of icy water. Other supernatural people . . . they'd probably heard everything. Oh, the utter mortification. *That deserves a jump off a building.*

"I put a secrecy charm over your room when Tyler left earlier." Axel answered my inner fears with a smile. "I'll go downstairs and let you get ready."

I nodded and stayed in bed until I heard the door close with a soft click.

Twenty minutes and two obnoxious reminders later, I made my way downstairs to face the waiting group. I found Axel immediately. His eyes took in my appearance before locking on to mine, unyielding. Desire pulsed somewhere deep inside me, threatening to burst with each passing second. We needed to talk about him staring at me like that in public, and how it was *not* okay.

Joshua hugged me silently, pouring all his worry and relief into that one gesture. He'd gone through hell and back, I could tell. He looked as bad as Axel. Cassie squeezed me in a warm hug and handed me a steamy bowl of chicken noodle soup. I inhaled deeply, letting the salty aroma fill my senses.

I took a seat next to Axel, my legs curled under my butt. He, however, had a different idea. He pulled my feet onto his lap and urged me to relax, not caring about the prying eyes in the room.

"Thank you."

He shrugged, massaging the balls of my feet, deep in discussion with the group. I fought back a moan from the simple pleasure of his touch.

With every sip of soup, I indulged in his flawless features. His golden skin glowed from the light in the room. His jaw clenched and his eyebrows creased when he spoke, answering questions or asking them himself. His fingers teased his silky brown hair when he felt annoyed. All the things I'd taken for granted before now brought a smile.

He occasionally glanced at me, giving me a delicious grin.

"And all mine," he'd said.

Yes, I was all his.

He jerked his head toward me with a smirk on his face. Heat coursed through me.

"Ren."

I didn't see Axel's lips move. Hell, I would've noticed if they had. I bit my lip.

"Ren."

Axel stifled a chuckle, pressing his lips together and shaking his head. He jerked his chin toward Elijah.

"Ren."

I peeled my gaze from Axel and glanced to Elijah. He smiled with affection as I heard snickers from around the room. There were more people here than I remembered. Including two new people I'd never seen.

I moved my legs off Axel in a swift motion and felt my cheeks flame. He moved closer to me, placing his hand over my shoulder, pulling me toward him. I relaxed against his touch.

"I understand you've had quite the last few days, but we need to hear your side of the story."

"Um . . ." I looked around the room, then to Axel. He gave me an encouraging smile and a soft squeeze on my shoulder. So I began retelling the story and answering any questions.

CHAPTER TWENTY-NINE

"DEAD. AGAIN!" DIMITRI YELLED.

It had been a little over a month since my initial intro-
duction to the art of one-on-one combat training and two
weeks since the incident in Chicago. Dean and the rest of
the group practiced with weapons a couple yards away. But
both Dimitri and Axel had agreed that I was nowhere close
to training with weapons. I'd been getting my butt handed
to me on a silver platter with rose petals every time I stepped
into the training room, so I was secluded from the group.

That didn't keep them from stopping to watch Dimitri lecture me without mercy, though.

"Repeated mistakes, princess." Dimitri yanked me off the mat, nearly throwing me across the room. "Attacking isn't the only way. Defend yourself. You're leaving holes, making yourself an easy target." He was in my face, staring me down. "What's the first thing you do when attacking?"

"I . . . I . . ." I stammered, unable to think clearly.

"Keep your guard up." His voice grew furious. "On guard."

Dimitri's right leg flew toward my face in a roundhouse kick. I deflected with a sweep of my hands, the impact ricocheting up my arms. I threw a punch of my own to his open gut. He swerved and grabbed me, pulling me toward him. When he punched my ribs, I bit down on my tongue, holding in the pain. I stumbled away from him, the metallic taste of blood pooling inside my mouth. He attacked, using a flashy butterfly kick to close the distance and a leg sweep to take me down, finishing me off with a mock kill.

I was flat on my back, panting, after just a few seconds.

"Do you understand how important it is for you to stay alive, princess?"

I hated being lectured. And I hated that he did it in front of everyone. Anger clouded my vision. I shot up and went after him, hoping to catch him off guard. Without hesitation, he took me down again. I lay there with my cheek crushed to the mat, his knee between my shoulder blades as he pulled back on my left arm.

"Get off me. Get off me." I flapped my body and legs, trying to get free.

From the corner of my eye, I noticed Dean sprinting toward us, his fire magic ready.

"Don't get involved," Dimitri threatened Dean, raising his arm without taking his eyes off me.

Dean let out a menacing growl. Fire simmered on the tips of his fingers. Although he was good at masking, I had a nagging suspicion he could feel my emotions on a cellular level. Kinda like my pain was his pain, my joy was his joy.

He knew this was just practice, but while I lay there help-lessly, his bond wouldn't allow him to stand by and watch. I could tell from the look on his face and his bulging biceps that he was trying hard to control his rage.

"Stop wasting my time, princess. You need to take this shit seriously before you get us all killed. Or worse, get your-self killed." Dimitri eased up, pulling me to my feet.

"I'm *trying* to get my shit together," I yelled back, making myself sound tougher than I really felt.

Dimitri scared the bejesus out of me. That was one of the reasons I'd wanted him to train me. He also never held back. I *wanted* his dominance to induce fear. I knew he wouldn't dampen my training because he worried about hurting me, but sometimes, it was too much.

"It's not like I've been training my whole damn life to play the part." Anger surged through me, making its way to the surface. "Do you think this is easy for me? To be the weakest link? I hate that I'm just a big letdown. I fear the day someone loses their life because I'm so damn weak." I poked him in the chest. "So don't you *frigging* tell me I'm not taking this shit seriously."

I turned around and stomped from the training center. As soon as I got to the bathroom, I let all my frustration and anger out through tears. I hadn't realized those were my true fears until they'd left my mouth. Their anxiety, hope . . . their very lives rested on whether or not I succeeded. They strongly believed I was something I wasn't. And that responsibility terrified me.

The bathroom door creaked open. I tilted my head up and saw Trinity leaning against the wall. Her arms were crossed under her chest and she stared ferociously back at me.

I wiped my tears with my thumbs. "If you're here to mock me, don't let the door hit you on the way out."

"No." Her eyes softened as she looked down at her feet. "I understand," she said. "My whole life, I've been working hard to prove myself to everyone . . . to my father. He always wanted a son." I could hear the hurt, the rejection in her voice.

It was the last thing I'd expected out of her.

"I don't need your pity. Wipe that look off your face, princess." There was a hidden smile in her voice. "We need a leader, a warrior that can set us free. So don't let the little things get to you. We all need *you*."

"I'm not built for this, Trinity. I'm not who you think I am."

"It's not fair, but you're defined by your enemies, and hell, they believe you're the one. So it doesn't matter who you are. It only matters that you accept your role and play your part in the grand plan that was created for all of us."

She pushed off the wall and walked out of the bathroom without another word, leaving me to my thoughts.

No, I make my own choices. I choose my own path. I'm not a puppet in some grand scheme. She's wrong.

"*Angel, you okay?*" Axel's voice cut in.

"*Yeah, just give me a minute.*"

I washed my face with cold water and looked at myself in the mirror. My body had changed over the last few weeks—toned arms, abs, and legs. My jaw had lost the stubborn baby fat I'd carried all my life. I had always been fit, but with more of a runner's body—packed with lean muscle. Now, I saw a fighter, strong and determined.

When I walked out, Axel was waiting for me. He wrapped me in his arms and kissed my temple. I sighed. No matter how miserable I was, his touch had a way of soothing me.

"You're doing amazing, angel. You know that, right?" He lifted my chin with his finger. When I didn't respond, he continued looking deep into my eyes. "Dimitri's the type of person that takes his trainee's failures as his own. I'm not making excuses for his behavior, but I want you to understand where he's coming from. He gets frustrated because he wants you to be successful."

"Sometimes it's hard to be told I suck over and over again. You know?" I hugged him, burying my face in his chest. "I'm really trying, Axel. I am. Even though I don't believe it, I'm still trying my best to be what everyone wants me to be."

He kissed my forehead. "Ah, angel, I wish you wouldn't try to be someone you aren't."

"But everyone expects it. I don't want to disappoint anyone."

He pushed me away so I could look into his bright blue eyes. They spoke everything but disappointment.

"That's impossible. You're strongest when you're you, Ren." He looked at me thoughtfully. "The greatest success always follows epic failure. We've all failed, disappointing someone in our lives, but we rise above it because we learn from those mistakes. Don't get too worked up about it, okay?"

"Wait, are you telling me *you're* actually capable of disappointing someone?" I asked, smiling.

"I'm only Dracian . . . and I'm most afraid to fail you."

"That, my dear Alexander, is impossible." I gave him an airbrush kiss, standing on my tippy-toes.

"Yeah?" His eyes grew dangerously dark, but his tone was teasing.

He gently pushed me against the wall, hands placed on either side of my shoulders, boxing me in with his body. He looked at me with a crooked smile and leaned down, pressing his lips to mine. When he kissed me like that, slowly, flirtatiously, and tenderly, nothing else existed. I burned deep inside, yearning for more.

"Princess."

Axel growled and buried his face in my neck before pulling away, panting. I giggled, glancing over his shoulder to find Dimitri looking at us.

"Can we talk?" he asked.

"No," Axel said, the same time I said:

"Yes."

"Fine. I'll see you soon," Axel said, looking at me with creased brows. "Remember where we left off," he whispered with an unquestionable promise in my ear. My cheeks burned.

He gave me a quick peck on my forehead and walked toward the training center. I waited, watching Dimitri shift uncomfortably. He rubbed his hand across the back of his neck and sighed.

"I shouldn't have been such an ass," he said.

Was Dimitri actually *trying* to apologize? He never apologized.

Like. Never.

I smiled. "Dim, are you apologizing?"

"Don't get used to it, princess." He looked at me lazily, smiling back. Abruptly, all traces of that smile disappeared. "You're doing tremendous for someone raised human."

"Holy cow." My hand went to my chest. "I must've died and gone to Heaven. I get an apology *and* a compliment?"

"Yeah, well, this is a once in a lifetime thing." He held out his hand. "Friends?"

I squeezed his fingers. "Only if you promise to continue being an ass during training."

"Well, I can't promise that." I'd grown used to seeing that mischievous grin on his face. "I'll be an ass regardless of the time and place."

"Deal." I used my grip on his hand to pull him into a hug. "Thank you."

"So, you ready to get back?"

"I can't," I said. He gave me an annoyed look and I rolled my eyes. "I have a life beyond training." I elbowed his gut as we walked back to the training center.

"And here I thought you were an incredibly boring person."

"Ha! Ha! Very funny, *Dim*-wit."

"Princess," he said, like an insult.

"I see you're both alive," Tyler shouted across the room. He turned to Dean and Marcus and said, "Easiest hundred bucks I ever made."

"What the hell, Pernell?" Dean growled. "You just cost me fifty bucks."

"And me," Marcus added.

I shook my head, reaching for my duffle bag and flip-flops.

"Everything okay?" Axel asked, pulling me into his arms.

I sighed into his chest. "Now the world's perfect again."

"Kill me now." Dean gritted his teeth. "You guys are disgusting."

"Let me walk you out." Axel kissed my forehead, ignoring Dean's disgruntled attitude.

We exited the building hand-in-hand. I shivered in the cold December weather.

"You know, if you learn to control your elemental magic, you could make the air warmer around you."

I instantly felt warmer, and eyed Axel suspiciously. Since I'd awakened magically, I could somewhat control the earth element, mostly communicating with plants. But I'd been told, with the proper training, I'd be able to do a lot more than that.

"Hmm . . . I'd like to have as much normalcy as possible, like shivering in the cold, and getting yelled at for not cleaning my room, or for leaving the patio door open."

"You're so irresistible when you speak human." He leaned down and gave me a lingering kiss that made my heart thump faster. I heard a honk in the background and he growled.

"*What does everyone have against us kissing?*" he asked in my mind.

I smiled against his lips.

"That's my ride." I walked down the steps and turned to him. "Do I need a babysitter all the time?"

He traced my cheek with the back of his hand, like I was a delicate crystal that could shatter if mishandled.

"It's for your safety, until you know how to control your magic."

He cleared his throat and walked me to Cassie's car.

"Cassie." He nodded politely. "What're you girls up to today?"

"Last minute things. We leave for the wedding in a few days."

"I still need to take care of the guest reservations. Weddings are so frustrating," I added, turning to Axel. The next words left my mouth before I could stop them: "Promise me we'll have a very simple, small wedding?" I slapped my hand over my mouth in utter mortification. Heat filled my cheeks and my throat dried up. "Um . . ."

Is there an undo button somewhere?

Axel chuckled as he took my face in both hands. His eyes were brighter than normal.

"Your wish is my command, *Meus Aeternus.*" He kissed me slowly, pulling me under his spell once again.

"How about you lovebirds make out later?" Cassie said, tugging on my jacket.

I bit my lip, trying to hide my embarrassment.

"Never get in the way of a bride, unless you have a death wish," Axel said, standing by the door, waiting for me to slide in. "Right now, I love my life way too much to get murdered by Bridezilla."

"I heard that, Knight." It would've sounded threatening if she wasn't smiling so brightly.

CHAPTER THIRTY

"Rise and shine," Pey and I said in unison.

"Wakey, wakey, eggs and bakey," Serena—Cassie's best friend—sang, walking in behind us like she owned the place.

Serena pulled the covers off our beautiful bride, then jumped on the bed next to her, giggling. In less than six hours, Cassie would be married to my brother, and tomorrow, we would all be entering the New Year as a family.

"Is it that time already?" Cassie asked groggily, rubbing her eyes.

"Like you'd ever forget," Serena said. "You've only been drooling over Josh for decades."

"That's no worse than my brother. He's been infatuated with her since . . ." I stopped, looking at Cassie, her eyes shining with glee. I smiled smugly. "Well, it doesn't matter."

"Since when?" Cassie squealed, jumping out of bed. "That's not fair . . . tell me."

I raised my eyebrow, teasing. "Maybe after you get in the shower."

We spent the next three hours providing royal services to our princess-for-a-day. Pey did Cassie's makeup and hair, completely in her element; I made sure the bride-to-be was well hydrated, fed, and pampered; and Serena was in charge of shoulder rubs and entertainment, regaling us with tales of their high school and college years.

A knock sounded on the door as another story came to an end, interrupting our giggle-fest.

"Just a minute." I opened the door a crack and peeked through. Sandy and John waited in the hallway. I motioned them to come in and quickly shut the door behind them.

"Tight security," John said, giving me a sideways hug and a kiss on the temple like my father always had.

"Joshua's been trying to sneak in all day." I looked at my soon-to-be sister-in-law and smiled with pride. I inched closer to her and whispered, "Who can blame him? He can't wait to get you alone and out of that dress."

Cassie turned a lovely shade of red. I stepped to the side, grinning. *Yup, my job here is done.*

"Sweetie." Sandy gave her daughter a tight hug. "You're breathtaking. Here . . . something borrowed, blue, and old." She handed Cassie a beautiful, blue-jeweled tiara. "This was your great-great-great-grandmother's. It's been passed down for generations."

Pey let out a frustrated groan. "Ah . . . not the hair . . ." She took the tiara from Sandy. "I can do this . . ." She stuck a comb between her teeth, eyeing Cassie's up-do with a thoughtful, appraising look before going to work.

Knock. Knock.

"Oh, for Christ's sake." Serena opened the door to find Dean on the other side.

He was gorgeous. His black suit, white shirt, and pink tie made him all the more attractive. The pink matched perfectly with the bridesmaids' dresses and the pink gardenia pinned to his breast pocket. Dean's eyes locked with mine and his cheeks flushed. His lips parted slightly.

I cleared my throat, looking away.

"What?" he asked the room full of spectators. "Don't I get to see my beautiful sister before she becomes a Pernell?" he joked. "Josh wanted you to have this."

Dean handed Cassie a colored macaroni bracelet. It was butt ugly. Her face flushed and her eyes glossed over.

"I know how you feel, Cassie. That's just . . . argh!" I said, looking at the horrid thing. "I'm ashamed to be his sister."

She was speechless. She traced the bracelet between her fingers like it was a precious jewel and chuckled.

"I can't believe he kept it all these years!" We all looked at her, confused. Tears threatened to run down her cheeks.

"Oh no, you don't." Pey was by her side, dabbing at her eyes, careful not to smudge the makeup.

"Thank you," Cassie said, sniffling, her nose turning slightly rosy. She smiled at our shocked faces. "Joshua and I made these for Valentine's Day, back in grade school. I thought I'd lost mine, but that pinhead had it all along." She slipped it onto her wrist and looked at it with pride.

In that moment, I understood what love was. It was blind, deep, and magical. It protected, preserved, and intensified. Cassie and Joshua were proof. It didn't matter the real value of the object, only the value of the person who'd given it.

"*I love you, Alexander,*" I said through our connection.

I heard him chuckle. "*And I you, my beloved goddess. I can't wait to see you.*"

A mental image of the first night he'd seen me filled my mind.

My hair was in a messy up-do, and I was wearing some god-awful clothes. I sat next to Julia, the homeless mom that had lost her job and eventually her child. She'd given up her baby in the hopes it could find a better life with a good family. That night, I'd cried harder than ever before.

"*Out of all the images you could remember me by, that's what you choose?*" I asked sarcastically.

"*That's the woman I fell in love with—so compassionate, so beautiful, so divine. I knew right then, you were going to ruin me,*" he said.

I blinked away the sudden moisture in my eyes. If he kept this up, he was going to make me cry. An arm on my shoulder shook me back to reality.

"*I'll see you soon,*" I said, holding back a sniffle.

"You okay?" Dean asked.

I nodded.

"Can I talk to you a moment?" He took my hand and walked me out to the balcony.

The sea breeze kissed my skin, sending an electrifying shiver through me. I looked out over the water to the distant, never-ending mountains and creamy white buildings. The breathtaking landscape, cosmopolitan atmosphere, and fascinating, historic architecture quirked my emotions, like being touched by the power of a volcano's aura for the first time.

"I wanted to give you something." Dean's voice snapped me back to the moment.

He looked nervous as he pulled a box from inside his jacket. He took my hand gently and placed the corsage around my wrist. I peeked up through my eyelashes, studying his face. He was extremely interested in the corsage and how it fit around my wrist.

He seemed aged . . . mature . . . his jaw was chiseled with hard angles, all the innocence in his face erased. His lips were set in a hard line and his bright blue eyes twinkled, studying mine with intensity. Slowly, he brought my hand to his lips, kissing it without blinking.

His affection poured into me through our bond, like rain on a summer day, coursing over my skin. It was impossible not to react to such a gesture. I cleared my throat. "Thank you. It's beautiful."

"We should probably go inside," he said, no louder than a whisper.

I nodded.

†

"You ready, beautiful?" Dean's warm breath teased my ear.

I laughed nervously as we readied to walk down the aisle, hand-in-hand. "As ready as I'll ever be."

When I entered the room, Axel's eyes immediately landed on mine. He smiled. I blushed worse than the bride. His lips parted and my heart jolted against my chest. A wide smile spread, splitting his features in half. He was dressed in a black, Armani suit with a crisp, white shirt, the top two buttons undone. December sun peeked through the windows, illuminating him from behind and making him look like he had a halo.

"*Now I know why God made women,*" he said in my mind. "*To teach man how to worship the beauty of an extraordinary miracle.*"

I melted into a puddle. "*Thank you.*"

He said the most beautiful things, and that was all I could say? *Pathetic, Ren.*

The bride's music started. When the doors opened, I heard Joshua suck in a deep breath, like someone had kicked him in the gut. I couldn't help but grin as I watched John escort Cassie down the aisle. She moved with grace and precision, like she walked on air. She never once took her eyes off Joshua, and he never took his off her. In that moment, they were the only two people in existence.

Love. Magic. Desire.

The look in her eyes when she saw Joshua's hand playing with the matching macaroni bracelet tugged at my heart in ways I couldn't imagine. My gaze flicked toward Axel. His eyes twinkled and his lips curved up, teeth in full view, beaming.

†

"Join us in welcoming Mr. and Mrs. Joshua Pernell to their first dance as husband and wife."

Joshua held his hand out to Cassie and she took it without hesitation. Soon, they were in the center of the dance floor, staring at each other. Tight coils formed in the pit of my stomach. I imagined my parents sitting next to me, holding each other's hands as they watched their son and daughter-in-law. I remembered how they used to tease Joshua about his obsession with Cassie, saying Cassie was the beauty that would tame his wild heart.

My throat tightened with heaviness. I wished, more than anything, that my parents could've seen this. I placed my hand over my heart, aching for them. A tear escaped, rolling down my cheek as a tissue waved in front of me. I looked up to find Dean, wearing a compassionate smile. I took the tissue, patting the rogue tear.

"Dance with me, maid-of-honor," he said, his hand extended.

He walked me to the dance floor and placed a hand on my waist, the other holding my hand to his chest.

"I wish Jim and Irene were here, too, Nellie."

I didn't respond. He pulled me closer. I placed my head on his chest and moved to the music. When the song ended, I pulled back, but Dean held me tighter. "This might be my only chance . . ." I looked at him, confused, but didn't complain.

Tingles vibrated along the back of my neck and I knew Axel was nearby. I searched for him without success.

"Mind if I cut in?"

Dean's eyes saddened as he handed me to my new dancing partner.

"Hey, Killer," Joshua said, holding my hand in his.

I placed my wrist over his shoulder and smiled. "Man of the day."

"You have no idea how much we appreciate your efforts with the wedding."

I hugged him. Dean danced with Cassie, talking and laughing. He glanced toward us and winked, giving me his famous heartbreaker smile.

"If they were here . . ." I choked, unable to finish the thought. "We'll always have each other, right?"

"One way or another." He kissed my forehead. "I love you, kiddo."

"I love you, too." The song ended. "Hey, enough with the sappy. Go enjoy your new bride."

When Joshua let go, a warm hand covered mine, pulling me to him with need.

I smiled.

"Do I get a dance with the most beautiful woman in the room?" Axel asked.

"Why, yes. Of course." I wrapped my arms around his neck and my lips sought his immediately.

"Mmhmm . . ." Axel licked his lips, grinning. "If I had known I'd be greeted in such a manner, I'd have approached you sooner, my lady."

I chuckled. "If you'd come any sooner, you'd have missed it. I have this rule about kissing my *third* dancing partner."

He laughed and twirled me around, making me giggle.

CHAPTER THIRTY-ONE

I LET MY HEAD DROOP ON AXEL'S SHOULDER AS WE WALKED toward our hotel. He lifted me into his arms, pulling me to his chest.

"What are you doing?" I asked, unable to stop giggling.

"Carrying my over-exhausted, beautiful girlfriend." He dropped a kiss on my nose.

I wrapped my arms around his neck, kicking my legs happily.

A cold breeze whipped through my hair. I took in the smell of sea, mixed with burning wood and olives. *Olives?* I listened to the low tide swishing and crashing over the rocks. Whispers echoed in its soft cries, secrets yet to be revealed. The black sky glistened, full of bright stars and a full moon that reflected over the restless waters.

I lifted my legs one at a time to peel off my heels. Axel gently set me down, letting my bare feet touch the cold sand before he, too, removed his shoes and pulled up his pant legs. He laced our fingers together as we walked toward the sea. Waves broke gently on the shore, sending sprays of water to sprinkle us.

I jumped in and out of the surf, running along its path. Axel chased after me, nearly catching me every single time. I giggled and squealed, running and letting him dash after me.

Déjà vu. A vision of sorts came into my mind. I'd seen this exact scenario when we first kissed. I came to an abrupt stop. Axel caught up with me, snaking his arm around my waist.

He spun me, pulling me to his chest. His arms wrapped securely around me and our toes touched. His eyes glimmered, bright in the moonlight, as his lips curved with admiration.

He reached inside his jacket and withdrew a single-stemmed rose, presenting it to me with a flourish.

"For me?"

He chuckled. "I don't see anyone else around, angel."

Heat rushed to my cheeks. I wrapped my fingers around the stem, feeling a cold, metal-like thickness. This wasn't just any rose. I looked up, locking my gaze with his.

"I wanted to give you something that's as beautiful as you, something that will last until the end of time."

My eyes prickled. I examined the gold-dipped flower in my hand, catching the blood-red inscription along the base of the petals.

"*I will love you until the day this rose withers.* Your *Alexander.*"

A shiver passed through me as I reread his endearing message and let the meaning behind it sink in. My grip around the flower tightened as I felt the full truth to the words.

I had no idea who moved first. All I knew was his soft lips consumed mine with hunger, the golden rose slipping from my fingers in the heat of the moment.

"God, what you do to me. I've been dying to do this all day," he said between each kiss as he continued to explore my lips. "*I've missed you so much.*"

Another moment of déjà vu.

"No freaking way!" I said, astonished.

"What?" he asked, without breaking the contact of his lips against my skin.

Low moans escaped me as I pushed him backward with my body, landing on the sand. I lay on top of him, kissing him more aggressively. He groaned and flipped me onto my back, taking full control.

His mouth left mine and I whimpered in protest. I tilted my head back, giving him easy access to my neck. Without missing a beat, his lips traveled to explore the bare skin. His fingers slowly moved the dress straps off my shoulders, his mouth following each curve. He growled when I bucked under him.

A warm, slobbery tongue grazed my face. Well, that was different. I didn't think Axel was the slobber type. I opened my eyes to find a golden retriever standing over us, licking Axel.

I bit back a giggle before getting to my knees. Axel turned to pet the furball, chuckling.

"Hey . . . you . . ." I said.

"Are you lost, big guy?" Axel cooed at the dog.

The dog rolled onto its back, giving Axel free access to scratch, its tongue lolling from its grinning mouth.

This was a side I hadn't seen from Axel. My heart filled with adoration. A vision I hadn't seen before came to mind: Axel playing with our kids, teaching them to crawl and walk and read.

"What?" He looked at me with amusement.

I smiled, feeling a rush of heat pool in my cheeks.

"Comet . . . I'm so sorry!" The owner ran toward us, sand kicking up behind him. "He doesn't normally run away like that."

"It's no big deal." Axel stood.

I continued to pet Comet, my hand lazily snuggled around his neck, and he licked me in gratitude. "He's adorable."

"You can keep him," the owner said, laughing. "I'm Van." He smiled and stretched his hand toward Axel.

Axel hesitated for a second before introducing us. "I'm Axel, and this is Ren."

I stood and wiped my hands over my dress, adjusting it to a more presentable length before reaching out to shake his hand.

"Sorry for the intrusion. We'll get out of your way," Van said, eyeing me carefully.

Axel didn't miss a beat. He took my arm and placed it around his waist, pulling me to him.

"Nice to meet you," I said, trying to soften Axel's protectiveness. "You too, Comet." I rubbed behind his ear, making his tail wag happily.

"Come on, Comet," Van called. The dog barked viciously, baring his teeth.

"Comet—"

Multiple things happened at once: Van flew a few feet behind us, hitting the ground with a thud; Axel took a protective stance in front of me; and I heard a voice that twisted the very core of my being.

"Well, well, well," the voice purred. "If it isn't the prince and his pathetic wench."

"*Prince?*" I asked Axel through our connection.

"No bodyguards. Well, this'll be easy."

Axel growled as he pulled a butterfly knife from his pocket and flipped it open, ready to attack. *Is he always this prepared?* He grabbed my hand tightly, cutting off the circulation to my fingers. Van groaned a few yards away. I prayed he had a sense of self-preservation and would stay down.

"Lyla," Axel said, spewing venom.

"You're losing your touch, Prince Knight." She laughed like a lunatic, raising the hairs on my arms.

Why does she keep calling him "prince"?

Axel snickered, as if to dismiss her threats. I trembled in fear. The last time I'd been face to face with *Lyla*, she'd infected me, possessing my body.

"*I'm right here, angel,*" Axel comforted me.

I squeezed his hand and smiled uneasily.

Lyla stared directly into my eyes and a shiver crept up my spine.

"Ren, love, how's Mummy?" she asked in a sarcastic British accent, subduing what little confidence I possessed.

"Still talking too much, I see," I snapped back, surprising myself.

"What do you want, Lyla?" Axel snarled.

She raised her eyebrows. Her laugh echoed along the open space, raising goosebumps over my entire body.

"You surely can't be that naïve, young prince," she said as a dozen figures materialized behind her.

I stiffened, my breath catching in my throat.

"*For the love of all things holy, angel, please stay calm. Whatever you do, stay behind me and follow my instructions. Got it?*" I was too shocked to respond. "*Angel, do you understand?*"

I sent him a mental nod. He let go of my hand and drew another blade from his pocket, flipping it open and handing it to me.

Where the heck does he have space to shove these things? And how the hell did I not feel them during our make-out session?

"If you're that stupid, then so be it." Lyla gestured with her hand and her dozen or so minions charged toward us, snapping their vicious teeth.

"*Ren!*" he screamed in my head.

I'd trained to defend myself, but I'd never fought Goarders. And the thought that they were once human wouldn't go away. I tried to retrieve my training, but my mind was completely blocked with fear and confusion, my judgment clouded.

"*Ren, run. Run!*" he pleaded.

"*No. I'm not leaving you.*" I could feel Axel's worry wrapping around my body. He wasn't afraid for his safety, but for my life. "*Don't you dare, Alexander. We'll get out of this. I love you.*"

"*I love you.*"

A Goarder rushed at me, teeth snapping. Out of nowhere, Comet jumped between us, knocking the Goarder off its feet.

Comet growled and advanced, but the Goarder was ready to strike back.

"Comet!" I yelled, my heart beating against my chest. To my surprise, he backed away, standing his ground in front of me, snarling, protecting me. I felt a wealth of gratitude toward the mutt I'd just met.

Axel's cry of warning reached me just as a painful kick connected to my spine. I fell face forward, the wind rushing out of me. I wheezed, feeling my lungs grasp at the bit of air I needed. I pushed up on my knees slowly, one hand clutching my chest.

Unable to find the strength to stand, I fell forward and rolled onto my back. My eyes widened and a strangled scream left my lungs as a Goarder's dagger descended toward my chest. I rolled several times, away from him, adrenaline kicking in. When I was at a safe distance, I got to my feet, ready to defend myself.

Another snarl came from behind, blindsiding me. Before I could react, he grabbed my hands and twisted them behind my shoulder blades. Out of instinct, I leaned forward, trying to pull away. His razor-sharp teeth grazed the skin over my neck and I yelped in pain. Comet once again came to my rescue, attacking the Goarder that had me trapped. A vicious kick to the head sent him flying with a yelp.

"Bastard," I snarled. Tears rolled down my cheek, but I knew time was of the essence. Using the moment of distraction, I pushed forward, stomping on his foot, and jerking my right hand free. I spun and slammed my open palm into the side of his face, feeling the bones crack. He stumbled back a few feet, his hands clutching at his broken cheekbone.

I rolled my shoulder to ease the ache and settled into a fighting stance, my hands up. I knew this was a kill or be killed situation. But I didn't know if I could be a killer. I just had to stay alive long enough for help to arrive. We mimicked each other's movements as we circled one another. He growled like an animal.

I spun around, connecting the heel of my foot with the Goarder's sternum. The blow sent him flying a couple yards. I took in several heavy breaths.

"Enough!" Lyla yelled, losing patience.

Three more Goarders appeared behind me. One grabbed me in a shoulder lock and I winced in pain. Little tingles rose above my skin like tiny zappers, getting stronger. The hair on my arms stood up. My magic, my essence was coming alive within me, trying to protect me.

The Goarder let go with a cry. Lyla's eyes darted to mine and she sneered.

With a gesture of her hand, I was suspended in the air, screaming profanities a sailor would have been proud of.

Axel's gaze connected with mine and his face twisted in unmistakable fear. His irises widened, turning into stormy blue swirls, and his brows fused together. He'd successfully dusted off five of the eight Goarders that had initially attacked him.

But the remaining three rushed him, pinning him down in his moment of his weakness, shoving his face into the sand.

Two grabbed his hands, pulling them out to the sides, while the third placed the heel of his foot on the back of Axel's neck.

"You know what we want. If you want your little wench alive, bring *the Echo*."

Axel turned into a raging wild animal. His body convulsed as he thrust and screamed, fighting to get free, trying to reach me. But five more Goarders materialized around him. I watched helplessly as they rained kicks over his body until he finally stopped struggling. They let him go and he fell limply to the ground. A trickle of blood pooled under him, seeping into the sand where he lay, motionless.

"No!" I cried. "Wake up, Axel."

His clothes were ripped and his skin oozed with open wounds. His face sported a ridiculous amount of cuts and bruises that dripped dark-red blood. My heart beat feverishly. How had our romantic night turned into a nightmare so quickly?

"No. Please don't hurt him," I begged. "I-I'll go."

Lyla laughed dismissively.

She turned to face Axel. "Tick-tock. Time is of the essence, young prince."

"*Please, Axel, don't fight back. Go. Save yourself.*"

"*No!*" he cried, trying to push himself off the ground, his face tortured. Another kick to his ribs sent him back down with a painful scream.

I knew what I needed to do. This was his only chance to survive.

"It's me you want," I yelled. "I'm the Echo."

Lyla's head snapped toward me and a devilish smile appeared on her red lips. "Well, is that right?" She sauntered toward me, cockiness in every step.

"Y-yes," I said, beating down the fear that was crawling up my chest.

"No . . ." Axel's voice came out in a hoarse grunt. I ignored him.

"I'm what you want. I'm the Echo," I repeated.

"*Don't do this!*" Axel's desperate plea came in my head.

I swallowed, not caring that tears were now falling freely. I trembled. "*It's already done.*"

"*I can't leave you.*"

"*You can find me.*" I looked down to my pendant. It was missing. *Crap.* "*Dean . . . should be able to find me,*" I reminded him.

Before I could say anything else, something yanked at my neck and belly button, like being pulled up after bungee jumping. The last thing I heard was Axel's scream. Everything went pitch black as my head whirled and I was unable to tell top from bottom.

Nausea churned in the pit of my stomach. A second later, I hit the ground with a painful impact to my knees and hands. Bile violently spewed out of my stomach and onto the black-and-white marble floor beneath my hands. I barely had time to register my surroundings before another round of contents left my stomach.

A sharp pinch in my neck made me jump. My hand went to the injection sight and I crawled backward, away from the needle. My vision blurred and Lyla's face came into view.

"Take her . . . the pit." Lyla's voice cut through my heaving. "Let's see if she really is the *Echo*, as she so willingly claims."

I struggled to keep from vomiting again. My breath came in short gasps and my heart beat erratically. I was pulled roughly to my feet by my armpits. I fought to get my body and mind to cooperate.

My painful cries echoed along the walls until something inside me numbed. I could feel it hiding within. Cowering.

Son of a . . . they drugged me, was my last thought before I was thrown into a bright white room.

CHAPTER THIRTY-TWO

A GLIMMER OF LIGHT SHONE INTO MY EYES, MAKING ME WINCE. I tried to block it out with my hands, but couldn't. *What in the hell?*

I was dangling over the ground, my wrists bound above my head with metal cuffs that hung from hooks in the ceiling. I whimpered as I squirmed against the bindings, pain radiating through my shoulders and up my arms.

I swung my legs from side to side, hoping to find a way out of my constraints. Warmth dripped down my wrists as the steel cut into my raw, burning skin. I cried out in pain.

"Look who's up." A cold voice froze me to the core and I stopped struggling to escape.

I zeroed in on the stranger before me. He made a show of his shark-like teeth—trying to intimidate me, I was sure.

My captor's hands went to his lips as he studied me slowly, like he was enjoying the view, glaring lecherously. What was he smiling at? I looked down at myself and gasped at what was left of my bridesmaid dress.

"Son of a . . ."

"Now, now . . . we don't want to be crass." He moved closer, until he was standing about three feet in front of me. "Especially when you're so conveniently tied up."

He wet his lips and walked toward me. He grabbed my waist, sinking his nails deep into my skin before dragging them across my stomach. I flinched and bit the inside of my cheek to hold back a yelp. My heart raced and the room spun. I raised my legs high, trying to get free of his disgusting hands. He laughed, not moving an inch.

His grip tightened and a sultry smile lifted the curve of his black lips. He dipped his head and licked the width of my abdomen, lapping at the red liquid oozing from the wound he'd inflicted. My stomach churned, threatening to erupt at dangerous speeds. I growled in disgust, thrusting to get away from him. The shackles cut deeper into my skin, but I didn't care. I just wanted him off me.

Off. Off. Off.

I wriggled helplessly. "I'll kill you . . . I swear to God, I'll cu—"

"That's enough."

Lyla walked into the room, outfitted in a blood-red, sequined dress that fit her like a second skin and showed off a generous amount of her chest. Who was she trying to impress?

"Summon Rod, Lavirus." When he didn't move, she yelled, "Now!"

Lyla smiled angelically, pulling a Victorian-style chair from the corner of the room with a flick of her finger. Lavirus quickly exited, closing the door behind him.

She sat back in the chair, crossing her long, lean legs, appraising me slowly. She drummed her fingers against the armrest like she was contemplating her next move.

"Why am I still alive, Lyla?"

Her fingers froze and her lips curved to one side. "Preparing you to meet your prince, love," she said carefully, watching my reaction.

I felt relieved, but didn't dare show it. Or, at least, I hoped I didn't. He was alive. He was okay. I pushed aside my insecurities and put on a brave front.

"So, what, you're just going to hand me back to Axel?" I scoffed.

She lifted her eyebrows.

"We both know I'm as good as dead, so throw me a bone here. Am I going to be delivered in a body bag, or are you more for the whole sadism thing and you're going to kill me after I think I'm safe?"

She stood and walked toward me. I grimaced as her sharp nail cut deeper across the length of my waist, drawing more blood. She slipped her finger into her mouth.

"Hmm . . . I knew there was something different about you the first time I tasted your blood."

"I want to know how I'm dying," I repeated, ignoring her comment.

She laughed maliciously. "You're the key to defeating the Dracians once and for all." Her eyes gleamed with greed, like she'd already won the lottery. "When you mate with Lord Telal, your magic, the *Echo's* magic, will bind with his, making him immortal, invincible. His children will be blessed with unimaginable magic. Making us, the Telalians, a force to be reckoned with. Your precious Dracians will finally be wiped from existence."

"He . . . that's genocide!" What she described, what Telal had planned was an abomination.

"No, my love, that's survival of the fittest."

Didn't she understand what was at risk? Nature's entire balance would be thrown off. Suddenly, the words Nala and Axel had said came back.

The balance is being disturbed. Power is a curse.

"Go. To. Hell." I spat in her face.

She looked at me in disgust. Her eyes turned into black globes and her hand tightened around my neck, cutting off the oxygen to my brain. I gasped, choking as I tried to breathe.

"Mistress." A thick, hoarse voice interrupted us.

The new guy easily towered over Lyla, even when he was on his knees. His head was bowed, his eyes trained on the floor. He wore black leather pants and heavy boots with buckles. Every inch of his exposed skin was covered in piercings and tattoos, making him scarier than a murderous clown. Thorn-like red chains crossed over his exposed chest and arms.

"She needs to be prepped and tested. I want to know for a fact that she is indeed the Echo. And Rod, darling . . ." I kicked and gasped, struggling to breathe as she said, "See that she is *very comfortable.*"

Rod nodded with a malevolent grin as his red orb eyes locked with mine. Lyla finally let go of me and exited the room. The door shut behind her with a loud thud, leaving Rod and I alone. I gulped as her words sank in. I needed to get out of here. Now. I didn't know what she'd ordered Rod to do, but I knew I didn't want to find out.

"Looks like it's just you and me, Dracian."

He withdrew a red rod from the sheath on his thigh. It was two or three inches in circumference, and wrapped in tiny, sparkling spikes. Beads of sweat formed across my forehead. My heart raced, slamming against my ribcage.

My head exploded in pain as he touched the rod to my wounded skin for a second, like he was testing it. My vision blurred, panic set in, and I hyperventilated.

This isn't good.

I needed out. Gathering as much strength as I could, I struggled, trying to free my thumb, even if I had to break it. The chains screamed with every movement I made.

Freedom. That's what I need. Control.

"Do you know why they call me Rod?"

He ran his finger across the spikes like he was caressing a lover's lips. My stomach lurched in fear.

"Clouth . . ." he purred at the rod. Red rays emitted through its spikes, reaching out like it was dying to connect to him. "Soon . . . lamb . . . very soon."

A colorful string of vicious profanity came out of my mouth. I didn't know what that thing was, but I didn't want it anywhere near me. I tried to push my thumb through the shackle. Pain throbbed down my arm as numbness slowly spread through my muscles. I didn't care. I pushed harder until I heard a crack. I winced in pain and bit my tongue to stop myself from crying out. Tears pooled in my eyes.

Freedom. Freedom. Freedom.

"I'm one of a kind, Dracian." He grinned, taking a few steps toward me, leaving an arm's length of space between us. "It's been a while since Clouth had a taste of Dracian. Not since . . . well, let's just say, she will enjoy this."

His lips turned up in a sinister smile that would frighten even the blind.

Clouth glowed an angry red. Like a lion ready to feast on its kill, it was enraged from having its needs denied for too long. Electric static vibrated against my skin as Clouth inched closer. When it finally made contact, the pain cut deep through my core, far worse than the first time.

I screamed, squeezing my eyes shut. Every muscle in my body tightened and convulsed. Tears spilled down my cheeks as the searing spread to my arms, chest, and legs. Red, angry veins pulsed from the point of contact as my skin burned.

Pain. Oh, so much pain.

My ribs felt like they'd exploded. I cringed with the last ounce of fight I had left. I felt my heart stop for the briefest of moments. My life flashed before my eyes.

Flash.

I was on Daddy's lap, my arms tightly wound around his neck. My head rested against his shoulder as Mom lectured me about how I should be avoiding strangers.

Flash.

My brother walked me to the park after he'd seen me crying over a fight at school, leaving his friends behind. He was giving me a piggyback ride as I giggled, saying, "*Faster, faster!*"

Flash.

Dean and I jumped off the tire swing by Cascade Lake, challenging each other to make riskier jumps. His smile was brighter than the brightest of suns.

Flash.

Pey and I scored guys passing us at the mall, ten being the hottest. I saw gorgeous baby blues pass us by, and said, "Ten!"

Flash.

Axel . . . the first time we'd kissed and the visions that had flooded my mind; our first fight before and after we were a couple; him playing with Comet.

Hours could have passed. I couldn't tell. Then, abruptly, it stopped.

Thank you. I sagged against the cuffs, shaking with the aftereffects. Maybe I wasn't as lucky as I thought. My lungs worked overtime, trying to compensate for the lack of oxygen and blood flow.

I opened my eyes, gasping for air.

"Intriguing." I heard Rod's voice as I struggled to keep my heart beating.

"Isn't that . . . a big word . . . for . . . you?" I asked, gasping down huge gulps of air, trying to keep myself conscious.

He laughed viciously as he forced Clouth back onto my chest. Piercing pain shot through me, drowning the walls with my screams.

A monstrous burst of red light exploded behind my closed eyelids and the pain abruptly stopped again. I felt raw, beaten and crushed like a car in a baling press.

Coherent thoughts were nowhere to be found. Hands grabbed at me, and the chains rattled above me. Weak protests slipped through my lips. My feet buckled under my weight as they finally touched the ground. A velvety-smooth cloth draped around my shoulders and a warm pair of arms circled me, pulling me against a firm chest. I let my head fall back as I was lifted, cradled in someone's arms.

"Nellie. Nellie." Dean's panicked voice called me back to reality.

Slowly, the fuzziness gave way to more defined shapes. "You're h-here," I stammered.

"Well, I really didn't have plans until later tonight," he joked.

"Is he . . . ?" I asked, trying to look for Rod. I flinched weakly and my eyes rolled back as residual pain throbbed through me.

"No . . . he escaped before we could get him. But I promise, babe, I'll make him pay," he said, running the back of his cool hand over my cheek.

For the first time in what felt like an eternity, I smiled. I was going home. I was safe.

He carried me out of that horrible place as cold, soothing ribbons wrapped themselves around me.

Dean's healing me.

There was a muffled struggle that trailed along the walls behind us. It sounded like someone being wrestled to the ground. Then a new set of arms wrapped around me, carrying me up a set of stairs. *Joshua.* I'd know them anywhere.

Shouts and clashing metal-on-metal erupted not too far from us. My eyes were half-open as he set me down in a corner, replacing the cover-up with his jacket.

"Killer." He gently patted my face to get me to open my eyes. With great effort, my heavy lids cracked open. His brow creased. "I need you to stay here." He placed a metal object in my hand and wrapped my fingers around it. "Don't try to be a hero; this is just a precaution." He lifted the cloth that covered me. "Shit."

He looked to both sides, running his hand through his hair. He cupped my cheek, looking at me like I was on the verge of death. Then he turned and disappeared. I cowered in the corner, trying to hide within the shadows. My teeth chattered and cold consumed me.

A thundering noise echoed through the corridor as the electrifying sizzle of magic filled the air. The cacophonous sound of steel colliding with steel penetrated my ears. I couldn't just sit here, waiting for my friends and family to die.

Using what little strength I had, I stood and walked the narrow hallway, using the walls for support. The sounds of battle grew louder, drowning me with their volume. Finally, I reached a grand, stone archway. Stepping over the threshold, I noticed a line of old-fashioned lamps burning here and there, illuminating the huge room.

I rubbed my eyes to clear the haziness in my sight and gasped at what unraveled before me. A staircase spiraled its way down to the main floor, where the Dracians and Telalians were locked in a furious battle.

I scanned the room, hoping to find Axel, Joshua, Dean, or any of the other Dracians I had come to know. I was so engrossed in my search that I didn't hear the hissing noise until it was a few feet away from me. I spun on my heel, fear sparking along every nerve, and came face to face with my worst nightmare.

A massive obsidian snake with a thick, scaled body and head . . . scratch that . . . *four* heads loomed over me threat- eningly. *This sucker would put the world's largest anaconda to shame.*

It reared its head back, opening its second head to its full width and struck me in the shoulder. I lurched back, falling down the grand staircase and sprawling face down on the cold marble floor.

I flipped on my back and groaned, placing a hand over the increasing burn in my right shoulder. Before I could fully comprehend what had happened, red eyes stared down at me, ready for another round.

I let out an ear-splitting scream and scrambled backward, trying to keep distance between us.

I swear, karma is out to get my ass.

Its jagged teeth glistened in the brightly lit room. I fumbled for the weapon I no longer possessed as the monster reared back, red venom dripping from its fangs. It snapped forward, striking at me for the second time.

Joshua and Axel skidded in front of me, their swords held ready. As the serpent's head drove down, the shiny metal in Joshua's hand moved at a blurring speed. He jumped to the side and ducked underneath. The edge of his sword sliced through the demon's head, enraging the remaining three.

The serpent pulled back and came down again with full force. Axel slid under the creature, disappearing inside its mouth. Screams rang in my head as I watched Axel become a meal. But then the head split open and he made a grand reappearance from the remnants of dead snake.

With two heads missing and two attackers, the serpent was clearly distracted, its heads whipping from one direction to the other, hissing. Axel called forth his elemental magic, and for the first time, I watched Joshua summon his as brilliant blue fire consumed the length of his arm.

They easily lured the beast away from me, cornering it between two giant pillars. The snake hissed with anger, lashing out at its attackers in desperation.

Joshua's eyes became slits as he brought his palms together, creating a ball of fire. One after another, he threw the energy toward the monster, grunting, keeping its attention on him. Axel ducked around the outside pillar, carefully moving, unnoticed, toward the creature. He sprang into the air, latching onto the beast's head with his legs. He placed the dagger across its neck and slit it open, his face stoic.

The one remaining, really pissed-off serpent head snapped at Axel as he slithered down its back. The moment its attention turned, Joshua took the opportunity to slice clean through the last throat.

With a thud, the demon crumpled to the floor, spraying venom. The serpent vanished, crumbling into black ash.

"Do you ever listen?" Joshua said, extending his hand to me.

I placed mine in his. "Just living up to your expectations."

He smiled and held me in a tight embrace as he led me toward the warzone. "You okay, kiddo?" he asked, facing me.

I nodded. "Those were some super bad-ass skills, Muskles. I never say this enough, but you are my freaking hero. I love you." I threw my arms around his waist, hugging tightly. I winced at the numbing pain between my shoulder blades, but ignored it for the moment.

"I love you too, kiddo." He chuckled, pulling me into a bear hug. "But we need to get you uninfected."

Axel's hand wrapped around mine, squeezing reassuringly. I felt warm blood trickle onto my hand and my eyes widened in horror. Axel was hurt.

Before the words left my mouth, Axel pulled me behind him and Joshua. I turned and saw six Goarders rushing toward us, snapping their teeth and swinging their weapons.

Joshua and Axel formed a protective wall between me and the oncoming horde, each taking on three at once.

Soon, I was left unguarded, tucked in the corner between two pillars.

My eyes darted, searching for Joshua. I saw him fall forward with a huge gash across his back. He rolled, bringing his sword up, blocking the Goarder's attack in the nick of time. With a quick kick to the gut, he sent his assailant flying. But before he could find his way back to me, another Goarder blocked his path.

Thinking I was unprotected, one came at me, its sword aimed at my chest. Panicked, I looked around for a weapon.

Abruptly, he froze, his sword mere breaths away from piercing my skin, his eyes wide with shock. I looked down. Joshua knelt on one knee, his dagger thrust into the Goarder's body. Shimmering red dust floated to the ground.

"We need to get you somewhere safe," he said, handing me the dagger.

He held my hand and led me through the crowd, shielding me with his body. A jolt of electricity came toward us. Joshua quickly blocked it by creating some sort of blue force field. Goarders rushed forward, trying to get around Joshua's magic. With each attack, Joshua was pulled further into the massive pool of fighting bodies, attacking and defending from all sides. Once again, I was left to fend for myself.

A surge of . . . something . . . a buzzing elation coursed through me, like I was high. My veins hummed and strength uncoiled from the base of my spine. The numbness from my fall down the stairs increased, and my body ached, but I ignored it.

Everything slowed, like someone had hit slow motion on the TV remote. I watched my injured comrades struggling and my lips curled in a snarl. I didn't want to kill, but injuring wasn't out of the question. I stepped back and yanked an oil torch from its mounting on the wall, slamming the end into the back of the nearest Goarder's head. The Goarder crumbled to the floor. I locked eyes with a surprised Trinity for a split second before she stabbed her dagger through the center of its body.

I nearly fell forward as my strength wavered. Trinity grabbed me by the shoulders, steadying me on my feet. She peered into my eyes for a moment, then gave me a curt nod, understanding that I wanted to be here. After she let me go, she tossed me one of her double-edged swords.

"Might as well protect yourself, princess," she said.

We circled with our backs against each other. I settled into a fighting stance as a Goarder ran at me.

Everything slowed again. Tendrils of power seemed to crawl through me, like I drew energy from the earth itself. Like my magic had finally reared its claws to protect me.

Was this how Legions felt? Was I finally learning to become a Dracian in the midst of crisis?

My attacker's weapon, a bladed claw, hung like an extension of his arm. He swung it high. I raised my sword, protecting myself, making contact with deafening steel-on-steel vibrations. Using my full strength, I pushed him back.

Another Goarder flung himself at me. As a kneejerk reaction, I swung my sword swiftly, meeting his suspended body with a quick stab to the gut. Red dust glimmered all around me and I trembled.

Holy shit! I just killed someone!

I couldn't breathe.

Murderer. Murderer. Murderer.

I took a few deep breaths. My strength waned. I knew that if I hadn't, I'd be the one lying dead. But that didn't ease the tightness in my chest. I'd still killed someone. I'd willfully taken their life without hesitating.

I'm stronger than this. I have to be.

"Watch out!" Trinity yelled from behind me.

I whirled, bringing the sword up, and quickly blocked the claw swiping at my head. I grunted, trying to keep the Goarder from skinning me alive. As I struggled, my sword got caught between the fingers of his claw. Angling his weapon, he ripped the sword from my grip. I lost my balance, falling to the ground. The Goarder moved in, dropping his knee on my chest, pinning me to the floor as he raised the claw high. My heartbeat accelerated as I stared death in the face.

He lurched forward suddenly, his eyes going blank before he disintegrated. Red dust rained down around me.

"You could've at least waited till my mouth was closed," I said, trying to cough up the nasty particles. I took Trinity's extended hand and she pulled me to my feet.

"We're even," she said stoically, unaffected.

"Whatever." I rolled my eyes.

Aaand we're back to being enemies. Great!

I turned around, ready for the next encounter with death and sucked in a horrified breath, my stomach twisting with fear.

Cassie stood twenty feet from me, fighting a Goarder, completely oblivious to the Proxy eyeing her with a smirk, his hands raised.

Rolium.

I recognized him immediately. My parents had died by his hand. I wasn't going to let him kill another one of my family members. Not while I was still alive. My eyes connected with Dean, who was ten feet to my left.

"Nellie," Dean yelled, the fire surrounding his body deflating. He knew what I was about to do. "No!"

Before he could reach me, he was intercepted by a Proxy and a flying fireball. I pushed through the pain as I ran along the seam of bodies, weaving and ducking with one destination in mind.

Right before the burst of red sparks hit Cassie, I jumped between, blocking the attack, taking it full-force in my gut. Time seemed to freeze as I flew across the room in slow motion. I saw every detail of every struggle in those few precious seconds before I hit the ground with a thump.

Joshua's eyes widened in horror. Cassie pivoted on her heel, her face registering shock and terror. Axel's blue eyes found mine and I saw the blood leave his face, his mouth wide open in a silent scream.

Before I knew it, two pairs of hands held me. I could hear murmuring, but my ears were dull from the buzzing of blood rushing inside me. Warmth poured out of my waist as an icy coldness settled over everything else. Tears ran down my face. I couldn't move, quaking as I felt my blood spill. Numbness crept over my skin, and my eyes grew heavy.

"Why . . . ?" It was Joshua.

I looked at him with blurred vision and smiled. "You . . ." I closed my eyes.

I felt raindrops fall on my forehead. No, not rain. I looked up. Axel held me against his chest, his hand holding one of mine as he kissed the top of my head, tears falling easily. He didn't speak; he didn't need to speak.

"I have to do this. You understand?" Joshua asked, looking at me, then to Axel. The look on his face was tortured. "I love you, and I promised to protect you, whatever it takes." He glanced at Axel and nodded. "Whatever. It. Takes."

He kissed my forehead as he placed his hand on my chest and started to murmur something I barely understood. A stream of energy penetrated my skin, my muscles, intertwining with my blood and organs. I became light as a feather as my body worked with Joshua to repair itself at the molecular level.

Boom. Boom. Boom.

Vibrations shook the ground beneath us. My eyes opened to find my brother struggling to keep his concentration. My gaze traveled to Axel and followed the direction he was staring, his eyebrows furrowed.

Everything around us had gone eerily quiet. The fighting had ceased.

My eyes narrowed in on the tall dark man that stood before us, commanding the attention of everyone in the room.

"Telal," Axel whispered.

With a grunt, Joshua shot to his feet, working hard to breathe. His chest heaved and he trembled uncontrollably.

"I did as much as I could." He gave me an apologetic look before turning around and addressing Telal. "It's been a while, my *friend*." His voice was anything but friendly.

"That it has, *friend*," Telal said, cold and emotionless.

My heart accelerated. His voice felt familiar, like I had known it all my life. But how was that possible?

"I have you," Axel whispered in my ear, steadying me.

I tilted my head and glanced at him, my vision slowly clearing. Axel's face was haunted, darkness written all over it. He wore a weary smile, and his eyes looked tired and puffy, but determined.

He put his arms around my waist, helping me up. I was surprised to find the wound on his hand hadn't healed yet.

"*You're bleeding,*" I said in panic.

"*Don't worry. I'll have it taken care of soon.*" Although he spoke to me, he concentrated on the threat before us.

Strong. Resolute. Powerful.

Another hand slid into my right palm and squeezed it lightly. *Dean.*

"You will not have her," Joshua said. He stood unyielding, but his hands clenched and relaxed like he was trying to control himself.

Telal laughed. His eyes connected with mine and my heart hitched with fear.

His expression softened. *Is that . . . adoration?* I felt my skin slither like tiny, slimy eels clutched to my body. I shivered in revulsion.

Lyla's voice echoed through my mind. "*When you mate with Lord Telal, your magic will bind with his, making him immortal, invincible.*"

"She's as beautiful as I remember," Telal said.

I stiffened. He remembered me? When had we ever met? I tried to think back, to place his face with people I knew. Nothing. One thing was certain, though—something inside me stirred at his voice. His lips curved into a smile.

"I promise, no harm will come to you," Telal addressed me directly.

Axel went rigid. I took a step toward Telal, unknowingly, before Axel's hand pulled me back.

Telal's draw on me was too strong. No, not on me, but on something inside me. Something ancient. Something old, powerful, and dying to be unleashed. I shook my head, forcing the feeling down, burying it.

The tension between Joshua and Telal increased by the second. Joshua pulled throwing stars from his sleeves and chucked them at Telal. The stars flew every which way with force, like someone blew them out of the air before they reached him.

"You've lost your touch," Telal barked sarcastically. What was stopping him from attacking us?

Joshua drew an object from his pocket that looked like a heart intertwined with a triangle. His lips moved silently as the object glowed bright white.

I felt part of my essence trying to reach out to it as the white glow enveloped Axel and Dean, their eyes wide. I gasped in shock.

"Dean? Axel?" I poked their shoulders. Neither responded.

Swallowing, I swept my gaze around the room. Nearly everyone in it—Dracian and Telalian—was frozen, wrapped in the same white cocoon as Dean and Axel, unable to move.

Panicked, I turned to Joshua, who was unaffected. "Joshua, what's going on?"

He didn't respond, continuing to mumble in a language I didn't understand. His eyes were locked on Telal.

"Your brother believes he can stop me," Telal said, his voice lacking any trace of hatred.

Confidence? Yes.

Cocky? Very big yes.

But hatred? Absolutely none.

The white light burst from the object like concentrated, sprinkling stardust, shooting straight at Telal. It pulsed rhythmically, targeting Telal's heart over and over again. Each hit boomed like thunder between the walls of the colossal room. The vibrations hummed through me. My knees weakened, buckling as I cuffed my ears, attempting to muffle the overpowering sound.

Telal managed to deflect a few hits but fell to his knees under the power of the attacks. He roared in agony, and then disappeared without sound or smoke. A hush fell over the room, like everyone waited with baited breath. Joshua scanned the room cautiously before rushing to my side.

"Promise me, Ren. Promise me . . ."

I looked at him, wide-eyed, as Telal appeared behind him, his chest rising and falling in an erratic pattern.

"This is for us, love," Telal said, grabbing Joshua's neck, tilting it back as he raised a snake-shaped trident. For the first time, I saw fear cloud Joshua's eyes. They widened and his lips parted. I screamed, and Joshua grabbed my hand. In the same moment, Telal plunged the trident into my brother's chest, missing his heart by mere inches.

I fell to the ground with Joshua, holding his hand.

"No, no, no, no, no, no!" Tears spilled easily over his failing body. "Joshua. No. This can't be happening. Please."

"I-t-t's okay, Killer . . . we'll b-b-be okay. I p-p-promise."

There was something in his eyes that gave me hope. I wanted to believe him.

A shadow cast over Joshua's limp body.

"You've always been so weak, son."

The voice, deep and harsh, came from behind me. I turned to find a well-groomed man with an abundance of bleached-white hair that needed to be tamed. He looked anything but old, though, and his shirt fit perfectly against his muscular body.

"A-Armen," Joshua rasped.

Armen's lips curved up in a sinister smile as he looked at me. "If I want something done right, why do I always have to do it myself?"

He kicked Joshua and a slew of blood spattered onto the white marble floor.

"No," I cried. "Don't hurt him, please."

I threw myself over Joshua's body, blocking it with my own. Armen grabbed my hair, tugging at it with force. I fought back a whimper as I covered his hand with mine, trying to break his merciless hold. He swung me around and threw me into the hard edge of a table in the corner.

"Father," Telal growled. "You promised no harm would come to her."

From the corner of my eye, I saw Armen twist the trident. Joshua's body writhed in pain, and he screamed in agony.

"This is how it's done," he said, his voice controlled and filled with hatred, venom. He twisted the blade counterclockwise in Joshua's chest, whispering in his ear.

"Noooo!" I got to my feet and ran toward Joshua, warm blood rolling down my face.

The ground beneath me shook. I skidded to a stop, sliding on my knees, reaching Joshua's hand in time to hear him say, "Everything wi-ill b-b-be fine, Temperance. . . . Trust i-in me. *Sarajeha Lavetri.*"

I knew the exact second I lost my brother. A single tear slid down his cheek as the light faded from his eyes. His fingers went limp and I was thrown across the room in a burst of blue and white sparks. I fell to the ground with a thud, cracking bones in multiple places. But I didn't even have time to register the pain before my body started to repair itself.

"You soulless bastard!" I screamed at Armen.

I wasn't sure how, what, where, or when, but I wanted vengeance. For the first time in my life, I *wanted* to kill.

As I moved toward Joshua's body, I stepped over the object he'd had in his hand before he was killed. It was still glowing blue. I picked it up, rage filling every inch of my existence. Warmth seeped through me, inching its way toward my cold heart. The air around me heated as my palms crackled with white sparks.

The suspended bodies around us unfroze, falling to the ground as they registered what had taken place. I didn't care. Joshua had been murdered, and the murderer stood in front of me, looking directly at me. Alive. Very much what my brother wasn't.

He. Will. Pay.

I squeezed my eyes shut, and when I opened them again, I felt nothing but grief-filled rage. I advanced toward Armen. The earth shook beneath my feet, the air filled with static, and my entire being burned. Every inch of me ached to combust into a million pieces.

"Tame your bitch." Armen turned away from me, scowling at Telal before disappearing.

"You stole everything from me," I shouted, discharging every bit of my hate.

"This wasn't how it was supposed to be," Telal said calmly.

How could he be so calm? He and his father had murdered the only remaining member of my family. Axel's hand reached for mine. I snapped my eyes to him, willing him to let me go. Instead, he fell to his knees, holding on to his body. I didn't understand why he was in pain, but now wasn't the time. I turned and stalked toward Telal.

He stood patiently, like I was a child having a tantrum over a broken toy. When I was in close proximity, I placed my hand on his chest. He flinched a little. I stood on my tippy-toes, inching closer to his ear.

"I'll never be yours," I whispered before falling back on my feet.

I glared into his eyes, leaving the palm of my hand over his chest as I felt my elemental magic mix with the rage in every cell of my body. Telal's expression softened with regret, love, and desire. His eyes widened and his nostrils flared as I stepped closer to his body, putting pressure on his chest. I didn't know how, but I knew this would hurt him.

And I wanted to . . . *kill* him.

White energy burst from my hands. His screams filled the room as the flames that surrounded him flared with my anger.

Vengeance held no mercy.

My heart smiled and my lips curved up in satisfaction. I stepped back, letting him cry in agony.

"I love you. I always have. I always will." I heard his voice reach my ears.

The room lit brightly with a final burst of flames. Then darkness fell like a black hole, sucking the light out of the room, taking Telal with it.

I turned around to find Cassie holding my dead brother, her beloved husband, her soul mate, cradling him as if he were falling asleep.

"*Soon, your strength will be tested as others take your place in the universe—others that hold the most influence in your life.*" Nala's words rang in my mind.

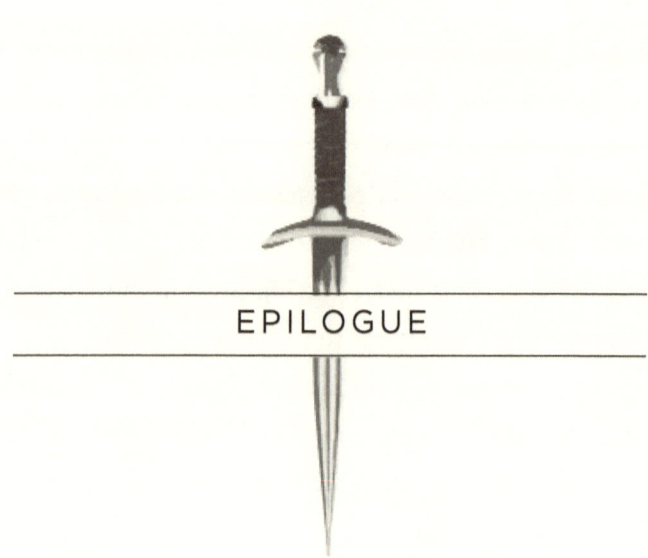

EPILOGUE

MY PAST. MY PRESENT. MY FUTURE.

They all had one thing in common: death.

I get that now. I didn't before. But Armen had made sure I understood. Unlike the day of my parents' funeral, today was much different. There were no chirping birds, no warmth from the sun's kiss. Even the trees were lifeless. Dead. So appropriate for the venue.

People had once again gathered to cry over the loss. The loss of my last family. A soft, cold hand slid into mine and squeezed gently.

Cassie.

I looked at her. "I'm so sorry," I said, hugging her. "So, so, sorry."

She was the only one I owed any kind of apology to. If it weren't for me, Joshua would be alive. If it weren't for me, Cassie wouldn't have lost her husband. And if it weren't for my very existence, none of this would've happened.

"It is *not* your fault," she said, choking with emotion. She cupped my face between her hands and kissed my forehead. "Joshua knew what he was doing. I knew what we had to do. No one blames you, Ren. We would make that same choice all over again, if it came down to it." She tucked a strand of hair behind my ear before kissing my forehead again. "I love you."

I nodded with a tight-lipped smile.

"*You okay?*" Axel's troubled voice asked in my head. But before I could respond, I felt the hairs on the back of my neck rise and turned around. Even in the gloom and doom, he was a pleasant sight to see. I watched him make his way toward me, his gaze never wavering from mine.

"Hey." Axel leaned down and kissed my temple.

"Hey." I leaned into him and he wrapped his arms around me.

These days, he seemed to want to touch me every chance he got. I didn't complain. He stayed over every night, but slept on the couch downstairs.

Since the incident in Greece, I'd fallen victim to irregular sleep patterns and regular nightmares. I would wake often, screaming, but never crying. The dreams were so vague. The only thing I'd remember at the end was falling. Falling into an abyss. And Axel was there to catch me—both in my dreams and in reality.

He was a dream boyfriend. He was patient and encouraged me to mourn my loss so I could start the healing process. But however hard I tried, I couldn't.

This time, I had no tears to shed, no sleepless nights. I ate well and remained healthy. There was nothing in my behavior to indicate Joshua was gone. When my parents died, I'd felt a part of me was torn apart. This time, none of that. Perhaps I'd given up hope, or I'd been better prepared. I didn't know which. I think that was the part that scared Axel and everybody else the most.

"*You okay?*" he asked.

"*I will be.*"

Pey stood before me, her eyes bloodshot and puffy. Joshua had been as much her brother as mine. Her arms wrapped around my neck in a death grip, pulling me away from Axel and Cassie.

I flinched, holding on to my stomach. Although Joshua had healed me using his own essence, draining him of the power he'd needed to fight Telal, the battle wounds hadn't healed at the rate they should have. Rod's black magic and my near-death experience hindered me from properly healing.

"Ah, Pey . . . I can't breathe." I patted her back as she swayed me back and forth, still not easing her grip.

Against everyone's advice, I'd decided to tell Pey about the Dracians and what was expected of me. She was the one person I wanted to keep alive *and* still be honest with. I'd been pleasantly surprised by how well she'd taken the news, considering.

"They're ready for us," Dean said, walking up behind us.

"You ready?" Axel asked, his hand once again laced with mine.

I nodded, slumping against him. His arm draped around my waist, taking in most of my weight. We followed behind Cassie, who was being escorted by Dean, much of her body slanted into him. He whispered things in her ear and she nodded. He kissed her forehead as they stood by their parents.

Their healthy, lively family.

"I've got you." Axel squeezed my shoulder.

Father Jacob looked up as he took a step forward, his eyes connecting with mine for the briefest second. The tightness in my chest made it hard to breathe.

This hadn't felt real until right now. But now that I was face-to-face with the reality of the situation, I didn't think I could do this. I stepped back, running into Axel.

I looked up, silently pleading him to take me away. I didn't want to say goodbye. Not again. "Please."

"If you really want me to, I'll take you away from here, angel. But I don't think you should go. You need closure. You need this. You're stronger than you know. And I'll be right here as long as you need me."

"Me, too," Cassie interjected. "You're not alone, Ren. You have us. We're in this together." She offered her hand, waiting for me to accept it. Swallowing the thick, Texas-sized lump in my throat, I took her hand with my free one and let her lead me toward Joshua's casket.

Father Jacob nodded as he began the ceremony. Words bounced off me. I couldn't concentrate on them. Instead, I studied how beautiful Joshua's final resting place was. The deep mahogany finish with purple and white floral accessories.

"Temperance," Father Jacob called.

My gaze lifted to his. I nodded and stepped forward. My knees gave out, taking Axel with me as I fell to the frozen ground.

"I'm right here," he whispered. "I have you."

"I know." I patted his arm. Grabbing a handful of dirt, I made a silent promise. *I'll make them pay. I swear to you, Muskles.* I kissed the fisted dirt in my hand. Vengeance-filled tears made an appearance as I stood.

"Let go, angel," Axel whispered. "I promise, I won't let you fall."

Holding my fist over the lowered coffin, I slowly let the dirt roll off my cold fingers.

I'll never let you go.

ABOUT THE AUTHOR

Clara Stone lives in the beautiful city of Boise, ID. Unlike what most believe about Idaho, it's more than a sack full of potatoes.

When she's not writing, you'll catch Clara reading mostly YA books and enjoying time with her family. She is a proud CW TV addict.

The Dracian Legacy is her first YA paranormal romance series. She strongly believes that true love conquers all and that's a common theme you'll find within her novels.

Get in Touch with Clara!
Email: AuthorClaraStone@ gmail.com
Snail Mail: P.O Box 2652 Eagle, ID 83616

Connect on Social Media:
Website: www.authorclarastone.com
Amazon: www.amazon.com/Clara-Stone/e/B00N53DX8U
Newsletter: www.eepurl.com/bK-HEz
Twitter: www.twitter.com/authclarastone
Facebook Group: www.facebook.com/groups/TrueLoveJunkies
Facebook Page: www.facebook.com/authorclarastone
Instagram: www.instagram.com/authorclarastone
Pinterest: www.pinterest.com/authclarastone
Goodreads: www.goodreads.com/author/show/7857676.Clara_Stone
Wattpad: www.wattpad.com/user/authorclarastone

ACKNOWLEDGEMENTS

Thank you to my amazing boys, Rajesh, Jay, & Koda who supported me day in and day out allowing me to immerse myself in my fantasies when creativity ventured.

Big thank you to Kisa Whipkey, my editor, master of action choreography and the person who put up with my craziness with a smile! Thank you so much for investing your time and brain cells into this book.

A super thank you to REUTS Publications and team, who produced unbelievable design and branding for this book. And for believing in my story.

A heartfelt thank you to my Critique Partners who had originally made this story ready for readers' eyes!

A huge thank you with a cherry on top to all the bloggers that supported me for my debut novel. Second time around as well! Your support and constant encouraging words have been a true blessing.

An enormous thank you to the readers! You bless me far beyond any words can describe.

Finally, to the person that holds the universe together. Thank you for your consecrations in keeping everything together in my life. I owe you everything.